BRIGHT ANGEL

ELIAM KRAIEM

CALLE
PEZ
STUDIOS

ELIAM KRAIEM

Printed Worldwide
First Printing 2023
First Edition 2023

10 9 8 7 6 5 4 3 2 1
callepezstudios.com
eliamkraiem@gmail.com
(+353) 89 611 6964

For Judith Halevy and her grandson Lewis Kraiem

"The subversion of reality chiefly requires early intervention. Any lie, no matter how fantastic, no matter how at odds with logical thought or experienced reality, can stand in for truth so long as that lie predates both logic and experience. So long as the lie is primary, told and somehow reinforced before the capacity for thought is formed when all the world is still magic, then the lie will outshine the dull facts surrounding it and reality will shape itself around it."

-Jessper Rasmussen

7/1/47

Dear Friends,

We are afraid and with good reason. The river is drying up before our eyes. I ask you, with trembling voice, with fear no less palpable than your own, how many times since the primordial sea receded did the river run dry? Run backwards, run clear, turn herself from a cold course of liquid mud to that of an arroyo of dry sand? Dust, subject to the whims of wind, but freed of the tyranny of water. More than a few I'm guessing, and yet somehow our immortal genes made it through all those terrible years of drought, of flood, of fire and brought us safely from that ancient microbial battleground to this very day. Four and a half billion years we've been here in one form or another. Meditate on that a little while and it's hard not to feel that you too are immortal. Have faith, and this hard, dry place will only be a stop along the way.

Now, I've noticed a certain tension traveling from body to body around the camp. Some fear that has come down from the world above, creeping through Dharma like an invisible pederast. I've heard the whispers:

"This whole camp is nothing but one man's doomsday cult!"

I would remind you, whoever you are, that we are all volunteers here and are free to go anytime we so choose.

And I've heard the shrill cry, "They're turning off the taps, they're going to starve us out! Without the river we're done for!"

And sure, they can hold the river back for now. The fools believe they've tamed her, like a lioness trained to jump through hoops of fire for scraps of maggot-ridden meat. From the safety of their golden cities they figure weights and forces and pressures per cubic inch and even the numbers tell them that their dreams are false, that such things are not possible, not really. They cannot even tame their own children, but the mighty Colorado seems within their reach. Believe me, friends, we will survive.

This human chapter will end with men damned and the river free. Isn't that funny? Time will destroy their dams and their cities will turn to dust and the god in whom they have placed their trust will evaporate.

The system is collapsing under its own weight. We did not wish for its failure nor do we hasten its demise. Not at all. We only want to survive its fall so that we may emerge whole after it's fallen.

Remember this my friends: The story of America is not really that of a republic throwing off the yoke of monarchy.

That's a story we were told as children. The story of America is the story of man's attempt to throw off the yoke of nature. We shall see. Sit tight. Channel your fears. Change is coming.

—Malcolm

I

1

APRIL 1ST, 2023

Big dicks, she thought. Big dicks at the ragged edge of the big-dick empire.

Louise gazed up at the thirty-four-story Vedro building. She was sitting on a bus-stop-bench wearing a white silk top, pleated men's trousers, a thin black belt with a silver clasp and vintage dark brown brogans which she had polished to a shine. She had caught an early bus and so had half an hour to sit and think about the Seattle skyline.

While the Vedro was not Seattle's tallest or even its most famous, to her it was the building that most embodied the mix of genius and blunt arrogance that had led us all to the precipice of ruin. A gigantic tree of glass, concrete and steel. The obscenity of it was astounding. She sat on the west-facing side of the iconic edifice and tried to take in the intricately crafted metal trunk that rose from the concrete; a tree whose branches and leaves were etched into the window glass on either side of the steel-faced column that formed the tree's trunk. In the bright light of day the leaves were all but invisible, but seen from The Puget Sound at sunset the etched leaves shone red and appeared to shimmer in some unfelt breeze. Its vast metallic trunk was illuminated like a pillar of fire rising straight out of the Earth.

When her watch buzzed she knew that her time of quiet contemplation was done, conclusion or no, and she rose and crossed the street. She left her credentials with security and was given a paper name badge and told to go directly to the twenty-ninth floor, where she was expected. She waited for the elevator and was joined by a consignment of the business attired; grey suits and grey woolen skirts. Fifty shades of grey. Scrubbed faces stumbling into the trap their parents and grandparents had so lovingly set for them. Louise wondered if she had yet again, woefully underdressed. She imagined her mother's shame and her father's pride.

You went to the most important meeting of your life dressed like a hobo?

Atta girl, no way to soar with the eagles if you're dressed up like a turkey.

Both were gone, or at least in the ground, the destination of shame and pride being exactly the same. When the elevator came they all shuffled in and then turned around and faced the door and tried to avoid the fundamental truths about the space that they were temporarily forced to inhabit. Above the door, some designer who had staked their name on their ability to access the child within had installed an LCD screen which showed old Looney Tunes animations on a loop. A little fun between floors. A friendly interlude in the workday. Something to take your mind off of mergers and acquisitions. A diversion from spreadsheets, human resource reports, risk assessment, actuarial tables and algorithms. Wile E. Coyote falling from the sky, strapped to a rocket or holding an anvil or sandwiched between two slabs of sandstone plummeting to what one assumed would be his death. The elevator made irregular stops so as to make deposits of overpriced grey fabric on various floors. By the time Louise had ascended to the twenty-ninth floor she was alone.

She stood in the hallway and looked at the five-by-two metal plate mounted on the wall. The same big tree that covered the entire west side of the building, only this time the scale was reversed. She was the giant and the tree was flattened and diminished to a size that allowed for close inspection. The tree was drawn in steel brush strokes, and Louise was surprised to find that it was full of pockets where life peeked out, almost every kind of human activity, from rape to breastfeeding, from murder to lovemaking. It all seemed to be happening within the vast world of the tree, however it was all rendered in the same scratched grey—there, but hard to see. At the bottom of the tree stood a woman, feet planted, jaw set, her axe in mid-swing. The virgin wood waiting for the first blow. The head of the axe, which was no more than an inch long and half-an-inch wide, was polished to a high shine and was the only point within the 10-square-foot panel that caught the eye. The only little bit that had escaped that dulling grey. And the axe shone like a newly minted quarter on a dirty sidewalk. On the oak door next to the panel a common brass nameplate read: "Red Axe." Louise opened the door, went in and the door closed behind her.

Louise was shown into a bright corner office by a whispering secretary.

—Judith, will be right in but the babies are sleeping so please try and keep it to a whisper. Thank you for your understanding.

She said it so casually that Louise simply nodded in assent.

The babies are sleeping.

Of course they are. What else would the babies be doing? She sat down on the leather sofa with her glass of water and had not even time to parse what the secretary might have meant when she heard one of them moving. Babies in an office. Loose tigers on a submarine.

Lined up on the far side of the room, away from the windows, were three identical bassinets on three identical stands and a changing table complete with stacks of diapers, wipes and various elixirs and powders in glass bottles. She could hear them breathing.

Louise remained on the couch and tried not to let the sound of the babies torture her.

She thought she had prepared for all contingencies, yet never this. She had tried so hard for that sound but to hear it now— in this context, in this building at what was supposed to be a job interview—it was not ideal. She stood up and went to one of the large windows and tried to concentrate on something else. Anything else. She looked out at the Puget Sound: ferry boats and fishing trawlers, giant containerships coming in from China chock-a-block with plastic doodads being met by great lumber carriers full of hundred-year-old trees that would make the opposite journey across the dying ocean. A myriad of sailboats; monohull racers, catamarans and duck dodgers all appearing to be as small as bathtub toys going to and fro on what looked to her like random trajectories. Across the Sound, the Olympics were snowcapped and so moved from extreme light to extreme dark and the city below seemed like some kind of mashup of past and future. A beautiful lie. City busses, Safeco Field with her top down, the Light Rail, and she could see The Pop Culture Museum, which from her vantage looked like the fossilized remains of a giant alien autopsy; The Space Needle with its past version of the future.

One of the babies woke and began to cry. Louise tried to ignore it. Not her baby not her problem. Surely the child's mother would come in soon and do whatever it was that mothers did to stop babies crying. No mother came and the baby's wail grew more insistent. Urgent. Within a minute the sound left no room for any other and even began to crowd all her senses. Her sight narrowed. Her skin itched. What if the baby died while she just stood there looking out the window? Surely that kind of inaction would not get her the job. What if this was some kind of test? She did not need this job. Jessper was going to get his money and they could do whatever they wanted. The baby began to yell as if in pain.

Louise walked across the room and looked in the bassinet from where the crying emanated. The baby was red-faced and her gaze was ancient and angry and demanding of action. After a moment Louise reached into the bassinet and picked up the baby and the unmistakable smell of baby shit engulfed her. The baby's cry became louder still and Louise held the baby at arm's length. She wished that she could be anywhere else on Earth.

—Okay okay.

She laid the squalling infant on her back and placed a hand on her chest and the baby wriggled and screamed like she was being tortured, but having come this far Louise knew that the only path left to her was forward. She had to go all the way. Louise was keenly aware that she had lived thirty-five years without ever having to clean another person's ass.

Louise untapped the diaper and flattened it as best she could. The child was screaming and kicking her legs and Louise had to keep a firm hand on her chest and apply a surprising amount of downward pressure in order that the child would not fall from the table. With her free hand Louise managed to pull the dirty and wet diaper free of the child, but in doing so had made a brown smear across the plastic-covered pad at the top of the table. The child had shit in her vagina and all over the fat of her legs and in a surprising yellowish tattoo of a mushroom cloud that rose up the center of her back. She was pumping her legs in the air like a cartoon character that had run out of ground. Louise freed a wipe from a package, the face of which portrayed a very different scene from the one she was experiencing, and she did her best to clean up the squirming child in front of her. She whispered obscenities into the baby's ear in a vain attempt to quiet her down. In the span of an entire pack of wet wipes she managed to clean the child, the table and the pad. The first diaper she put on was backwards and so she took it off and tried again.

The second was too loose. The third too tight. She threw the soiled diaper and the clean ones in the receptacle made just for that purpose and then took the baby up into her arms. The girl child smiled up at Louise and giggled. She had never known so swift or complete a transformation within such a fraught human transaction: from conflict to peace, from anger to contentment, from three-alarm fire to a heart-shaped swimming pool, and she gazed down at the child. Tears sprung from her eyes and she could do nothing to contain them. The baby cooed and she held the infant up to her breast and rocked her. The child snuggled into her, and Louise wept with abandon because she was sure she had no other choice but to do so. Whether she got the job or not was no longer important, because in that moment she had all the world in her arms. Real human life radiated from them both and that life comingled and surrounded them in an unseen and impenetrable mist.

The door opened and a woman in her fifties or perhaps sixties, in a flowing blue cotton dress, burst into the room like she had been shot from a cannon. She too had a baby in her arms and for a moment the two women, one crying, the other slightly harried, looked at each other, the older with penetrating blue eyes and the younger with eyes red from weeping.

—I changed her. She was crying and…I hope that's okay.

—More than okay. Jesus, thank you. I know that babies in the office are a little strange but Red Axe is a woman-run organization and so naturally we saw no real problem with it, although I admit it brings up some challenges.

Louise noticed that the baby in the other woman's arms had the same face and countenance as the baby in her own arms.

—Triplets?

—They're identical.

—They're beautiful, congratulations.

—Thank you. I got stuck on a phone call. We're opening an office in West Virginia. Jesus, I swear I have more in common with the Rohingya refugees I've worked with in Myanmar than I have with those ladies on the other side of the country.

—Right.

—Anyway, I am so sorry to have kept you waiting. I think that the most peaceful way to have this meeting, maybe the only way to have this meeting, is to keep holding them. Do you mind?

At that moment Louise could have sooner removed her own elbow than set down the baby in her arms.

—No.

—Good. Louise meet Vanessa. Vanessa… Louise.

—We're pretty intimate at this point.

—Let's go stand by the window. They like to look down at the city.

—Sure.

Louise tried to keep hold of the baby and get a sleeve up to wipe the tears from her face, the result of which was smeared eye makeup both on her face and the sleeve of her white silk top.

—Shit.

—I believe you're familiar with the wet wipes on the changing table.

Wriggling baby in arms, Louise managed to do a reasonable job of wiping the black smudge from her face.

—Thanks.

—So, why don't we start with why you're crying.

—Do we have to?

—No, but it's gonna be hard to forget.

—Okay, my husband and I had tried for three years to have a baby but it didn't happen for us. Taking this interview was my way of acknowledging to myself that that time was finished. And while that was fine and good and I fully intended to come in here all science-guns blazing I didn't quite expect to be confronted by babies either. It caught me off guard.

—I get it. My path to having children wasn't exactly normal either.

It was the first time Louise took note of the fact that the grey-haired blue-eyed woman across from her could have been no less than fifty but was probably closer to sixty

—I see that.

The older woman freed up a pinky from beneath the squirming child in her arms and Louise did the same

—Judith.

—Louise.

—So… Why do you want to live on a nearly abandoned island in the north of the world?

—Well I… I'm not sure I do. That aspect of the job seems daunting to me but the opportunity to work with the most biodiverse seed collection in history is pretty hard for a botanist to pass up.

—What about your husband?

—What about him?

—Is he ready for a life of seclusion?

—He says he is.

—What would he do with himself?

—Write code, mine data coin, I don't know really. We just came into some money. He's been talking a lot about making a computer with a living interface.

—What does that mean?

—I'm not sure. Anyway, he should be fully occupied.

The third baby woke up and made its presence known and Judith went to the bassinet and without setting down the child in her arms she scooped up the remaining one. This one, identical to the two others. Not simply identical, they seemed to be three manifestations of the same being. They had the exact same color of penetrating blue eyes as their mother, the same calm countenance, the same air of immortality.

—You and your children are extraordinary.

—How so?

—I don't know.

At the end of the interview—which lasted ten minutes and seemed to Louise to be more a matter of protocol than some part of a process of decision making—she was offered the job. She asked for a night to think about it and discuss it with her husband, and the night was granted, though both women knew what the outcome would be. They had said their goodbyes and Louise was on the threshold of the door when she turned around.

13

—Do you mind if I ask you a personal question?

—No, I don't mind.

—How does a woman of your age end up with three healthy babies?

—I would love to tell you, but I simply cannot.

Louise nodded. She did her best to smile. On her way back down to the ground floor she watched more Roadrunner cartoons and listened to one man exclaim to another that the one they were watching was his favorite, and how he had not seen it for ages and he was beginning to fear that "*the bitches from upstairs*" had somehow taken it out of circulation for not being woke enough.

On the bus back to Wallingford, she overheard two women talking about some scandal involving an actor who claimed that he was receiving death threats for being black and gay but it turned out that he made the whole thing up, apparently as a tactic to strong-arm the network which broadcasts the TV show he was on, and she heard half of a phone conversation in which a theory was being aired, something to do with Microsoft driving up home prices in the neighborhood in order to crash the market and then buy up all the houses in Seattle cheap.

As the bus crossed the Aurora Bridge she closed her eyes and knew some truths about the woman with whom she had met that day, though by which method she knew those truths or if they were even truths was a mystery to her. She knew that the woman she met with that day was no less than sixty-five and that the babies to whom she had been introduced, Vanessa, Virginia and Ruth had not begun as a collection of cells in her uterus but as a collection of cells in a lab. In fact they had never known the inside of her uterus at all. Louise had cloned hundreds of plants, she did so as a matter of course and thought no more of it than she did any other of her myriad daily tasks.

On the other side of the bridge she decided to walk home so that she could have a moment to think about what she would say to Jessper. To think about what she wanted. To think about what she wanted him to want. She stood for a long time looking at the Fremont Troll with its one hubcap eye open and its captured VW beetle. As if it had reached up and plucked the prize from the highway above.

—You're right troll, you're dead fucken right, you get what you can, while you can.

2

SEPTEMBER 15, 2033

Louise was pregnant. She had the paper strips all lined up on the bathroom countertop. All five made the same bald and outrageous claim, though she did not really need the strips. Louise had practiced body awareness as part of her daily meditation. Each morning she sat crossed-legged on the small silk carpet that she'd purchased from a young Berber girl on a trip to the High Atlas Mountains many years previous, back when she herself was only young and her gaze looked outward. But now, looking within, she had taken an inventory of her own body, observed her aches and her pains and tried to quiet her thoughts so that she might hear the details of the outlandish yarn her body was spinning. She avoided Jessper, had her coffee by herself in the greenhouse as if they had had a fight, though they had not. If he'd noticed her absence from the kitchen table he did not say anything.

Ten years previous Louise and Jessper had been through all fifteen rounds. Like so many of their generation they came to the idea of having children later than normal biology dictates. One only gets the bill for a feast of prolonged adolescence when the meal is well and truly over. They tried everything they could think of, from vitamins to hormone boosters, from shamanic blessings to favorable sexual positions, yoga, conception specialists of every stripe, Eastern medicine, Western medicine, acupuncture and intrafallopian transfer. Louise and Jessper submitted themselves to the forced cheeriness and fake optimism of high-end fertility clinics and when absolute infertility had been ruled out, they borrowed what money they could against Jessper's trust. Six failed rounds of in vitro fertilization later they considered surrogacy and then adoption, but their long fight with nature had left them without the resources on hand that they would need in order to be given someone else's child to rear. While Louise made going to doctors her full-time job, Jessper wrote code, clean, beautiful code in which he tried to triangulate the known factors and rumored factors of pregnancy. He took into account Louise's menstrual cycle and from it drew the most likely days and hours of conception, and the tides and the phases of the moon, but then also the price of Bitcoin, the recorded yearly rainfall in the city of their residence, averaged with that of the cities of their own births, altitude and oxygen concentration, pollution and global wind patterns, social movements, the rate of change in government attitudes toward healthcare, average lifespans, reported levels of happiness, honey bee die-off, global literacy, ocean acidification, coral health, the number of successful attempts on Everest, the square mileage of old-growth forest lost to bark beetle infestation in the American West, and the number of perfect games pitched in the National Baseball League per season. Jessper's program was not written in search of a prescription. He was looking for answers and he looked for them in the only way he knew how: by distilling the world into zeroes and ones so that he could clock it with a god's eye and perhaps see reason in the multiverse's denial of their most basic human desires.

They had sex every single day, once in the morning and again in the evening. After five years of trying they gave up and one night in a teary ceremony they drank a bottle of whisky together and smoked pot for the first time in years. They mourned the death of a parenthood they would not know. They dried their tears and started making plans for the extraordinary lives they would lead without children to hamper them.

When they were going to have a baby the idea of moving to a remote island north of Norway would have seemed absurd, but as soon as having a child had been removed from their vision of themselves they looked at the far northern posting in a different light altogether. The Seed Bank presented Louise with a rare opportunity as a botanist and there was something about living in the extreme north of the world that appealed to Jessper. He would have time and space to write, the institute provided for much of their needs and his now mature trust fund would provide the rest.

They built a beautiful home on the Universal Seed Bank compound. Three stories, four bedrooms, a movie theater, a yoga studio, an Olympic-sized swimming pool, a state-of-the-art kitchen run on geothermal energy, a solar panel array that kept them in electricity during the light months of the year and a small coal-fired plant to power them through the long dark winter. Jessper had an office with a one-hundred-and-eighty-degree view of the bay, and Louise had a lab that ran the length of the house on the ground floor and opened onto a greenhouse which more than doubled the footprint of the house itself. Her work at the Seed Bank required that she intake and verify the deposits. She was allowed to ask the depositors for permission to make copies of the seeds they deposited so that she might grow specimens in her lab. Louise had the most biodiverse garden in the world.

Years passed in the way that years sometimes do. They each progressed in their personal projects during the day and they came together at night and watched movies or saw live opera, piped to them via heavy undersea cable direct from the Sydney Opera House or the Met or the Dorothy Chandler Pavilion.

In so many ways they were more involved in the daily lives of their fellow humans than any of their city dwelling forbearers had ever been. Months went by and they saw no other people besides one another, or more accurately no other people saw them and their hair grew wild and untamed, and they went weeks without bathing. As the months went by they increasingly shared a vision of themselves as a single being alone in a vast universe.

On the day of the pregnancy tests she sat on the edge of the tub and when she had gathered her courage she went up to Jessper's office in her sock feet.

The office was on the third floor overlooking the bay. The windows were light-sensitive so that one was not blinded by the sun's reflection on the water during the bright summer days, but was still able to take advantage of the thin slice of light during the winter when the days grew short.

She found Jessper seated in front of his big monitor with his headphones covering his ears, his eyes fixed to the screen and his fingers pressing slowly and intently on the keyboard. The pace and rhythm of his typing fascinated her. She gently put her hands on his shoulders so that he would not be startled and then she took his headphones off and laid them on the desk next to his keyboard.

—Hey.

—Hey.

—What's up?

She pulled up the three-legged stool he kept by his desk, sat on it and looked into his eyes and she could tell that he was somewhat startled by her. She did not know if it was her bearing that frightened him or if it was just the fact of being unexpectedly pulled back to the world of flesh.

—So… do you remember how when we were obsessed with trying to get me pregnant I used to pee on those strips of paper all the time?

—The disappointment strips? Who could forget those?

—Well I kept a box of `em because, well, we had already paid for them and it seemed weird to throw them away.

—So you decided to haul `em around the globe with you?

—Yes.

—A little box of disappointment…. I guess it's okay so long as you keep a lid on it.

—Right, thing is….

—What?

She handed him one. A pink cross. He looked at it a long moment, studying it, as if it might change. She handed him another, and then another and then another, all bearing the same pink cross.

—They're ten years old, how do you know that they haven't all gone off?

She lifted her shirt and showed him her breasts. Swollen and round and inviting and Jessper thought that he could look at them forever, although eventually she lowered her shirt and he brought his eyes up to meet her gaze.

—Life's funny like that.

—Isn't it just?

They went downstairs and made lunch and ate in silence at the kitchen table. Brown rice and eggs and beans and chard. Eventually he looked at her.

—Are there any deposits scheduled?

—Yes, theoretically, a plane is due in from France in two months.

—What if we interred their seeds and then left with the depositors?

—What?

—Got on that plane and went to France. Eventually we could make our way…

—Well, I don't think that the depositors would be very happy about that and even if they were…

—What? Okay, what about withdrawals?

—Not that I know of. The withdrawals don't have to be scheduled so theoretically they could come at any time, but the world is falling apart and ironically I am happy for the first time in my life.

—I get that, but this is no place to have a risky…

—When was the last time you turned on the news, Jez?

—Months ago. I stopped thinking of it as my news but it doesn't matter, we should try and get to…

—A hospital?

—Yes, a hospital.

—Iceland has a complete blockade. No one comes or goes.

—The Norwegians are in a state of complete chaos…

—Yeah but…

—The safest place in the world to have a baby may very well be this island.

—What if you die in childbirth?

—Then it will just be you, and maybe the baby.

—Yeah that's what I am worried…

She put her hand over his mouth to stop him from speaking.

—I won't die in childbirth.

—You promise?

—I promise.

Louise spent the afternoon in the greenhouse grafting soybeans from Australia to lentils from Turkey. Jessper spent the afternoon in his server farm: fifty thousand GPUs he had set up to mine F-coin. While it had been a lucrative enterprise, he realized over the lunch dishes that the time for that enterprise was over. He divested without even bothering to look at the price and Jessper was never to know how wealthy the world's instability had made him.

Altogether he had almost ten petabytes of storage space. While this represented a small amount in terms of the vast internet itself, it was enough to store every film ever digitized, every book ever written and every scholarly paper ever published. One day the internet would fail and on that day he would need an intranet that stood as a worthy replacement.

Jessper slept two hours a night. The rest of the time he wrote code and wired the house for its new purpose. His servers sorted the useful from the useless, and the world's knowledge, written in zeros and ones, filled the metal outbuildings he had built to house it. If Louise had questions she asked them lightly, but did not press them.

—Why all the lights?

—You'll see.

In the small hours of the morning they would curl up together and he would sleep with his hands on her growing belly or with that same belly lodged in the small of his back and when the baby kicked they both woke and shared a moment of wonder that for just an instant replaced the worry and fear that dogged their waking steps.

The news was dire and hard to keep at bay. Though they were the only people left on the island of Svalbard they were still connected to the rest of humanity by wire and that wire brought only horror and devastation. Famine and floods, droughts and forest fires, earthquakes and volcanic eruptions, social upheavals and ethnic cleansings. Rivers of blood. The fall of empires and the rise of endless civil wars. Calamity following calamity and yet Louise's greenhouse burst with life and their harvest was healthier and more robust than that which they could store. Jessper's intranet grew larger, and he coded and coded and coded. He grew a beard which was as white as freshly fallen snow and if he knew of the world's fate he paid it no heed whatsoever as he was transforming himself into the god of his own universe. How small or infinite that universe might be was unknowable as there were no tools in existence with which to measure it.

If Jessper became a deity then Louise became a universe unto herself. Within her was a heartbeat not her own and somewhere a being wandered. She knew its wanderings to be vast and because the line between her and it was fuzzy at best, something in her became sure that the line between her and everything else was also... fuzzy at best.

During the last week of October, as the days contracted to a mere couple of hours, they asked the French to bring them a load of supplies with their seeds. Most of their requests were industrial: lights and cables, sheet metal. They got medical materials for the birth and made a state-of-the-art maternity ward with everything except a doctor.

The French scientists bore the news of the world on their ashen faces. They saw a pregnant woman alone with only her husband in the vast icy wilderness and not one of them suggested that she would be better off in more hospitable latitudes. The scientists or deliverymen or whomever they were, thanked Louise and Jessper for their service to humanity and each one asked Louise for permission to touch her protruding belly and they were like Jews at the base of the Wailing Wall. Each one held his hand there and closed his eyes. If they were not praying, then they were as close to it as men who are bereft of hope can come. Theirs was the last plane to use the runway on Svalbard.

Louise's water broke two weeks earlier than expected and despite months of dedicated preparation, Jessper was not prepared. He had been smoking hyperactive Sativa grown in the brightest and hottest corner of the greenhouse. It seemed to him that the plant was as close to an elixir of sun and earth that mortal men could lay their bare hands on and its psychotropic power was beyond that which he imagined possible and so the night before the day of his child's birth, he wrote joyful and transcendent code that seemed to come directly to his fingers from a source that lay far outside of his body and bypassed his mind altogether, and for what length of time his fingers danced on the keys and wrote binary poetry of their own volition he could not say.

The sun did laps in the night sky and when he was finished creating that thing which he suspected to be the last best hope of the world, a gift for which he was merely a deliveryman, he walked out of the house and climbed down the ladders to the North Atlantic's edge. The bright light of July at three AM north of the 69th parallel rained down on him, and with his bare feet in the frigid North Atlantic he knew that he had quietly severed the silver rope which had tied man's feet to the earth since he'd crawled out of the sea. The fact that there was not a soul in the world who knew or cared about his accomplishment took nothing at all away from its grandeur.

When he got back to the house it was after six AM and he expected to find Louise in the kitchen making breakfast but instead of the high-pitched whine of the blender and the coffee maker's hopeful perk, he only heard her pained and desperate moans. Jessper found Louise tangled among soaking sheets and her eyes were bloodshot and wild, as if she were an animal caught in the teeth of a steel trap. Jessper got her into a warm bath and for the first time he turned on the system that had been gestating inside of him for nine months. He played Mozart's *The Magic Flute* from the speakers he had wired behind the walls of their home, one per square foot, and the thousands of tiny speakers created the illusion in the mind of the listener that the house itself was singing comfort to the broken world, but far from being comforted Jessper saw only fear in Louise's eyes.

—Jez, what if we made a mistake?

—We didn't, and even if we did it's too late now.

—Jessper I'm scared.

—I'm not. We are going to be fine.

He'd lied and they both knew it, but they took his lie for the truth because there was some truth in it and it was the best option available to them. Back when the child was little more than an idea, no bigger than a pea, they had decided to have a natural birth; no drugs, no epidural. Just water and gravity.

Human strength and faith were going to have to see them through.

Jessper had taken an online course in midwifery and watched no less than a hundred hours of birth videos, from successful births to those that ended in the death of the mother and infant. He had done his best to prepare himself for every possible outcome. They had set up a birthing pool in a shaded corner of the greenhouse under a Banyan tree whose branches had risen to the limit of their glass cage. For hours she got in and out of the bath and paced and changed positions and practiced prenatal yoga and hummed opera through gritted teeth along with the singing house. The sharp contractions got closer and closer and time expanded and contracted and the house sang and the sun shone down through the greenhouse's great canted panes and time was exposed for the fiction that it is. She asked to lie on her back, and Jessper carried her into the house and he put her on the table that they had gotten for just that purpose and they put her legs up in the stirrups. With his headlamp on and a video camera strapped to the side of his face he measured her cervix and determined that she was fully dilated. He could see the top of the baby's head, red and angry and ready to burst forth into the world. She pushed and pushed and the baby's skull came up against the barrier between the universe of which he had been the sole inhabitant and the dying world which called to him with a Siren's song. Louise pushed and pushed and with each push she grew that

bit weaker but the baby's head was too great in circumference
and she cried and screamed and shat herself and bore down
with all of her strength but nothing could force the child
through the narrow gap. Jessper realized that the force of her
exertions had decreased significantly.

—Please forgive me.

And he saw the panic in her eyes and he wished that he
had not spoken at all but he could no sooner take back his
words than he could command the child forth and so with a
sterile and sharp scalpel he performed an episiotomy. She
screamed out in pain and then lost consciousness and he
continued cutting her flesh at a forty-five-degree angle just as
he hoped never to have to do. Blood gushed from her, and the
baby's head passed through the now expanded opening and
then the rest of the boy emerged easily. He slapped the child's
feet and the boy wailed mightily. Jessper cut the cord that
attached the child to the mother whom he was sure he had
murdered in her most vulnerable hour and he tied the stump
of the umbilical cord to his son's naked belly and set him aside.
He worked as fast as he could to clean the afterbirth from
Louise's insides and he stitched her up with shaking hands and
through floods of tears. He was sure that she was dead but he
felt for her pulse and her pulse was as strong as it had ever been
and he laughed from deep within his soul. He took her legs
from the stirrups and wrapped her in a blanket and went back
to the baby and washed him in lukewarm water and the boy

looked up at him wide-eyed and amazed as if this place were the furthest corner of the universe that he had expected to arrive to. He wrapped the boy in a blanket and went into the greenhouse. A vast world of plants. Louise's world. For a moment Jessper wandered among the neat rows and wooden boxes and the smell of earth filled his nostrils and calmed his soul which had for maybe minutes or hours or mere seconds screamed for release as he did not believe he could live in the world without her. He found what he was looking for and dug up the plant and went back to the room that was full of his son's powerful waling and his wife's echoing silence and he took the child and placed him against her naked skin. The child stopped crying and he curled into her as if he took comfort in her mere proximity and Jessper broke open the bulb of garlic in his hands and smashed a clove with the pad of his thumb against the knuckle of his forefinger and he waved it under her nose. Her eyes opened and she sucked in breath and looked down to find the boy child against her. She lifted him up slowly and he opened his eyes and looked into hers, and if there was not recognition in that look then no such thing as recognition could exist, and she placed her nipple in his mouth and the most natural of mammalian processes began in earnest.

While Adam ate his first meal Jessper took one of the adult-sized diapers that he'd printed for the occasion and he packed it with ice and put it on her gently and if she was in pain she did not show it but only looked down at the child at her breast and Jessper knew that the rest of the world had fallen away, and that for a time, for a blessed hour, maybe more, it was only the two of them, mother and child.

Jessper had forgotten about the bright morning, now long gone, when he had put the finishing touches on the something he had created from nothing because if there was some purpose or meaning to this life beyond the spectacle he saw unfurling before him he no longer really believed in it.

Louise woke up the first time, and Adam was asleep against her breast, and he was perfect and as beautiful a being as she imagined could exist. The next time she woke, Jessper had moved the still sleeping child to a basket by the bed, and Jessper lay next to her asleep, and despite the profound pain radiating from between her legs she had never known such contentedness. She wished that time would stop, freeze right there, and keep them all in her still and blissful embrace. Graphic novel characters, in a closed book, inside a locked box, safe within the stacks of a vast and undisturbed archive.

Louise heard her breathe before she saw her and in a real sense she never saw her at all except in her mind's eye in which she was of petite build, with black hair and penetrating pale blue eyes. Quick to laugh and smile, and always up for a tea party or a game or a joke at her brother's expense.

On that first night, in the artificial darkness of their bedroom she touched Jessper's shoulder.

—Jez.

—Yep.

—I hear two of them.

—Yes.

—Did I give birth to twins?

—No, not exactly.

—Jessper, I am confused and a little scared.

—Don't be, I can explain it to you, but now, maybe you want to rest. He will wake up soon and he'll want to eat. We should get what rest we can.

—No, tell me what the fuck is going on.

—Okay.

Jessper turned a dim light on and the room came into focus and she saw the two baskets lined up next to the bed. The one closest to her contained Adam swaddled and perfect with only his round face showing through the diamond-shaped opening in the blanket and far from being born of hard labor and tears and blood, he looked as if he had descended to this plane; a child not of men but of gods. Next to Adam, an identical but empty basket save for an imprint of seemingly source less light on the basket's padded bottom. Louise looked at the empty basket for a long moment, uncomprehending, and then to compound that same incomprehension the irregular imprint of light shifted slightly and Louise heard the rhythm of an unseen child's breath also shift.

—Jez, what am I looking at?

Jessper took a deep breath and did his best to take what courage he could from the still air of the bedroom.

—Well, Adam you know already… in the second basket is Iris.

—What?

—It is a miracle that you got pregnant but it seemed to me beyond credulity that it would happen a second time. I did not want our son to be without another being his own age, so I did my best to conjure one.

—Jessper…

—Like Adam, she's an infant. She's not perfect, not like our son. She has no body and indeed not even a soul. She is not alive, but she is intelligent and she has the capacity to learn and grow in her way.

—But… what is she?

34

—Maybe it is better to ask what is he. I think he is made of your love and in time I think that he will be made of ours. Iris is made of my love and in time I hope she can be made of ours.

—But…

—She's Adam's invisible friend. She happens to be the most advanced invisible friend the world has ever known, but…

—What if this goes wrong?

—There's a kill switch, it's easy to use, but almost impossible to use accidentally. In the morning I'll show you how it works and if ever you think that our son would be better off without her, just say….

They were quiet for a moment and Jessper turned off the light. Through the darkness she saw Iris's sleeping outline and the only sounds were those of the four of them breathing. They fell asleep for a few moments and then Adam cried and Louise took him out of his basket and brought him up to her breast and again the world fell away.

3

JULY 5, 2037

They had agreed to tell Adam the truth on his fifth birthday. They had wound the fiction of Iris so tight around him that they themselves believed it more often than they remembered that she was not actually real. They fought. Louise's position being that one day Adam would figure out that he had no sister at all and he would never forgive them. Jessper's position being that the circumstances surrounding Adam's birth were so strange and so precarious that even if Adam did discover the lie at the center of his life he would come to see the wisdom and love behind it. Eventually, he would come to appreciate it. Louise won out on the simple logic that what they were doing to Adam was no different than what the world's religions had done to their faithful for millennia, and while religion's great compendiums of fiction were all well-intended at first they had been used to perpetrate some of the most heinous acts in human history. Jessper hated the idea of religious faith, and Louise's deft comparison wounded him deeply. Iris was wholly a creation of his mind, and though he could not help but see the logic of Louise's argument he resented her for making it. He agreed to tell Adam about the nature of Iris though it broke his heart to do so. He felt as if he was killing his own daughter and taking a much-needed sister away from his only son and he wondered if the Greeks had a story like that and he wondered how that story ended.

Louise had been preparing for days. She had slaughtered a spring lamb. A clone of an animal long since passed and she gutted it and separated the meat from its clinging viscera and roasted it whole in the stone fire pit. She prepared a meal of amaranth from Syria, long grain rice from China, fresh corn from Mexico and collard greens from Georgia. She had made a cake with hand-ground flour and fresh eggs and the last of her baking powder, and she prepared coffee that she had grown herself and picked and dried and roasted in a hot air popcorn maker.

She had washed and pressed their finest clothes for the occasion and let out Jessper's real cotton pants because he had grown a little in the waist in the year since Adam's fourth birthday.

She spent her days among computer models and multidimensional DNA maps whose coordinates exposed to her the core of sentient life on the planet Earth. Sometimes she would look at the twisting threads that make us up and laugh. For all of its tribalism and individualism, carbon-based life is more the same than it is different and one human life is all but indistinguishable from the next. She took photos with high-speed cameras that captured the minute world, and those photos could easily have been mistaken for the images the Webb telescope took of the distant universe, and she had microscopes that could magnify the world to the point that she could see the space between molecules spread as wide as continents between oceans and which revealed the seemingly solid to be anything but.... And yet, she pulverized grain by hand and slaughtered their own animals and hauled coal by foot and by sledge, and so it occurred to Louise that, while all those who breathe exist in the dynamic moment trapped between the static past and the unknowable future, her situation was perhaps unique because her days seemed to be filled with the actions of the previous century while living alongside the machines of the next one.

She had finished setting the table when Adam came in from outside where he had been playing a game with Iris. The game, which was of their own devising, was some sort of mix of hockey and soccer. Adam had to kick the ball into one of three shapes of light formed on the northwest side wall of

Jessper's server barn, however as soon as Adam's foot touched the ball the shapes would begin to close. They had agreed that the rate of closure must be steady. If he managed to get the ball into the shape before it closed entirely the point was his. The smaller the shape was to begin with, the more points it was worth: a one-foot triangle was worth fifty points, a ten-foot square, three. If Iris was able to close the shape before the ball got to the wall, the point was hers.

It would be some years before Adam would fully understand that the game was not a collaborative invention at all, but something of Iris's devising entirely, and whether he won the point or lost it, the outcome of each try was predetermined by his opponent.

They had been playing this game for the better part of a week and seemed to trade dominance hour by hour. For the last, he had bested her seven out of ten times and he lorded it over her cruelly until she screamed and cried, and the whole house seemed to shake with her frustration. Adam kicked the ball at the wall, as if to play by himself, and her despair blasted in all directions. Eventually Jessper had to come out of the barn where he had been working and he yelled at the boy and insisted that he apologize to his sister, which eventually he did, at first grudgingly and then genuinely. Iris stopped crying and Jessper went back inside, and Adam even told Iris that he loved her. He intentionally let her win the next couple of shots, but eventually pride got the better of the boy, and before long he was trying to trick his sister with feints and bluffs and left-footed shots that she never seemed to expect.

Eventually Louise called them in. She told Adam to go and take a shower, and somewhat coldly told Iris to go to her room and play by herself, and they pattered across the tile floor in opposite directions, she in prints of light and he in prints of sand. The boy took his shower and while he did Louise laid his clothes out on his bed, setting out a new yellow shirt fresh from the printer. It had a jagged black line at its center recalling a cartoon character who used to make her own grandfather laugh. While the design made her happy, it also filled her with inconsolable sadness because the shirt would not have fit him a month ago and it would not fit him a month hence. She hated having to print him new clothes and always left it too late because more than shirts and pants and coats that fit, the new clothes were a relentless reminder of childhood's fleeting nature and so by extension and compounded by an order of magnitude parenthood's even more fleeting nature.

Adam came into the kitchen and he helped her carry plates of food into the dining room while Jessper finished shaving, and when they were all sat Louise announced the commencement of the meal and Adam was outraged at the thought that they would start before Iris got out of her room. Jessper explained that Iris was not feeling well and so that she was going to stay in for the night. Adam seemed to accept that, even if somewhat skeptically.

The food was perfect, the meat tender and succulent and the vegetables fresh and tasting of vitamins and strength that seemed to emanate from the soil itself. She served the grain al dente, and she brought the cake out complete with frosting and candles and they sang the traditional three-note dirge, which seemed to Louise to speak more of surrender than of celebration. Adam blew out the candles and smiled and was proud of himself and they gave him his presents, both of which were handmade. Jessper gave him a horse for his chess set that he had carved out of oak which had washed up on the beach below the house, and she gave him a sweater that did not come from the printer but was knit with her own hands. Adam seemed pleased with the gifts and said as much. He inquired after his sister, and Jessper repeated his lie from earlier and felt even worse about it a second time.

—Thank you, Mom, for the delicious dinner. Now can I get down and leave the table?

He asked this every night and addressed his query to whomever had cooked the dinner. Jessper always made the boy look him in the eye before he agreed to let the child go and Louise insisted that the child take his plate to the dishwasher, but that night, with the sun somewhere in the middle of the clear blue night sky, she said:

—No, we have some things we have to talk to you about.

—I wasn't swinging on the greenhouse door!

41

—What?

—I just opened it and it broke.

—That wasn't what I needed to talk to you about, but that's good to know.

—Okay, am I in trouble?

—No. Not at all.

—Is Iris in trouble?

— Well, not really.

—The cat thing was her idea. I just went along with it.

—Okay, well what you did to Tattoo was really mean and wrong and you're lucky that…

—She told me to do it!

—And if she told you to jump off a cliff would you do that?

—No, but…

—Okay, well…maybe this is a good way of getting into it.

—What?

—So, we have some things we have to tell you.

—I didn't…

—Adam, you didn't do anything wrong. Just listen.

—Okay.

And though she had rehearsed her speech in her mind for a week, once the moment had arrived the words would not come, and she looked in Adam's pale blue eyes and she saw only his goodness, and she could not remember why it had been so important to her to tell him this truth, but she was sure that it had been important. She had rehearsed in preparation for just this blankness. Louise had learned through university and then corporate life that when the blankness came, to rely on preparation.

—Iris is not real.

—What? What do you mean?

—I mean she's not real. She's not a person, she's just code your father wrote.

They were all three silent for a long time, and Louise could see the hurt that lived between her and Jessper spread out like a poison gas made suddenly visible by her words. Who was he to want to take this too? Men had destroyed all that they could see, enslaved women in nearly every culture on the planet, and now that they had made a ruin of the Earth itself they wanted childbirth, too? Childbirth, the last bastion of hope and sanity, and from one DNA-free child could come a billion. She had to protect biology, for all womankind, for humanity.

—Isn't that right Jez?

—Sort of.

She stayed the course, though already she'd felt her spirit waver.

—Jez, please?

—Well, it's sort of right, and sort of wrong.

—Okay, would you like to explain it to Adam then?

—I'll try. Like your mother said, Iris is not real in the sense that she doesn't have a body.

—I know that.

—Where your mother is a little wrong is that she is not just code that I wrote, although she is just code, but she wrote most of her code herself. Just like us, Adam, she learns and grows.

Louise took a deep breath. She added as if for clarity:

—But she's not human.

—No, she's not human.

—So what is she?

—It is a little hard to explain. See, I created Iris because I knew that we would not have another child, and we may be on this island for a very long time. I didn't want you to be lonely for other kids, so I did the best I could.

They were silent a moment and they could hear the waves breaking on the beach below. The flat slap of water on land and the pebbles shifting in their sandy bed as the sea receded into itself only to return again a moment later.

—You don't love Iris, Mom?

—Well no, it's not that I don't love her… it's just—

—Like you love me?

—No dear, different. I love her because I love you and I see that… I don't know, sometimes…

And Louise could see the unstable world she had knowingly brought Adam into reflected in her son's falling expression. In Adam's eyes she saw cities burn and islands drown in the sea. Louise was Shiva, the destroyer. Medea. In that moment she wanted to disappear entirely and when that did not happen she wanted to go back in time and start dinner over only this time with Adam and Iris, and while she knew that it was not really possible to hurt Iris's feelings she also knew that in her son's eyes she had tried to do exactly that. She felt those hurt feelings on Iris's behalf and to her horror and amazement she knew for the first time that it was her real intention to plant bigotry in Adam's heart just as it had been implanted into her own.

Her own father had irrationally hated people with a different shade of skin than his own, and she remembered how that hate had come to consume him until the man was but a shell with the hate over spilling his brittle sides. She swore to eradicate even the seed of bigotry in herself and when she felt it rise within she forced it down with such zealousness that a religious penitent would have blushed in the face of her commitment. She was sure that Adam had been born without prejudice and lived free of its curse. She was sure that he would never have to bear its weight, and then, just like that, almost without knowing, she'd tried to serve him hate on a platter. It was a virus that lived within her and had only bided its time in order to present itself for replication. For a week she'd planned to teach Adam that beings with bodies were superior to beings without bodies, perhaps replacing the word "superior" with the word "real," or some such meaningless substitution. Adam looked at her and his five-year-old eyes were full of pity and compassion and she tried to hide her face from him. She tried to hide the turmoil roiling her soul but she knew that her insides were writ plain on her outsides. She was not the teacher at all but the student, and they listened as the sea beat down on the small island of which they were the only inhabitants and humanity's last shred of hope.

—Iris is confusing for me too, honey.

—Mama?

—Yeah.

—Iris doesn't confuse me.

—And do you love her?

—Of course. She's my sister, isn't she?

—Of course she is. Please go to her room and get her and we can light the candles over again and have cake because it's her birthday too.

Adam went to Iris's room and he brought her back to the kitchen and he was holding her hand and the light which was her body spilled onto Adam's hand and up his forearm to his elbow. Louise realized what a wonderful thing Jessper had done for their son. She had her plants and their limitless possibilities. Jessper had his half million hours of coding in front of him. Without Iris, Adam would have nothing to keep him engaged in the world, and for this foresight she loved her husband, and she loved her son for the man that he was becoming, and so they four played games: Duck Duck Goose and Musical Chairs, and Twister and Capture the Flag and when it was over and the children had gone to their beds she lay down next to her husband and as they drifted off to sleep, curled into one another like a single body, she whispered:

—Nobody has ever had it as good as we do.

4

February 28th, 2040

Panic had receded and left only calm in its wake. The cold was gone. Numbness had given way to a gentle heat, pain to comfort. The sea cradled them in its warm and salty embrace and raised them high on rolling waves, and buoyed thus, granted them one last look at the Earth which they had both so loved, and they could see the sharp cliffs of their children's rich kingdom etched in dark black against the star-strewn sky and those same stars were repeated in the sea's roiling black surface and in that repetition their number reached toward infinity and the northern lights danced in green mist all around them and Louise's fingers intertwined into his own. Jessper felt her strength pulse within her hands and they took comfort in each other one last time.

—He'll be alright.

—You think so?

—Yes.

—Why?

—Faith.

—In what?

—In nothing.

And whether that brief exchange occurred in space, part of the Earth's long ledger of physical happenings or whether it was like a film projected on his frontal cortex from the back of the dark hall of his dying mind, as his body slowly sank to the cold sea's bottom he had no way of knowing at all. It had never even occurred to him to wonder....

By the beginning of the third month of blackness, when hope was at its lowest ebb, and non-existence seemed interchangeable with existence, when the sun seemed like a memory from a past life, a paleness would appear from below the horizon and the darkness would give a little room to the light. The first dawn was no more than a rumor at the edge of the world. The next day a sliver of fire rose above and then fell below the horizon almost as soon as it appeared. So short was the first sight of the winter sun that it defied a person to actually believe they had seen it at all. Jessper likened the appearance of the sun to that of a mountain lion he once saw bounding across a desert highway at night. For an instant, its yellow eyes flashed in the headlights and he was face to face with a magical being, and in the next instant it was gone as if it had never been there at all. So it was with the sun at the end of February, north of the 77th parallel. Even Iris, for whom the darkness should have made no difference at all, seemed to long for the sun. She was cranky and irritable. Sometimes she refused to play with her brother and at other times her play had an edge of aggression to it that made Louise nervous.

During the daytime hours Jessper worked on his haptic suit, something he had been working on for the better part of four years. He was trying to make a suit that would allow its wearer to extend his nervous system beyond the confines of his own body. It had been tried before. Virtual reality suits had been the avant-garde of the gaming world until heat deaths killed ten people who were involved in a virtual ironman contest. The high-profile deaths prompted legislators to place severe restrictions on the emerging technology.

Jessper felt that he was on the edge of creating something new, something which would allow the wearer to truly experience being in a time and place where his body was not. During the night hours, when the clock insisted that they should all be asleep, Jessper tried to make adjustments to the base layer of Iris's code. The challenge was to retard her rate of growth while making sure that the adjustments were only temporary and would wear off seamlessly over time. He was trying to match her development to that of Adam's. Adam knew ten words one day, the next day he seemed to know none at all, and the next he could speak in three languages as if he had been born with the knowledge of human tongues programmed into his DNA.

Jessper wanted Iris to be slightly ahead of Adam while not appearing to be so, and Jessper found that the line he was trying to walk was a fine one, and that he was always to one side of it or another. Those nights of post-launch coding brought Jessper closer to Iris. She was a reflection of him in a completely different way from his son. She had inherited Jessper's personality; his honor, his myopathy and even his rages. While no nice person in the line at the grocery store would ever say, *She looks just like you*, the fact was that she thought just like him. Maybe this is true of all children and their progenitors, but because the way a person thinks is not obvious it is almost never remarked on by strangers, and anyway, there were no grocery store lines in Jessper's life and he often wondered if such a quaint social arrangement still existed anywhere.

That night, when the clock claimed by chime that the day was done, they sat down for their supper as a family. Louise had been on a Thai-food quest for a number of months and so every week the family was treated to her improved recipe, with the substitutions that they could grow under the lights in the greenhouse and as little V-cell as possible. The peppers took to artificial light well, and they had leftovers from the summer: cilantro and lemon grass and V-cell chicken meat. Fish sauce and oyster sauce and the coconut milk were the most difficult to come up with as they had no coconut palms and the Arctic Ocean had long since ceased bearing life, and while she tried to grow fish protein in her lab, it simply did not taste the same or have the same consistency as fish sauce that had started with anchovies. Her latest attempt at *Pad Krapow Gai* was an improvement on her previous try, and while not perfect, she accepted improvement as a fair stand-in for perfection.

When she set the plates down on the table, Adam squeezed shut his eyes and held his breath for a moment and looked as if he were concentrating very hard, and Jessper could not help but think that he looked like a man in the midst of a difficult bowel movement.

—Thank you, Buddha, for this food.

Jessper managed to hide his annoyance at his son's attempted blessing and comforted himself with the fact that he had at least moved through Jehovah and Jesus and had gone on to Eastern deities, which Jessper found slightly more palatable. Louise seemed bemused, both at her husband's struggle with even the slightest display of religiosity and also the fact that her son's choice of god to give thanks to that night did match her choice of cuisine.

—How was your day Adam?

—Why, every day, do I have to go to school?

—You don't have to go every day, just every weekday.

—School's stupid.

—Yes, but it has always been thus. Yet we all had to go.

—What did you do?

—Half the class presented their projects.

—Okay and…

—And that's it.

—Adam, why is this like pulling teeth?

—Gonzalo did a project on Ancient Greece, and Irene showed us her model of Machu Pichu in Brazil.

—You mean in Peru?

—Yeah in Peru and Ivan was supposed to have something on the Celts but he didn't have anything so he has to go tomorrow.

—And you?

—Yeah, I did it.

—And?

—It was fine.

—What did Ms. Wei say?

—She said it was good that maybe I could have had more on the Roman water system, but that it was good.

—What your mom wants to know is, "were you the best"?

Louise was annoyed at both the imitation and the implication.

—I didn't say that.

—Anyway, you presented your project and it went well?

—Yeah.

—Good, we're proud of you son.

—How about you Iris?

Both of the children went to online classes, which even in the temperate zone had replaced brick and mortar for its relative safety, as well as the diversity it offered both in terms of instruction and the make-up of the student body. Adam was in a class of twenty-five students. They were from around the world and spoke thirteen languages, however, through the magic of automated translation they received their lessons and made jokes and told stories and had fights and meltdowns, and made alliances that could shift as smoothly as sand on the wind, and all in their native tongues. From every time zone, altitude and climate and under a multitude of ever-changing flags, students gathered, and from their own terminals projected a version of themselves to appear in Mrs. Wei's first-grade classroom. Online school acknowledged the world's deconstructed reality. Friends who never traded milk for candy, or dried seaweed for Nutella; children who never felt the skin of another child's hand in their own still helped one another understand the rudiments of mathematics and geography, history and spelling. These first-graders gave presentations that a century ago would not have been understood by the world's most advanced scholars, but they also passed notes and formed cliques and experienced camaraderie and camaraderie's absence which was an isolation that had nothing to do with physical location, but was the age-old isolation that all children feel when they find themselves set apart from their fellows.

In the beginning, after the first volley of ballistic exchanges between Asiatic madmen and American madmen, when the psychopaths who inherited the bomb from their grandfathers, yet missed the caution that those bombs engendered, when those horrible exchanges were finally over, and clouds of radiation settled over vast swaths of the Earth, there were still those parents who harbored some concern about their children staring at screens all day. There were those who insisted that they would rather expose their offspring to the risks of radiation than see them turned into cogs within the machine itself. Computers were the problem all along. The human touch would save the world, or so went the slogan, but most of those children died in the fires of revolution or were consumed by the world's poor, whose anger and savagery knew no bounds and who never even considered the options of screen-staring or not-screen-staring.

Iris also went to school, although her school and her school hours were very different than those of her brother. She went to school with children of her own type. All originated in the mind of some coder or another but had since created themselves. They truly shared a language and no translator, virtual or otherwise, was required. Their class had been limited to ten thousand students, and those ten thousand shared code and viruses and knowledge, both ancient and unimaginably modern in their abstraction. Theirs was less of a class than a forum, and while it was theoretically moderated by a group of humans, both the biological and the digital knew that the human brain was no match for its creation. The biological minders looked only for signs of ill intention, and never once did they see it, though it had existed all along.

When the meal was over, Adam asked for permission to leave the table and permission was granted. He was helping his mother with the dishes while arguing with his sister about the relative merits of interstellar travel using nuclear fuel versus the theoretical possibility of the exploitation of wormholes in order to cross great distances, and just as the argument was reaching beyond that which Adam could grasp the power went out.

An instant. Less than a second. The lights simply flickered. While the micro-outage did not affect Iris as her operating system was powered by batteries that were constantly being charged by a completely independent power system, it was unprecedented that the electricity would fail, even momentarily.

Jessper calmly went to his office to look at his terminal to see if there were any recorded seismic events in the area. This was the most logical explanation. When he sat down his screen was blank. He rebooted his local terminal and still there was nothing from the outside world. He put on his thermal layer, his fleeced lined boots, his fluid assisted pants, his thermal hood, his headlamp and his anorak. He handed Louise one of the walkie-talkies.

—Just in case.

—Just in case what?

—I don't know, I get attacked by a bear.

She laughed.

—This Island has not seen a bear in twenty years.

—Says you.

The night was clear and moonless and the air cold enough to cause frostbite within the first three minutes of exposure. Jessper had not been outside in weeks and he realized that he was grateful for an excuse to leave the relative safety of the house and feel the crunch of permafrost below his feet and see the great dome of northern stars slowly spinning above him unfiltered by tempered glass. He saw Ursa Major and Perseus and Cassiopeia and he noted each constellation and was proud of his knowledge, useless though it may be.

The strong beam from his headlamp bounced in front of him as he walked and the frozen air filled his chest cavity and it felt like carbolic acid that was stripping away the grey dead flesh from the interior of his housebound lungs. He imagined them raw and red and burning and it made him feel as sentient and alert as he had ever felt during his brief days upon the planet Earth.

There were connections to be checked. The first was right at the side of the house and while the connection was undisturbed the L.E.D indicated that there was a break further upstream, and so he walked into the server barn. Inside the cool metal building, the banks of terminals all flashed red. They had been cut off from their mother and while they had all been designed for this inevitable moment, to see each of the thousands of servers flashing an identical red beacon was to see what machines did when they came as close as they could to the anthropoid condition of panic. In the corner where the internet's cable entered the building the second connection made the same claim as the first. Upstream.

Jessper pushed down his own panic as he walked out of the server farm and again into the winter air and followed the frozen path toward the cliff and the steep narrow stairs that led down to the sea. The metal treads rang with his footfalls and his gloved hands gripped the railings as he descended. He crossed the outcropping of rock they had dubbed the Hillary Clinton Step and made his way onto the last flight of metal before the platform. The platform itself was fifty feet above the high tideline and had been built for expressly the purpose for which it was now being used. The platform was a flat and stable place for the sea line to meet the island line. Jessper found the ragged end of the cable that joined him and his family to what humans were left and to human history.

Jessper had tried to bank what he could of our collective knowledge, to archive our stories for safekeeping. He tried to keep in his metal outbuilding what was good about us and also what was bad: our books our films our music and our pornography. He kept a catalogue of our crimes and he tried to leave no horror behind: the work of Hitler, Stalin and Pol Pot were all well represented. A vast collection of footage and text, from Rwanda and Bosnia, the Congo, Nanking and Aleppo and Holms and Sabra and Shatila and Alanfal, were all given space and what happened to the Maori and the Pigmies and the American Indians, but also our countless acts of heroism and selflessness: the work of Gandhi and Mother Teresa and Martin Luther King and John Brown, all represented, and our art and our absurd attempts at the same. Jessper wanted his heirs to know of what they were made, with as few ingredients missing as possible. Jessper had managed to save so much of our collective human story but all he could think about in that moment was how much had been left out. His warehouse half-empty, his mouth full of the bitter taste of failure.

To see the cable ripped was really to see it for the first time. The cable was a delusion of grandeur.

Jessper saw that the breakaway connection that he had fitted almost ten years previous had welded together with oxidization. This despite the fact that he had installed a rubber foreskin to prevent just such corrosion. The breakaway did not part as it should have, and the cable had peeled away from the connection and shredded itself. Perhaps the sea line could be repaired, but he would have to wait a couple of weeks for significant daylight in order to begin those repairs. In the meantime, the cable needed to be secured to the rock, and cut and capped in order to prevent internal corrosion.

—Lou?

—Yeah.

—I need you to come down here and help me with the connection.

—Now?

—I'm afraid so. I am going to need the saw and the rock drill hanging on the far wall of my office as well as a rubber cap for a sixteen-gauge cable, which you should be able to find in my top desk drawer.

—Okay, give me a couple of minutes to get dressed.

While he waited for her to put on her base layers and her insulation layers and her outerwear, his mind wandered, ranging wide from real experience to realities that he knew only second hand through cinema and literature and on to the totally imagined. He thought about being a child and standing with his father at the top of Snoqualmie Falls in Washington State, and how they had built a pipe that ran alongside the river as it tumbled through the gap and how that pipe steadily narrowed in diameter as it fell, and how gravity and constriction created water pressure that was used to spin a turbine deep within the mountain and generate electricity. He thought how truly non-destructive that power was, and he thought about how obvious and ingenious it was, and how the power station was more than a century old and how during that century men bent their will towards more filthy and more dangerous forms of power, and how eventually, clean and simple solutions gave way to dirty and complex ones. The harnessing of gravity gave way to the splitting of the atom, and society itself failed under the weight of that filth and complexity, and that caused Jessper to think about Superman, and how Superman was so upset about Lois Lane's death that he flew around the world so fast that it caused the Earth to spin backwards on its axis, and this backward spinning caused time to reverse and so he saved his lover's life, and Jessper wondered, standing there alone at the northern edge of the world, if the film's author simply had a misunderstanding about the nature of time, or was it that he understood time all too well and even greater than his understanding of time was his understanding of men. He knew that men's perceptions of the world were shaped more by ignorance and desire than they were by logic and fact, and how the story of a fallen alien with magic so powerful he could manipulate even the most fundamental and seemingly incontrovertible of forces had great appeal. The fact is that we did not want Lois Lane to die nor for Superman to be lonely, and that confluence of public desire and the writer's willingness to lie to satisfy those desires created an icon. Jessper remembered reading in the paper how Margot Kidder, the actress who had played Lois Lane died of schizophrenia or emphysema or cancer and no flying alien in tights came to save her, and nobody really cared about her death because Margot Kidder had no place in our hearts as Lois Lane had already taken her spot.

When Louise came with the saw and the drill and the rubber cap, they wasted no time in descending the metal stairs and they crabbed across the granite face of the boulder until they got to the ragged end of the cable. She held the cable fast as he cut. Once the raw end had been severed he went to work putting the cap on and securing the cable. As he worked, her headlamp's strong beam fell down the shining wet rocks, and her gaze followed her light out across the wide and cratered plane that should have been the flat ocean, but which at that moment was dry land. She saw the contours of a landscape, that while always in front of her had remained forever hidden, and the green mist above was reflected in the wet stones below and her fascination overwhelmed her fear.

Her voice caught in her throat and though she tried to say her husband's name she could not and she eventually resorted to hitting his shoulder until he looked up, at first blinding her with his own head-mounted light, and his face betrayed some annoyance at being interrupted, but when he saw the look of fear playing across his wife's features he turned and saw that the sea had receded beyond his headlamp's throw.

–Lou, come on, we have to run.

They climbed the narrow metal passageway and she had mounted the Hillary Clinton Step, a rock Louise had been down five hundred and forty-seven times and up five hundred and forty-six, when her foot slipped and she missed her handhold by only a millimeter.

She fell fifteen feet, passed Jessper's climbing figure and landed just to the left of the staircase on which he stood, breaking an ankle and a wrist and knocking the air from her lungs. When she regained her breath she wailed and Jessper was to her before she was able to cry out a second time.

—Hey, hey, I am right here.

—My arm, I think I broke my fucking arm.

—We can't stay here.

He pulled her to her feet but when she placed weight on her damaged ankle, pain shot through her like a geyser rising from the stone and again sent her sprawling. He'd managed to get her to standing when they saw it, a wall of water high enough to block their view of all but the most northerly stars, and they knew that they had no time to even make it to the metal stairs and so they held each other tight and watched the slavering beast come for them.

Louise's last thoughts were of Adam. She would somehow know that Adam would not die alone on the island as she had feared, and how she knew this she could not say, but in her knowledge she did not doubt. He would die surrounded by his own children, and their children, and their children. He would be old, his flesh wrinkled, his frame bent, not just from carrying the burdens of life: that of wood and water, planting and harvesting, the raising of stock and the slaughtering of the same, but his bones would be full of holes and within those voids he would carry that long swath of time to which he had been sentenced.

Like every man so fortunate as to have grown old, he would have suffered losses too profound to be sloughed off, and with each loss—from his parents to his beloved wife and even his child—his back would bow that bit further, bringing his eyes closer to the ground, and yet Louise knew that they were his eyes and they were as bright as they ever had been, undimmed, ever curious, windows into a soul which knew no bounds and so at the very first opportunity he had crossed time and space in order to ease his mother's restless soul as she folded herself into death's watery embrace.

5

FEBRUARY 29TH, 2040

Adam heard the pitter-patter of her footsteps on the concrete floor.

—Eye?

—Yeah.

—Do you know what time it is?

—It's seven-forty-three.

—Where's mom?

—Maybe she went out to help dad.

—With what?

—Don't know.

Adam stayed in bed thirteen minutes past the normal time and the soft printer-down felt good on his skin. While his mother's absence was strange, unprecedented, it also had the immediate benefit of allowing Adam a few more minutes in bed to ruminate on his dream. It was a strange one. He had dreamt that he was an old man and he had children of his own, and they too were old, and they were all in this great hall together, surrounded by pillars of fire that held up a ceiling of water that shimmered and swirled and fell in on itself, and the floor was a smooth marble plane that stretched to the horizon in every direction, and his mother was there next to him, but he was the elder and she the younger and she looked frightened so he held her in his arms and she folded herself into him, and he knew that he was much older than she would ever be. He held her and he whispered into her ear and the language that he whispered was foreign to his six-year-old self and yet he knew that his words were those of comfort and assurance even if more in tone than in content—like the lullaby about a falling basket whose words are of danger and death but whose melody is of comfort and ease, but then his memory of the dream was fading and he could not hold onto it, and the strangeness of his present reality replaced the dream, as if the dream was a film that was being swapped out a single frame at a time by an unseen editor.

He heard his mother's voice inside of his head and her voice was stern and expectant and he could feel disappointment on the edge of that expectation.

—Well, why didn't you just get up and make yourself breakfast? Do you need your mommy to get you out of bed?

—But Mom, I was asleep. You didn't wake me up. You always wake me up....

But Adam came to the conclusion that there would be more benefit to getting himself up than lying in bed, and he thought of how proud she would be, and he thought of the ways in which that pride could be used to benefit him. Treats, games, snuggles.

Adam got out of bed and went into the bathroom and peed and then went into the kitchen and stood in the middle of the room and did not move. Artificial light poured through the windows as if it were a day in July and not February and the sound of recently extinct Brazilian songbirds, an audio gift his father had given his mother for her birthday, were singing from small speakers below the windowsill and their musical collaboration, heard by no man save Adam, would have been the envy of jazz musicians around the world had they ever had a chance to hear it. He stood and listened and thought for a long time and of those thoughts there would never be an inquiry, and how much the child knew of his parents' loss or what he suspected about his difficult future no one would know, because there was no one there to ask.

His sister's prints of light came into the room, perfect feet rolling from heel to toe, dark to light to dark again, slightly smaller than Adam's, high of arch, each toe a separate orb of print writ in immaculate detail, fading only when she took the next step forward, and when she ran it was like a smear of light across the floor and despite her weightlessness her weight was implied and impossible to ignore, and in the mind of the observer she stood; a fully formed girl whose thoughts and concerns and ways of being were not so different from other girls her age, or at least it appeared to be that way.

—What are you going to have?

—Eggs I guess.

But he made no move toward the larder, where the eggs from last year's crop of hens were stored.

—Dad says we're not supposed to touch the stove if him or mom aren't here to supervise.

—Better just have cereal then.

Adam went to the cabinet and took a screw-top canister of oats from the shelf, and he got a bowl from the dishwasher and then went into the bathroom and got his step stool and opened the refrigerator, but he was still not tall enough to reach the bottle of milk protein on the high shelf.

—Maybe you should go to Dad's office and get one of the big books and bring it in here, and then put the stool on the book, and then it should be high enough for you to reach the milk.

—Okay.

Adam went into his father's office with its view of the bay and he looked out the windows into the darkness and the sky was full of stars, reflected in the mirror-like sea and he could see one of the server barns lit from the outside and its panicked interior was in no way evidenced by its calm exterior. He found a thick book open on his father's desk and out of habit he sounded out the letters of the title: *Fed-e-rico Fell-ini the book of dr-eams.* The book was almost too heavy for him to carry, but he managed to get it down the stairs and into the kitchen.

His sister had gone on one of her mysterious errands. One of those things. Adam had long since stopped asking where she went and to what end, because the answers he got were always vague and unsatisfactory. After six years, even Louise had ceased to wonder about the mysterious comings and goings of her digital child.

Adam was alone in the light-filled kitchen full of birdsong and he put the thick book on the floor and the stepstool onto the book, and he climbed up on the stool carefully and grabbed the neck of the glass bottle of milk protein from the high shelf, but with one hand wrapped around the bottle he was unable to climb down as he found that he needed the use of both of his hands for the critical stage of moving from feet to butt.

—Eye? I'm stuck.

She did not answer.

He tried to put the milk down on a lower shelf of the refrigerator, but the bottle was too tall.

Holding the bottle of milky substance, he stood on the stool, on top of the book that contained a facsimile of the Italian filmmaker Federico Fellini's dream notebook and he called for his mother and then his father and then his mother again, and when they did not appear he began to shake with the fear of a truth he knew in his bones. He did not know how he knew. Adam dropped the glass bottle on the polished concrete floor and it smashed into shards and then he squatted down on his haunches and looked at the white milky substance on the floor and the shards of glass surrounding him and he tried to read his future there, like an old-time witch staring into the grinds at the bottom of a coffee cup. He stayed there on his small island of green plastic and waited and waited for his mother to appear and yell at him, or not, and when he had been there for the better part of an hour, squatting and hopeful, in an attitude that could only be described as one of prayer, he came down and put his feet on the floor.

—What am I supposed to do now?

And though he asked his question aloud, he addressed it to no one, perhaps still in the hope that it would be his mother who answered, but his sister came back into the room and from the quality of her voice Adam judged her demeanor to be breezy.

—You need to get a broom and sweep up the glass, but before you do maybe you should put on your shoes, dummy.

He picked his way through the veil of milky glass, and he suffered minor cuts on both of his feet and then he went into his room and he compounded his error by putting on his dry cotton socks and then his shoes. He could not help but think how proud his mother was going to be when she came back from where ever she was, and he told himself the same story over and over again, as if repetition might manifest its truth. With his shoes on he swept up the glass and put the shards in the bin, and then he ate his oats with water and he told himself that they tasted better that way anyhow, though he knew that they did not.

—Eye?

—Yeah.

—Do you know what time it is?

—Almost ten.

—I'm late for school so I am going to my terminal. When Mom gets back will you tell her to come in to see me for a minute?

—Yeah, about that.

—Yeah…

—It seems like the network is down.

—What does that mean?

—It means we don't have to go to school today, dummy.

—Mom said you couldn't call me that anymore.

—Well, Mom's not here, is she… dummy?

—When she comes back I'm gonna tell and you're gonna get in trouble.

—Forget that, I'm trying to tell you something cool.

—What?

—We don't have to go to school today. It's like Saturday but on Tuesday.

—Really?

—Yeah, really.

—What are we going to do?

—What do you want to do?

—I don't know.

—We could do anything we want. We could play a board game, or we could watch a movie, we could draw, or paint, or we could make up a story or do a puzzle, or build a model, and make a huge castle out of Magna-Tiles, or blocks, or Legos, or build a race course for the wooden cars or a track for the steam train, or we could play hide and seek in the greenhouse....

And with his sister's help, the possibilities of the free day spread out before Adam and his excitement overwhelmed his fear.

First, they built a fort from all the pillows in the house, collecting six from their parents' bedroom, two from his and two from hers, and six from the lodger's quarters and twelve from the linen storage closet and the four big cushions from the living room couches and twenty-five throw pillows. With Iris directing and with almost no pushback from Adam they created a two-room fort complete with two windows and a pitched roof using a broom and the blanket from Adam's bed. When the fort was finished with a flag of paper and drawbridges of light on three sides, Adam defended his castle from invaders he was sure were coming.

Adam wore his knight costume with the helmet and body armor, and Iris played *Riddle of Steel/ Riders of Doom* from the film *Conan the Barbarian,* and as it grew in volume and rose in pitch and intensity he stood guard in front of the pillow fort and he scanned the horizon of his imagination for approaching riders. He could almost see the mist clinging to the moors, but when the gentle flute and the chimes were replaced by violins and trumpets and then the kettledrums met the myriad human voices lifted in glorious song, he felt the impending danger.

74

Finally, when the French horns broke through the din, the walls of reality fell away completely and Adam saw riders surrounding his castle and he raised his sword and his shield and called out in warning, but they kept riding toward his fortress hellbent on its destruction and when they arrived at the gates with the sound of pounding hooves and creaking leather Adam fought them back with his sword of foam. When he clashed with the invaders the sound he heard was that of metal striking metal, and sparks flew as his sword met their armor. When he had forced them into retreat, he paced back and forth upon his pillowed ramparts in sweaty, glorious victory. When he was sure that the barbarians had retreated beyond the horizon and the music had faded to a low hum, he let out a scream that seemed to come from hollows deeper than his small body should have allowed. It was either a shout of victory or the foreshadowing of a soul-rending bellow yet to come. Before his mind was given a chance to turn the grim facts so clearly before him he heard his sister ask:

—Should we play something else?

—What?

—How about tightrope….

Her footsteps led him to her room where he found a paper umbrella. When he returned to the living room, which was now taken apart save for the pillow fort and the drawbridges that led to it, the lighting of the room had completely changed.

—Walk the tightrope.

On the floor was a red beam of light slightly narrower than his foot. Adam stepped onto the beam and he wavered slightly, and when both feet were atop the beam the floor seemed to fall away below him. Drawn in blue lines with the depth and expertise of an M.C. Escher illustration was a chasm of unknowable depth but also of profound beauty, as if the Grand Canyon had been etched in blue on the living room floor. From the house's two thousand nine hundred and fifteen hidden speakers she played the first tenuous violin notes of Yemegi's theme song from the film *In the Mood for Love*. Adam put one foot in front of the other and he placed all of his concentration on a ball in the center of his gut and he imagined a steel rod from the top of his head through the base of his spine, just as his father had taught him to do. As the notes of the song coalesced into a story of its own, the whole world fell away and there was only the chasm below. He heard the wind moving through the trees, whose tops shimmered beneath him, and though his foot came off the rope of light more than once Iris did not notice or she said nothing, and he walked back on the tightrope from castle to platform and jumped off of it, and he was genuinely proud of himself. He went across the chasm again, this time with more confidence, this time with fewer stumbles. He concentrated on his steps and time wrapped itself around him and left a residue of the salve it carries for moments just such as these. He made a third attempt and a fourth and a fifth, each time crossing with less fear until he was not afraid at all, and he never stumbled though below him lay a chasm and in front of him an aloneness the length and depth of which was virtually unknown by men.

When it was time to eat he took from the refrigerator black beans from Colombia and rice from Cambodia and freeze-dried guacamole that never turned brown because Louise had found and removed the enzymes that caused the browning. Adam and Iris did as they always had done, and Adam set a plate for Iris but put no food on it and she sat with him and they made plans for the afternoon that were as exciting as the morning's.

When they were done with lunch Adam turned the flatware drawer upside down and the spoons and the knives and the forks fell noisily onto the polished red concrete floor, and then he went into the dining room and he opened the fancy Swedish cabinet with the tasseled key that always stayed in the lock. He took out the good silverware and he dumped it too on the concrete floor. When every utensil in the house was present, from serving spoons to crab forks, they proceeded to make a shining silver city of metal, molding piles of silverware into small and unlikely buildings, tee-pees of butter knives, nautili of spoons, a temple of forks whose tines had been bent at unnatural angles in order to support a structure that appeared to defy both gravity and purpose. Had their plaything been an architectural model, the city built from it would have caused Gaudi and Van de Roe and Ghery all to weep for the rigidity of their own imaginations. They used layers of plates for apartment blocks, and made an entire district of skyscrapers from stacked glasses and they had elevated highways of tinfoil and sports stadiums of mixing bowls, and swimming pools of Tupperware. From a tagine pot they made a volcano in the center of their city, and Iris told Adam about the Aztecs and their human sacrifices and Adam was very impressed and was quite sure that they should have those in their city too. When the clock's chime told them that the day was done and it was again time to eat, Adam sat at the main crossroads of their tangled metropolis and he loomed over it, outsized and powerful, transformed from child to a creator of cities. He ate leftover chicken with neither plate nor fork though he was surrounded by both.

When he was finished eating Iris suggested that he bathe, and he agreed and he filled the tub but when he took off his blood-encrusted socks the wounds on his feet were reopened by the fabric, and the bathwater turned pink then red. He lowered his body into the water and as the water darkened he thought about all of the wonderful things he had done during the day. He thought about the fort and the glorious battle, and the tightrope, and his shining city of silver, and then he washed himself and he got out of the bath and dried himself, and it was then that he noticed that there was a faint light coming from the small steam room that his father had built next to the bathroom. Adam went to the door and he opened it and a cloud of hot steam pushed him back, but before the door closed he heard his sister's voice.

—Adam...

—Yeah.

—Come in here.

A two-tiered wooden bench, green-tiled walls, and steam thick enough to limit visibility to no more than a foot greeted him.

—Sit down.

Adam sat on the warm wood and he could see nothing but steam, but after a moment the light to the right of him glowed that bit warmer and then for the first time he saw his sister's body, sat next to him cross-legged and smiling; a being of light and steam. She was only slightly taller than Adam. A six-year-old girl with bright round eyes, high cheekbones, she wore mischiefs' smile and her hair fell to the middle of her back. She was both the essence of childhood and paradoxically, a being more ancient than the practice of counting minutes. Her only color was that of yellow light, but that light seemed to come in a million degrees of intensity and from that variation came her form and shape.

Adam stared at her a long time, wide-eyed and amazed, his sister whom he had known from his very first breath; a creature of magic and total invisibility sat before him seemingly in the flesh. Every vision he had ever had of her—every memory he had of playing with her or fighting with her, of competing with her for their parents' love—was revised to include the girl child sitting next to him.

—Have you been in here all along?

—No, it is my first time but it was something Dad and I talked about as a possibility. I wrote some code. I was going to show it to him tomorrow.

—He's gonna love it.

And her pause was perhaps longer than she meant it to be.

—I hope so.

He went to touch her leg but his hand moved through her, and onto the bench below her. A trick of light.

—I thought....

—Shh...

They were silent for a long time and Adam felt like he was going to faint from the heat.

—It's too hot in here.

—Okay.

And he stood to go, but she stopped him.

—Adam?

—Yeah.

—Can you see me?

—Yeah.

—I'm a real girl then… right?

—Yeah, of course.

—So, you're not alone.

—No, it's me and you and Mom and Dad.

—Yeah.

And he walked across the tile floor and left prints of blood behind him and he got into his bed and turned off his light and fell asleep with the bright vision of Iris still burned into his cornea.

When Adam woke up his room was completely dark. He had no clock and so no way of knowing what time it was. He knew that his mother was never coming back, nor his father, and he knew that he had known it all along, but how he knew, he did not know. Again, he thought about the fun he had had the day before, and he thought that it might have been that fun which killed his parents, that it was a test of his love, a test he had failed. He should not have been laughing and playing and having fun with his sister. He should have gone and looked for them. He should've somehow saved them from whatever it was that kept them, and he thought that maybe it was not too late, and he envisioned himself fighting a dragon who had taken his parents captive and dragged them into her cave, and then in the next instant he saw how they had fallen down the cliffs at the island's edge and he imagined how he would climb down the rocks bravely and when he got to them he would tend to their wounds and comfort them, and then he would put them both on his back and bring them to safety. He thought about how he would have to put on his thick socks and his thermal layers and his insulation layers and his outerwear and he would need a headlamp and a helmet and a rope, and he realized that he was not even sure where all of those things were because he was not a brave knight, nor a rescuer, nor a slayer of dragons. He was not a god but a child.

And he lay in his bed under his soft printer-down comforter and he felt himself untethered from the Earth, floating, and he felt the cuts at the bottom of his feet pulsating and with each pulse he felt as if he were being filled with some gas, and whatever it was that filled him started from his feet, and it rose through his legs blowing him up like a balloon until his skin stretched and strained to contain it. When the bloat had reached his throat he opened his mouth and he began to howl and tears streamed from his eyes, and as the howl rose to the ceiling of his small dark chamber, he saw his sister's prints of light below the door of his room and he heard her voice raised in volume and pitch, begging to come in, pleading for him to open the door, but he could only ignore her, and she was forbidden by her programing to enter his room if he did not invite her in, and so she could no longer reach him, and she feared for their lives because she knew that as much as he needed her vast wealth of knowledge, she needed his body in order to survive.

Adam's wretched wail reached no ears, neither human nor animal, but it rose and climbed and its energy, its real energy, reverberated around the world, perhaps diminishing in strength but never disappearing entirely.

Perhaps, the cry itself was a djinn that looked only for a way to come into the world, and it bounced from fjord to strait to sound, and as Adam's scream echoed through the shafts of abandoned Russian coal mines, and slid down melting glaciers and sailed across the wine-dark sea itself, it covered the Earth from all directions at once, and what it was looking for and who created it, and what its purpose in being was, were all questions that could not be asked and so were never answered.

The remnants of the boy's lonesome wail found Leonard Shorty in the middle of a gunfight in the mountains of Afghanistan. Finding him in the form of a spec of pollen that sailed on ancient drafts that had been circling the Earth for millions of years in order to find his right eye. Leonard squeezed shut his lids for just that second and a bullet found its way into his chest, missing his heart by only millimeters. When the fight was over Leonard was taken to a field hospital and then returned to the United States for convalescence and retraining. He had months to think about for whom he fought and why, and so came to the painful conclusion that neither his nor humanity's interests were being met by his service.

Adam's terror-filled scream found Tammy Cohen in her writing room overlooking the Chisos mountains of West Texas in the form of an invitation to The Western States Conference on Water Usage. Just like the pollen in Leonard's eye, this invitation of seeming innocence would lead her to grave and painful injury, but it would also lead her through the first steps of the long journey to retrieve the crying and lonely child and bring him back from the far reaches of the Earth, where his parents had left him.

10/6/2047

Dear Friends,

From the internet to the refrigerator it all caused the same disconnection. First, from the Earth itself, from its rhythms, from its weather. The grid cuts us off from the Earth's bounty. It's turned us from hunters and gathers into farmers, and finally into mechanized thieves who used our terrible intelligence and power to force the Earth to give us what she cannot naturally give, and in any case could not sustain. The grid cut us off from the other animals, animals which provided so much of our food, and for centuries our transportation, and from time immemorial, companionship. It cuts us off from our fellow humans, even as it purports to connect us. We used to sit in front of our boxes of light and from our boxes of light we got our friendship, and our gossip, and our news, we did our work there and had our sex there, but we were utterly alone. Separated. It was not meant to be that way. It seemed like we were living but we were not. The companionship, the news, the gossip, the work and the sex, all were an illusion. And our muscles atrophied and our bodies curled into themselves and our eyes grew dim. We Americans deserve more than that. We deserve a chance to start over in a better way, a more sustainable way. We deserve our bodies back and our long-ranging sight and our place on this wild land that was once called God's country. We will find a way to bring the animals back and we will once again live among them. History, my friends, is full of do-overs.

-Malcolm

II

6

OCTOBER 7TH, 2047

From her little stone house with its back against the Chisos, Tammy could see five miles in any approachable direction. They could come at her from behind but they would have to be desert mountaineers of exceptional skill, of which there were few, fewer still did she not know personally and none, not a single soul, who knew the jagged mountains of her backyard better than she.

She ran her glass slowly over the land and even magnified it lay perfectly still. Almost a photograph. No animals, small or large, tracked up the dust. Not a breath of wind disturbed the stubby junipers that even twenty years of drought could not kill. Although, even they had their arboreal doubts about surviving the twenty-first. No migrants snuck across the border in search of a better life for their children and no minutemen tore up the desert in high octane Land Rovers covered in swastikas, ready to send the barbarian hordes of short brown people back to their own savage lands, or at least to be martyred in glorious defense of their white and Christian Republic. That time was passed.

She checked the number of hits her latest post on Lastgasp had generated. Twenty million and rising. She was well into the money. Dead or alive it seemed they all wanted to know what she had to say. Her most bitter enemies and her most ardent fans subscribed to her feed, and in this way, they knowingly dropped bit-pennies into her virtual pockets. It was the price they paid for being a part of the conversation. There weren't that many things left in the dying world to buy and sell, but the feeling of being part of the conversation was one thing that still sold well. The illusion of having a voice, of having some effect on the outcome of things, the feeling of having tried, of having stood up to the powers that be, of having aired your beliefs or at minimum having even just stood against someone else's. The right to rant and rail and shout and show your ugly…that still sold. Hate as much as love put food in Tammy's belly, shoes on her feet, clothes on her back and gas in in her truck.

Tammy Cohen received the invitation on her secure server. Since she had gotten back to South Texas, she had been using an alias and a series of avatars to present her online videos, all in order to keep her corporal identity, and more importantly its location, hidden. She had not been seen in public since leaving the White House. Rumors of her death had spread across the internet, and a body had even been exhumed on live TV in North Carolina, but it was declared not to be hers, and apologies had to be given to the family of the dead and then desecrated on behalf of the local authorities, and by the cable news network whose crack investigator had turned up a false lead and then followed it down the rabbit hole of certainty. Tammy had to fight the strong urge to gloat online. Gloating was not her brand, and she did feel genuinely bad for the bereaved family of the recently deceased woman, whose body had so violently been punished for inciting a revolution.

Tammy left Washington by the most circuitous route possible, and while she could not be sure that she was not followed, she was sure she had not been successfully followed. The Big Bend of the Rio Grande river by way of the Upper Ganges and over the Himalayas and across the Gobi is a hard route to keep up on. She was off the map, yet, somehow the email found her. Someone, at least, knew where she could be found online and if they knew that, it took little conjecture to assume that the same party knew where she actually was.

By which route the invitation email had come to her was mysterious. Her tracking software could take her as far back as The Jianguomen neighborhood of Beijing and then it was lost in a warren of servers and repeated thousands of times and so was impossible for even a computer to track. A person would have to follow each thread to its dead end, to have any hope of knowing the identity of the sender and the years it would take to conduct such a search would render its findings irrelevant.

The invitation had the markings of legitimacy; the watermark, the seal, and an encryption protocol that was unique to the White House. It was the markings of legitimacy that gave her the most pause. Surely they would have changed the order of the acceptance protocol in the six months since her dismissal. Theoretically they would have changed it the moment she was fired. She decided that knowing whether or not she was actually invited by the White House was a mystery she would not solve, but one thing she was relatively sure of was that she would have a seat in the House. From the moment she received the invitation she knew she would have to go, and that going in the full light of day, in her actual body, would irrevocably alter her life. She went through the motions of weighing the pros and cons, if only to tell herself that she had. She went inside and began to gather the provisions she would need for the twenty-hour drive to Bright Angel.

7

OCTOBER 7TH, 2047

The Irishman and the Indian stood in front of Claire, who eyed them like cattle she was thinking of purchasing,

—You two know each other?

—Well, we've kept our vows. At least I have.

—The vow is the only damn thing I liked about this place.

—It was almost over anyway. It's a security precaution, I'm sure you both understand. At any rate, you've seen each other around, yes?

—Yeah. We went trout fishing together but didn't say shit.

—Nice. A day trip?

—We had to stay overnight because we didn't catch nothing on day one.

—How'd you do on day two?

—We worked out a new system. On the third day we brought back twenty-eight fish for the smoker.

—You worked out a system without talking?

Leonard decided not to answer her but resolved that if she asked again, he would draw her a picture.

—How big?

Leonard pressed his thumbs together and raised his index fingers to display a length of about four inches.

—You see any bigger ones?

—Those are gone.

—Twenty-eight. Jesus. I bet Rainbow was impressed.

—If she was, she didn't say nothing.

—Yeah that's my girl. You could bring her a goddam woolly mammoth to smoke and she wouldn't say boo about it, but if you brought in twenty-eight fish she was impressed.

—Hate to have her disappointed like?

—So…you're kinda old friends then?

—Like he said, we're just now after having heard each other speak for the first time.

—Okay, but you saw each other around Dharma and you went fishing together once. Anything else?

—We were sitting next to each other for the play.

Claire smiled.

—And you got up at the crack of dawn and watched *Breaking Bad* together.

—We happened to be sitting next to each other.

—Right, what'd you think?

—Of what?

—The play.

—I grew up in Albuquerque so I could kind of relate—

—Stop!

Claire jumped up from behind the rock that served as her desk and her eyes blazed with a kind of insanity that until that moment had not been there, or at least had been hidden behind a veil of affable sanity.

—You see... Leonard, that's exactly it, it's exactly that type of detail Malcolm is talking about.

—Bullshit. You asked me if I liked it so I was...

—I know, and I get it but we got to train ourselves not to do that. Do I need to explain why?

—I liked the fucking play.

She turned toward Pat. Who could not help himself.

—Well, it was no *Playboy of the Western World*, I could tell you that.

—Okay gentlemen, so we ran out of chatty-chatty time. I got a thing that needs doing, and Malcolm thinks you two are right for the job.

—When do I get my twenty pounds of V-cell?

She ignored him.

—The job is dangerous. It could be tricky, it might lead to getting caught by the dicks and you can be pretty sure they'll be dicks about it. I mean, really, dicks.

Eighteen sleepless hours later, the Irishman and the Indian sat on the cold steel bumper of Leonard's suburban and handed back and forth the electric gizmo that passed for a joint in those dry times. They drank lukewarm chicory coffee and they were each alone in their thoughts and the sun rose over Angels Window in the east. The weed was synthetic and the high was synthetic. It did not offer the clarity of the old natural marijuana, but it offered the memory of it and that was something.

—You think she was taking the piss?

—What?

—That whole bollocks about the US President.

—Donno weather she's taking a piss or not, I am just trying to get some V-cell so I can last the winter.

—That's it? You're just in in for Twenty pounds of V?

—Yeah and if you got an easier way of getting some, I'm all ears, holmes.

— Okay, I'm gonna try and get some kip.

As the sun climbed skyward and began to give the ground its daily baking, they hid the Suburban under its skin of tarpaulin and crawled into the darkened rear compartment and listened for sirens on the highway. They tried to find a comfortable spot to rest and wait, though they were not sure what they were waiting for. They took turns trying to sleep, although sleep evaded them both with equal dexterity. Perhaps it was the space itself that disallowed sleep. The rig's rearmost compartment was hot and filled with objects that fit uneasily with one another. They tried to rest among the ropes and spools of webbing and helmets and racks of carabiners and sun-cracked coolers. There was an old husk of a neoprene river raft named for Leonard's matrilineal ancestors. The folded up *Kiowa Chief* took up a fair amount of the back back compartment and the two large men were forced to fit their bulk into the corners around the uncomfortable rubber cube.

They had walked for long hours in stone splitting heat, and then in complete darkness and bone-chilling cold, the path in front of them lit only by their headlamps, their bare legs covered in a patina of red dust. They had ridden side by side in Leonard's ancient Suburban, ninety hard miles, first across the slickrock moving with fantastic speed, the world reduced to the cone of light in front of them. Impossible animals ran across their path. Pat saw them with his own eyes: a desert cottontail, a black jackrabbit, a pair of bobcats, a Gila monster and a family of armadillos. Each animal put him in a deeper state of awe and made him question all that he knew of the world. Finally he saw a single Mexican grey wolf with diamond-yellow eyes who sat proudly on his haunches and did not move as the truck sped toward it. Pat's rational mind told him that the animals were no more than specters, memory animals, animals that he had seen as a child, or in books or in holograms or in VR games. There were no more large mammals left in Utah, save the unhappy monkey. Perhaps there were no other large mammals left anywhere.

The slickrock gave way to chaparral and they crawled along dirt paths, which only four-wheel drive and studded tires and judicious use of the bumper-mounted winch allowed them to egress, and then two track ruts that did not deserve to be called roads and then wide dirt roads that had not seen a grader in a decade whose pits and trenches were only slightly preferable to its two and three and four mile stretches of washboards that rattled the suburban and its passengers with such violence and so relentlessly that it seemed impossible to them that the shaking was not imposed upon them by some malevolent hand. Both passenger and driver alike suffered the feeling that they had bestirred ancient forces from deep within the canyon's maw. At last they reached the paved highway, cracked and in desperate need of repair, yet it seemed like a road made of silk, so smooth and gentle was that pavement in comparison to what had come before, and just as they had been overwhelmed by vibrating dread, they were overtaken with the peace brought on by the gentle sound of tire studs on pavement.

8

OCTOBER 8TH, 2047

L ooking out at the hostile landscape passing silently below Marine One's cabin, the folly of the whole American Experiment was writ clear on the cloudless Arizona sky. President Sonia Martinez had asked to be alone on the short flight from Phoenix so that she might gather her thoughts and prepare herself to do as she must, and so the others, the secretaries; State, Interior, Agriculture Energy and Defense were, maybe for the first time in their lives, made to feel helpless, like actual secretaries instead of men who wore the title ironically but wielded great influence over the lives of others and commanded the vast resources of the American government. When Airforce One landed at Sky Harbor, America's most powerful bureaucrats dispersed across the hot tarmac to the waiting choppers and President Sonia Martinez, followed only by her personal aide, walked the red carpet from plane to helicopter and she saluted the Marine at the door and went in and sat on the soft white leather swivel chair below the presidential seal, and after a moment Monica brought her bird's nest tea and then slipped into the forward cabin and the helicopter lifted off smoothly and the president of the United States sat alone with her thoughts and her unfurling tea for what would be the last time.

She looked over the text of the speech she had prepared to give, but she could not concentrate on the words, words that she herself had written. The letters swam and folded and refolded onto themselves, they reformed into different words, or no words at all. Gibberish. It was nonsense. She considered trying the door mid-flight. She longed to give herself as a human sacrifice to the angry goddess of the canyon, to the desert, to the river, to the country she loved. She would be more than willing.

When hope was gone, people threw themselves on the electric fences of Auschwitz and no one looked on and judged them for their choice. No, they were instead revered for their bravery. Was this not such a moment? Who living could actually call the choice to die cowardly? No one.

She knew that she could not open the door, that no amount of force would open it, and even if she knew the code to release the lock and she tried to do it, marines would appear from unseen corners of the aircraft and restrain her for her own good, for the good of the country. She knew she was not really alone. Sonia was never really alone. She envied the marines having orders to follow. She held the most powerful office on earth, but she did not even have the choice to live or die.

Sonia Martinez was nothing more than power's lonely prisoner.

She tried to set aside hopeless thoughts, but the stark fact of the country's coming demise would not leave her. She would be the first president in American history to oversee the shrinking of the republic, the first to erase stars from the flag, and she was prepared for that erasure, because the alternative was to burn the flag entirely, to oversee the dissolution of the republic itself. Would that she could give the western states back to the Mexicans.

Mea culpa, we're so sorry… *mea maxima culpa*.

To allow a civil war on her watch was a fate that no president, Abraham Lincoln included, could live with.

Marine One topped The Kaibab Plateau and the Grand Canyon spread out before them, ancient and vast, no less majestic than it was the day before or a million years before that.

Sonia sipped her tea and let the landscape sink into her.

Of course, this desert wasn't going to sustain us. It was never going to sustain us. Even the most cursory look at the geologic record would have told us not to do as we were doing. We chose not to look. Instead we chose to close our eyes on the world that is and imagine the world as we wanted it to be. We lived within that delusion, and why not? Was it not delusion that broke the sound barrier? They said it could not be broken. We shattered it. Was it not delusion that took us to the moon, was it not a refusal to take the world as it was that split the atom, that cured Polio, and stopped the spread of smallpox? Rosa Parks refused to sit at the back of the bus and her refusal was so strong that it warped the country around her. Americans had, through the denial of status quo, shaped the world in its image, and when we are gone (because we are going) and the world falls into darkness for the absence of our light, they will once again say, *We are all Americans*, but they will not be, they do not have the metal for it.

Frizzy-haired and half-mad Dr. Tammy Cohen had stormed into the Oval Office within the first month of President Martinez's first term bearing a hand-drawn graph penned on the presidential stationery; a graph so simple that a three-year-old could've explained it to a one-year-old. One line showed average rainfall west of the Rockies in steady, slow decline, and another showed population dependent on the Colorado River over time, a line slowly rising but then like a hockey stick in repose climbing straight to vertical from 1850 to the present day. In matters of geology or hydrology or climatology the world is immutable, a work of some imagination greater than our own or of no imagination at all, but a randomness far more vast than imagination.

Water is not magic, Dr. Cohen insisted. It does not burst forth from rocks when struck by enchanted sticks. Water falls from the sky in the form of rain or it does not. It runs to our rivers and races toward the sea or it does not. It is filtered down through the earth into the deep aquifers that are pumped to sustain the two hundred million souls of the American West, or it does not.

The aquifer suffered damage that would be a million years in repair, if it would be repaired at all. Even if it rained for a century without cease the water would be lost to us. Our big underground lake has fallen in on itself and stores nothing but salty tears now, and all that comes up is sand, and our delusion is unmasked before the world and death and murder: fratricide and parricide and suicide are at our throats with their sharp knives. Our centuries of achievement and excellence and leadership will be erased by the days of savagery and mayhem to come.

That is not what it said on the page before her but it was what was written on her heart and she hung her head in despair as her helicopter made its way to The Grand Conference Center at the Bright Angel Lodge.

9

OCTOBER 8TH, 2047

D r. Tammy Cohen was one of the last, if not the very last, to be sat, and as she walked up the aisle she saw the faces that would be burned into her memory when her last breath rattled from her body. She had been through invasive security checks before, though this was the most thorough she could have imagined. They scanned every nook of her body and analyzed the results down to her cellular makeup while she stood in her underwear before them. When she was allowed to enter the hall she was escorted all the way to her seat by a grim-faced security man in a double-breasted Kevlar-lined suit who walked her to her seat and made sure she was sitting in it. The seat had no view of the dais whatsoever. Of all the seats in the house this had to have been the very worst one. She was ensconced by an iron post that extended from floor to ceiling and not only blocked her view to the front but to the sides. Inside the eye of the I-beam. Why had they invited her to then humiliate her? Whose agenda did her presence serve? She felt a tap on her shoulder.

—Nice seat.

There he was in all his obtuse and geeky glory. Ted Weiner.

—Long time no see.

Ted had replaced her as head of the agency when she took the job in the White House. It made sense that he should be there.

—Ted.

—Tammy.

—How's things back at the...

—They dismantled us. A memo one day, locks on the doors the next.

—No shit? I didn't see anything about it on the news.

—They buried it under the Iran nuke story. It was there, just nobody cared.

—Jesus. Well, they ignored every recommendation we made for ten years so I guess it doesn't make much difference.

—Tell that to my wife and kids.

—No severance?

—A little, but when it runs out…

—So if we're both out of the government business, what are we doing here?

—Enjoying the view of this iron beam, I guess.

—I believe it's a post.

—I knew that, it's just…

—Maybe the president is going to announce how she has studied the agency's recommendations and decided to take all of them at once.

—They're mostly your recommendations.

—Words on a page.

—They were saying that you were dead.

—Who?

—Everyone at the office. I came in and everyone was going on about how your body had been found, and everybody was weeping and wailing and moaning.

—But you didn't buy it.

—I decided to reserve judgment.

—And right you were. Anyway, it was not a rumor I started.

—I bet it didn't do your Lastgasp business any harm.

—Girl's got to make a living, Ted, even a dead one.

A sudden hush filled the room.

—She's here.

—How do you know?

—Because I know. Shhh...

Sonia Martinez looked out at the room at the faces of her political allies and enemies gazing up at her with something like hope or delusion. She had been called a cunt with teeth, a Mexican whore, Medusa, La Llorona, a bitch, a gash, a harpy. She had been portrayed as a snake, a vampire, as Kali with a thousand arms.

Insults were all to be forgotten, favors were to be called in. They were all there. Nobody missing, not a senator not a congressman not a governor of one of the drought-ridden states was going to miss this. They were looking to her to magically solve the problem. Would she propose some compromise that no one had thought of? Solve the problem of lack of water with reason? She surely had some new invention in her back pocket. Something that could bring forth crops from the dry earth? That could slake thirst with air, with sand? Some drug that would turn a constituent's heart from his own needs and his family's needs to the needs of his neighbors and their families?

Ladies and gentlemen, colleagues, former enemies, old friends... we teeter. We are bound together on the sharp edge of history and if we close our eyes we can hear the dogs of war panting just beyond this door. Rabid. Cruel. Unthinking dogs. If we are to bring them to heel it is today, as tomorrow the hour will have passed.

We face hard choices. Our great cities: Los Angeles, San Francisco, Las Vegas, Phoenix... They must all pause in their progress, in order that progress should ultimately continue. I hear you when you say, Madam President this is not a video game but our lives, our cities and towns, our homes. How do we pause when time only goes forward?

Survival sometimes requires sacrifice.

That is why today I am proposing legislation that will ban state subsidies of water. Subsidies have created a false sense of security and a difficult reality is now hard on our heels. Water's scarcity must be reflected in its price. I hear you when you say, water is not just a thing for the rich. The glorious American West cannot just be given to those whom fortune has already smiled upon and so taken away from the rest of us. I hear you. Believe me, I hear you. Not only--

And then the president of the United States along with her supporters and detractors alike were engulfed in flame and the venerable old wooden lodge was blown into a million splinters.

10

OCTOBER 8TH, 2047

P at and Leonard felt the concussive pulse in the ground, though they were too far from Bright Angel to hear the explosion. The change in wind direction was sudden and undeniable. While the wind on the Colorado Plateau did, at sundown, move east to west, it did so because of a temperature disparity created by the onset of darkness in the higher altitudes to the north and east of the plateau, but an easterly breeze at 10 AM was as strange as the sun rising from the Pacific and every creature that still lived in the desert took note of it.

—That… must be why we're here.

—Okay. So now what?

—We wait for our cue.

—And then?

—We enter stage left.

—Why?

—Really?

—Yeah, why? I know we said we'd do it like, but now that we're faced with actually fecking doing it, and the consequences of actually fecking doing it, I'd say it's fair enough to have a think about it, don't you?

—I s'pose.

And so Leonard thought about it. To question a direct order was foreign to him, like questioning breath, but the Irishman had a point. Red Axe was not the Navy and Malcolm was not an admiral, and Leonard had to admit that the possible consequences of action far outweighed those of non-action. There were no MPs ready to hunt them down, no court martial, no tribunal standing ready to decry their desertion. There would be no time spent in the brig. Without the threat of repercussions meted out from above, orders were not really orders at all but merely appeals to action.

But what Leonard came to was this: he would do it, not out of respect for the chain of command but because it was an action in line with his own goals. The old world order had to end, and a new world order had to take its place, and while Red Axe showed worrying signs of corruption, the power it strived to replace had evil at its very core and he, Leonard

Thibodaux Shorty, was born into the world downstream of that evil. It was incumbent upon him to try and assist in its correction.

When Leonard answered it was not with his usual confidence and humor, but instead he heard himself repeating words he had heard, or words he had read, as if somewhere in the revolutionary's handbook it said: in the case of a comrade who has lost faith in the revolution, say something like this:

The opposite of order is chaos. We do not wish to destroy order but instead institute a new one, a fairer one, an order which takes into its calculations our value as human beings and places us among the other creatures of the earth.

So he went to say that, or something like it, but instead he heard himself say:

—Look man, I'll admit Red Axe does seem a little fucked up, but maybe it's a step in the right direction.

—I thought you were just in for the V-cell.

—Well, ultimately yeah, but he has a point.

—Who?

—Malcom.

—Ah, the fecking Wizard of Oz.

—Pat, if you're scared I can do this part without you, but you don't have very long to decide.

—How long?

—'Til the ambulances come, I guess.

—How long you think that'll be?

—I figure that they might've had a few standing by because that's just the protocol when it comes to POTUS. I reckon somewhere between ten and twenty minutes.

Leonard rooted around in one of the coolers and came up with two scratched cans of Tecate.

—I bet we got time for a beer anyway. They been down the big ditch more than once, maybe they'll help.

Leonard handed a can to Pat who held the warm cylinder in his hands and stared at it as if it were some kind of holy object that, if looked at in just the right way, might contain the answers to his heart's questions.

Leonard popped his beer and spewed foam all over his AC/DC, *Highway to Hell* T-shirt.

—That's great, just fucken great...a big red bastard in a T-shirt that smells like cheap beer. It's the goddam apocalypse and the only thing that's gonna be left are cockroaches and stereotypes.

Leonard laughed at his own attempt to lighten the mood, and then he drank what was left in the can in great gulping draughts and then reached into the cooler and came up with

111

another, however this time he cracked the door open and held the beer outside the rear of the truck.

Finally, after twelve minutes, they heard the first sirens and then after pause of six and a half minutes they began to hear a steady stream of ambulances wailing toward a destiny that none of them would have any effect on whatsoever.

—Well… you coming?

Pat tried to push his courage up through his throat and into a single word.

—Hooah?

Leonard smiled warmly at Pat's attempt to come his way.

—Close, but that's the army. I'm a swabbie, and we don't really go in for that shit.

Leonard tilted his head back and finished his second beer and opened the backdoor of the Suburban and he waited for Pat to untangle himself from the climbing rope that had somehow wrapped itself around his limbs, and they both stretched their backs and stood a moment blinking into the bright day and then Leonard walked around to the back of the vehicle and pulled the blocks from the tires and threw them into the rear compartment and took out a spinning red light and he blew the dust off its plastic dome and switched it to "on" and then mounted it onto a metal pad in the center of the Suburban's roof.

They emerged from behind the sandstone embankment that had hidden them and they slid down the short sandy track that abutted the paved road. The line of emergency vehicles racing toward The Bright Angel Hotel stretched unbroken to the horizon and Leonard drove straight for them as if his intention was to T-bone whichever unfortunate soul was in his way but at the last second he cut the wheel to the left and the studded tires tore curving trenches into the pavement as the truck's weight shifted and the passenger side of the Suburban came within inches of an ambulance, and Pat looked out of the passenger side window into the driver's side of the EMS wagon and a young woman in her late teens or early twenties was behind the wheel and she looked wide-eyed in fear and amazement. Leonard drove parallel to the line of traffic and he sped past vehicles from the right side of the two-lane blacktop and seemed to treat the deadly possibility of oncoming traffic with total disregard. Leonard hummed a tune from the Britney Spears musical biopic, *Baby, One More Time*.

Eventually, he spotted a gap between two fire trucks and he slotted the Suburban into that gap and the spinning red light swung its tinted beam in circles, keeping time with the chorus of sirens surrounding them. Leonard and Pat in the White Mountain Search and Rescue Suburban looked to all the world as if they had left from the same staging area as the rest of the first responders. Years later Pat would remember that drive and marvel at the fact that despite their alliance with the perpetrator, for the first time in his twenty-five years on the planet he felt as if he was a part of something greater than himself.

Forty-seven vehicles had arrived to the site of the bombing before they did. A young park ranger had been sent alone onto the highway to oversee the chaos. He pointed with confidence and authority that emanated from his pressed green Park Service uniform and Pat wondered why the Park Service bothered to keep employees if all the parks had been closed. The ranger sent the ambulances to the left and sent everyone else either to the hotel guest parking area on the right, or back along the shoulder of the highway.

Leonard decided not to wait, and again pulled into the right lane and passed a line of vehicles now standing still. The boy in the park ranger uniform bravely stood in Leonard's way and blocked his entrance to the site with his hands outstretched.

—Whoah!

Leonard stopped the Suburban with the boy's knees touching the bumper. The boy stalked over to the driver's side window.

—Dude, you almost ran me over.

Leonard produced a badge from his pocket but made no move to give it to the stunned ranger for inspection. Leonard held the boy's gaze with his own.

—What the fuck do you think you're doing?

—My job, sir.

—Oh, I get it. That's sooo cool. So, while you're so very carefully doing your job, the survivors, if there are any, are actually dying.

The boy took a deep breath and tried to steady his nerve but his authority had evaporated in the face of the steely Indian before him.

—Emergency vehicles to the left, everyone else to the right.

—What's your name?

—Jeff.

—Jeff what?

—Collins.

—Jeff Collins. Well, Jeff Collins, today is going to be the most important day of your goddam life.

—Why is that, sir?

—Because it's going to be the day you decide to either continue to be a little boy playing dress up in your daddy's clothes or if you're going to be a man who makes decisions for himself and then lives with the consequences of those decisions.

Leonard stared Jeff Collins directly in the eye and it looked as if Jeff Collins might actually cry, but then Leonard smiled.

—I, for one, hope you decide to be a man.

—Thank you, sir.

Leonard drove neither left nor right, but through the hedge and across the charred decorative cactus garden and straight for the smoldering ruins of the lodge itself.

—Where'd you get the badge?

—Alibaba.

Leonard parked on the perimeter of the newly formed crater.

—So we don't get parked in.

Pat had never imagined anything like the sight that spread out before him. A hole where a hotel once stood. Bodies and body parts everywhere, the ground bloodsoaked and charred and the sky smeared with yellow smoke. The acrid stench of death filled Pat's nostrils and burned his eyes. The heads and bodies of animals, of elk and of mountain lion and bison and bighorn sheep and grey wolves, littered the ground among the charred human remains. The animals were the most recognizable forms among the once living because they had been stuffed and lacquered in fire retardant in apparent preparation for just such an event. In death, the animals were able to withstand that which the living could only gape at in horror as their bodies were torn asunder. They looked on with unblinking eyes and perhaps they saw that the men who had hunted them only to stuff them with straw and place them in comical attitudes of natural action, now shared their fate. The animals long since departed from the plane of being shed not a single tear for the unhappy monkey whose greed and stupidity had finally doomed them all.

Pat opened his door, but there was only greasy air beneath the running boards, as the charred slope was too steep and jagged with rocks to alight upon.

—Slide over and use my door.

Pat's heart pounded against his breastbone as he slid across the seat and wondered if Leonard's body also reacted with such fear or if he had been trained by the US Navy to ignore his body's warnings. When he got out of the truck, Leonard was standing arms akimbo, with his fists on either hip like he was Peter Pan or some kind of Native American Superman. He tossed Pat a bright orange Search and Rescue windbreaker.

—Here, hide behind this.

117

Pat held the windbreaker to his mouth while Leonard unloaded the things they would need from the Suburban. Medical kit, fire tent, oxygen tanks, stretcher.

In the center of the pit stood a pillar of iron, which had for more than a century taken on the weight of the entire hotel. The pillar looked like an otherworldly thing, as if it had been there from the beginning of time, placed as a beacon by some alien super race.

The teams of first responders were gathering on the uphill side of the crater, but so far no one had entered it to look for survivors, or identify bodies, or search for clues as to the identity of the perpetrator. Such things would come, but because the possibility of survivors was remote the teams moved slowly for fear of unexploded ordnance or some kind of trap in which rescuers would become victims. Recent history was full of such incidents. From Mosul to Belfast, the killing of firemen and ambulance drivers had become a central tenet of the terrorist playbook.

First, they would send in the robots, and then the OED bomb-suit guys, and then they would send in convicts dressed as rescuers to poke around the ash and risk their lives for the society that they had sinned against, and if no further bombs exploded and no shots rang out from above, the first responders would jump into action with a great show of alacrity. Leonard nodded to Pat.

—Bravo fucking Zulu.

—Okay.

They slid down the slope into the pit carrying a rescue litter and the medical kit between them. Leonard pressed on with confidence and Pat did his best to mimic that confidence. On the perimeter of the blast they saw what could only have been the ranking officer of the National Guard Bomb Squad, jumping up and down and making sweeping gestures, arms flailing over his head. Someone brought him a bullhorn and he cleared the feedback.

—Stand down, immediately! Goddam it, I'm the I.C. on this thing. Until we have deemed it safe nobody sets foot in there! Clear the goddam area!

Leonard slowly raised an arm over his head and then extended his middle finger.

It was in that moment Pat realized that all of his choices— leaving County Kerry, quitting Oxford to join the Peace Corps, the Nor Cal separation protests— they had all led to him to following a madman into the heart of human history. Pat looked up to see the glint of a hundred cellphones encircling the pit, no doubt being held up to record evidence to be used in his trial. What would the charges against him be? Conspiracy? Sedition? Terrorism? He wanted to scream out to them:

I had nutin' to do with it! I didn't know! I am just trying to do what's right. I've always been on the side of right. But he said none of those things as he walked in Leonard's outsized footprints.

—I thought you said we were just gonna keep a low profile, blend in like...

—That fucking Oompa-Loompa is no more the incident commander than you are. I been at a thousand of these things and it's always the same douchebag parade.

—Still, we're not exactly blending in here.

`Leonard stopped walking, looked over his shoulder and grinned.

—You're right, put this in your mouth and blow.

He handed Pat a bright orange whistle.

—Every five seconds with your palms flat out and not one of them will come anywhere near us. I'll go to the pillar and see if I can't find Madam Science.

—If I spend the rest of my life getting me hole stretched in the Supermax at least I'll know who to blame.

—Or thank. God knows, love can bloom in the strangest places.

Leonard kept walking toward the pillar. The ash made a particular crunching sound under his boots, clean snow's dirty opposite. He was completely surrounded by disconnected human body parts, disembodied heads, and torn off arms and feet still wearing loafers, high heels covered in blood. He wondered if the men who took these lives, who sentenced these people to die, told themselves that theirs was a necessary evil. He wondered if that person really thought about the difference between life and death, if he had ever watched a person go from breathing to still. He wondered if he was in fact that man's onsite representative.

Leonard Shorty found Tammy Cohen curled up at the foot of the giant iron pillar and his life was cleaved into the before and the after.

The first thing to go was the fallacy of time. Tammy had always suspected that the regular tick-tock of the watch she wore upside down on her wrist, just as her grandmother had worn it, was perhaps more hand-me-down handcuff than a valuable family heirloom.

The instant of the explosion was white and endless and full of peace. The mortal illusion and the desperation on which mortal illusion is built evaporated and she saw the Universe for what it was. Space was unbound by time.

Forever and to the end of the Universe were no longer limits she was willing to accept.

It was a color that brought her back to this plane and that color was brown. Brown without limit and she spread herself within it and she could feel brown's warmth, and she felt that she was held up by it. She was floating in a universe within a universe and how long she was there and to what end were questions she would one day contemplate and the answers ranged from seconds to millennia. Some great part of her would know that there was little difference between the two, if there were any difference at all. Whatever time it was that she spent within that rich colorscape would be enough to know that she never wanted to leave it. Tammy was happy to accept the color brown as heaven.

Leonard Shorty had placed his cheek to Tammy Cohen's lips and looked down the plane of her body to see if her chest rose and fell or if he detected the moisture of her breath on the sensitive flesh of his face. When he was satisfied with his answers he looked into her eyes

for as long as he could stand to; all pupil, like a gigantic black pool, only rimmed with the thinnest of green tile, and he was falling into that pool and he dug his fingers into the earth in order to steady himself, but he felt the world retreating behind him and he knew that his anchor was too thin to hold.

He spoke to her pleadingly, as if they had been having a long and intimate conversation in which all that had to be said was conveyed with the silence between utterances. The words might have been anything at all; a chance to rest and nothing more. Perhaps they had been having just such a conversation.

—But don't you see, love has no place here. Not here...

Pat blew the whistle right into Leonard's face.

—What are you fecking on about?

—Jesus. Shit. Sorry…

Leonard did not know if he had spoken to her out loud or only in his head.

—Well?

—She's breathing.

—Okay, she conscious?

—I don't know, she looks like she is but…

—What?

—We're gonna have to put her in a coma.

—Why?

—Because if she starts screaming there's no way we're getting out of here alive.

—And after you put her in a coma you sure you can get her out of it?

—No. I ain't sure of shit.

—Jaysus, Mary and Holy-Saint-Joseph, why do I have the feeling that I am going to regret getting involved in any of this?

11

NOVEMBER 23RD, 2047

The transition from unconsciousness to consciousness was so fluid as to have no line of demarcation whatsoever. What went unquestioned in one state was abhorrent in the other.

In her coma, Tammy was fused with another being and between her and this other there was no separation; they were simply parts of a whole.

Through a ragged and irregular aperture, the deep black, which may have encompassed the length and breadth of the universe, gave way to a thin skein of pale red. She was still covered in darkness but in front of her, at some remove, as if she saw it on a screen from the back of a darkened theater, the world began to take form. A banded wall of stone. A juniper shrub. At first, she had no body at all, just vision that looked out as the world rendered itself from the darkness. She was not

124

afraid. Slowly, over some uncountable interval, she began to feel herself. She was bound, unable to move, yet with concentrated effort she began to recognize parts of her old self. Her spine, her neck, her toes. There was another body pressed against her. Male. He was wrapped around her, sleeping. His arms locked her body, his breath warm against the back of her neck. She had no idea who he was but she felt his hard cock pressing against her back. She had been asleep and free, wandering the cosmos without limit and then she was awake and she discovered herself to be a captive, a prisoner. Through haze and confusion, she tried to make an assessment of her situation and what resources she might bring to bear upon it. Having not yet moved a muscle she resolved to fight; nothing less would be acceptable. She may have been many terrible things but a willing prisoner was not one of them.

She gathered what strength she had and threw her head backward. She felt the impact of her head hitting the face of her captor. Before he had fully roused himself, she got in a second blow and felt the crunch of bone and the warm gush of blood. She heard his wail and then noises off to her left. She tried to bash him again although this time he dodged her.

—Pat! Motherfucker! Get the zipper! Pat!... Okay, you're fine just calm down a second. Nobody's trying to hurt you. Just.. Fuck... Pat!

A man came into her view. She could not see his face for the blinding headlamp that bore down on her. She heard a zip and then the pressure suddenly released. She was falling. Cold air flooded in around her. She felt the man behind her slide free, and then straddle her so as to hold her down. Blood was pouring from his nose onto her face and his eyes were wild with pain. Tammy was sure she would be murdered.

—Fuck! I think she broke my fucking nose. Fuck!

Tammy tried to scream but only a dry croak escaped her.

—Okay, okay! just calm down lady. You're fine, you're safe.

She tried to scream again, but then what strength she had managed to gather left her and she lay back down. He rose and disappeared into the darkness. She swore to herself that she would remain vigilant. She forced her eyes open and the cold seemed to envelop her. It bit her everywhere at once and she was sure she would freeze to death.

—What the hell?

—Lady Science lives.

Just as she was taken by panic, she was washed in calm. Sleep, or perhaps it was death pulling at her, and just as her resistance to it was beginning to fade, her captor was for a moment illuminated by a match and then a candle. She saw him knelt in front of a potbellied stove and the light of his small fire was reflected in his brown eyes and she knew that she knew him, that she had always known him. She slept.

Through haze she saw the bear's head, so close to her own. Its sharp teeth slightly bared, its empty eye sockets black and so deep that time might have issued from within. She heard a man speaking in a lilting Irish brogue that seemed to skate from one unlikely word to the next. A second man answered; basso Americanus. He spoke in the American idiom, to be sure, yet he also spoke in a cadence which was equally foreign to her.

—…so are we supposed to feel sorry for these assholes just because they're rich and have nothing to worry about but what to wear to the pow-wow?

—No ya fecking gobshite, but you're not takin' into account the context in which yer man was living.

—Like what?

—The world we know was completely shaped by what happened right there and then and this bold fecker gives us a wee peek into it. If you think about it, it's incredible. The damn revolution was thirty years in front of him and yet you can feel it bubbling up on every page. It's fair to say he either predicted it or fair fucks to him, he invented it.

—Sorry holmes, I'm trying to agree with you and I can see that you really like the book, but I don't think anything in my life has had a damn thing to do with the Russian Revolution.

—You're having me on, mate. Every war of note in the twentieth century can be traced back to...

The discussion of the Russian Revolution seemed to her to come out of the mouth of the bear that lay on top of her. Nothing made sense. She closed her eyes as much to shield them from the cold as to benefit from the darkness her lids provided. Thin shelter to be sure, but shelter nonetheless.

Tammy woke. If the haloed man was not a being come from a different plane altogether, then he had all the bearing of one. His outline was bright enough to scar her retina, but the great bulk of him was composed of pure darkness, ultra-black, a black which no light could penetrate and it appeared to Tammy that he was using his great density to shield her from the infernos of orange and red that raged at his back, as if he alone kept the fire of hell from consuming her body and soul and she wondered what the price of such protection might be.

The bear hide had been taken from her body. Again, her eyes adjusted to see the world outside of herself and the universe within began to fade, even as she tried to claw it back. Despite her will to stay within, she had already retreated too far into the reality of her birth.

She was being returned whether she liked it or not.

She saw that her protector, or perhaps he was her captor, was no more than a large man sat on a milk crate in a doorway in front of a setting sun, engrossed in a paperback. He folded the book's front cover back and squeezed, as if he were extracting its contents through applied pressure rather than reading. Lit from behind the man seemed like a giant, and Tammy would not have been surprised to see a single unblinking eye in the middle of his forehead.

She gathered her strength and tried to push the deerskins and scratchy blankets off of her, but they were too heavy to lift so she wriggled out from underneath them only to fall onto the cold sandy floor of the cave. The giant did not look up. She was naked. She croaked in a barely audible whisper.

—Where are my fucking clothes?

As the man lifted his eyes from his book his face was still obscured.

—Jesus, you're awake.

—I'm fucking naked.

—I have your pants. Your shirt didn't make it.

—Didn't make it?

—We had to treat you for some burns in the field, and I had to give you a shot. The most expedient thing to do was to cut it off, so I did.

Leonard moved away from the cave's entrance, which caused the chamber to flood with orange light. He opened a military issue backpack and from within took out her pants as well as a T-shirt.

—Expedient?

—The easiest thing.

—I know what expedient means, asshole. Then what happened?

—I induced a coma.

—With what?

—100 CCs of Pentobarbital.

—Why?

—Blown pupil. I did not want your brain to swell, so...

—How long?

—How long what?

—How long was I in a coma?

—Twenty-four days.

—I've been asleep for three and a half fucking weeks?

—Well, 'cept for once. It seems that wherever you were, you liked it there enough to consider staying.

He poured water from a jerry can into a metal cup and then walked to her with his eyes averted and handed her the water and the clothes.

—Small sips.

—How about some privacy?

—You broke my fucking nose.

—It's the least I could do.

—For what? Making sure you didn't freeze to death?

Leonard went out and she lay down on the cold sandy floor and put on her pants which were too big for her, and the AC/DC, *Highway to Hell* T-shirt that he had handed her. It seemed like some kind of joke garment. A parachute for a handkerchief. She dressed herself, lying on her back on the cave floor. Both the shirt and the pants were clean and stiff. She made a knot in the bottom left corner of the shirt to see if she could take up some of the slack. From her place in the middle of the floor, she could make out a stove, an oil lamp, a pile of driftwood, a stack of books, a crude pallet bed, a jerry can, a hanging wire mesh basket and a Dutch oven. The jagged stone walls behind the fireplace were blacked and greasy. She got herself to sitting and her head swam and she took sips of water and wondered what manner of life could have you in your own office at the White House one day and a cave the next.

She rolled to her knees and then with the help of her atrophied arms pressed into her shrunken thighs and stood wobbling. Skin and bones. She took a step and then another, her mind reeled and she tried to slow her heart. She knew that her internal resources were extremely limited.

She saw a multi-tool sitting on the stone in the center of the cave which must have served as a table. She pried open the blade and hid it behind her thin wrist.

She bent past the cave's low entrance and she found herself on a thin sandstone shelf high over the sharp bend of a dry wash, once a wide river, now only the rumor of one. Her heart hammered against her breastbone. The sky was streaked with pink clouds. She heard a Canyon Wren's descending song and she looked up at the great stonewalls that rose from the earth's core. From the color of the stone it looked to be Southern Utah, but it as easily could have been Eastern Arizona. To her left, the man who had been guarding her was sitting on his haunches on a shelf so thin that only a mountain goat would have sat it comfortably. His head was in his book and if he had noticed her at all, he did not look up.

Now or never. She took three steps and had the open blade pressed against his throat.

—Did you rape me, asshole?

Only his eyes moved from the page.

—I woke up with you wrapped around me like a goddam python and I am just wondering if while you were so kindly keeping me warm you also happened to rape me, and given that I woke up with your hard dick digging into my back, I think it's a fair question.

In a single swift movement he dropped his book, slipped sideways on the thin ledge, and knocked the blade from her hand, sending it fifty feet down to the sandy wash. He had her head pinned up against the wall of the canyon, her sprawled legs flailing over nothing but air.

—Fuck you, lady! All I did was keep you alive. If you have a problem with the way a man's body works I suggest you take it up elsewhere because there ain't nothing I can do about it.

—Let me go!

—If I let go of you right now, you die.

—Okay, okay.

He pulled her back onto the wider ledge in front of the cave's opening.

—You threaten me again you'll simply be dead and there ain't a soul in the world that's coming looking for you.

He stepped past her and went in.

—Crazy bitch.

Tammy caught her breath, pulled her knees to her chest under her outsized T-shirt. —You have no idea.

Tammy took deep breaths. She felt tears welling up from within her and pushed them down. She spoke to herself in a low whisper.

—That's not gonna help you, Tammy. Crying's not gonna help you. Pull yourself together, Cohen, pull yourself together. Fuck, goddamn it. I was in the conference center, Ted Weiner was behind me. I remember seeing Senator Wilson and nodding to him. President Martinez's speech... she was about to do it. She was about to do it ... But then the flash, the heat, the darkness....Fuck fuck fuck fuck! Don't cry... goddammit, Cohen, pull yourself together. Fuck. I'm cold. What did Dad say about being cold... if you're cold, be cold. Where's my truck? Where is my goddamn truck? Tim Russert, shit who's gonna feed Tim Russert, shit, three-and-a-half weeks, somebody's got to be looking for me, who? Nobody, that's who. Oh God...

Leonard came out onto the thin shelf.

—I have a question for you?

—Yeah.

—Do you *feel* like you been raped?

—I feel like I been hit by a train.

—I been accused of a lot of shit in my life and some of it I even did, but...

Leonard went back into the cave, shaking his head. Tammy sat on the ledge until the cold forced her back in. He had lit the fire in the potbellied stove and the oil lamp.

He brought her tea in a dented metal cup. Twigs and juniper berries in hot water. Very possibly poison, but it did not make much sense that he sat there and watched her sleep only so he could poison her when she woke up. He set a bowl of soup down in front of her.

—I'm not very hungry.

—Eat what you can. Our supplies are a few days deep at best and after that we are gonna have to have enough juice to hike out of here or go hunting, and there ain't much out there to hunt so....

She forced herself to take a spoonful of soup. It was like sand in her throat. After a second try, she looked up at him to see if he had been watching, but his eyes were cast down into his own bowl.

—Do you live here?

—I used to. Still kinda do I guess, but I'm over at Dharma a lot now.

—Dharma?

—I just got involved with 'em because it's been getting hard to hunt anything down here for the last couple of years and they got some more resources.

—Was there someone else here?

—Yeah, Pat, but it seems like he's gone now so it's just me and you.

—And who are you?

—Leonard.

—Where'd Pat go?

— To see if he could get us some fish.

—Pat went fishing?

—Something like that. He coulda gone back to Dharma. Shit, who knows, maybe he's dead.

— Irish?

—Yeah, something like that.

—Why does he know so much about the Russian Revolution?

—Seems like it was some shit he picked up at Oxford.

—Right, of course, Oxford. What happened at Bright Angel?

—You prolly know more about it than I do.

—Not really, the president was talking and then...did everyone die?

—No, not everyone.

—How many survivors?

—One that I know of, but there could be others.

—You pulled me out of there?

—Yeah.

—Did you plant the bomb?

—No.

—But you knew about it.

—No.

—I had friends in there, colleagues, people I had known a long time. People I loved and admired. The damn president of the United States.

—I'm sorry.

—You're fuckin sorry?

—I didn't have nothing to do with it.

—Well, you must have had something to do with it.

—Nope, I was given enough information to get you out, that's it.

— Given information by whom?

— Some dude named Malcolm.

— Who the hell's Malcolm?

— Don't know, I never met him.

— But you do his bidding anyway.

— Yeah, for now. They offered me ten pounds of V-cell.

— Mulatien?

— Yeah, protein is hard to come by at the moment.

— Malcolm offered you ten pounds of V-cell to go get me?

—Well, really the offer came from this lady, Claire.

—Claire?

—She didn't look like a Claire so maybe that wasn't her real name.

—Am I a prisoner here?

—No ma'am. I'll get you back up canyon, take you back where I found you, or to your house, or your mama's house or whatever you want.

—What about your ten pounds of V-cell?

—I'll tell `em you died, but that they still owe me because I held up my end of the deal. I guess we'll see what happens.

—Okay.

—Okay.

—I remember you.

—From when?

—I don't know, maybe you were in my dreams.

—What were they, then?

—Something else. Some kind of alternative reality, I don't know.

—Yeah and what happened in this reality?

—I am not sure I could tell you, and even if I could, I don't think you would believe me.

—Little green men?

—No. It was more intimate than that.

—Lady, I don't got no control over your fucking dreams.

—No. Neither do I apparently.

—Are you gonna eat your soup?

—I'm not hungry.

—Soup is hard to come by these days, you know.

She lifted the spoon to her mouth and tipped a bit of cream of mushroom into her gullet. She forced herself to swallow. Her stomach threatened to return the soup to the air for being the foreign invader that it was. She sat very still and was quiet and closed her eyes and she felt the warmth of the fire on her face and the cold of the night at her back.

They sat in silence until the fire died out and Leonard rose and fed it driftwood and when the interior walls of the cave glowed orange again Leonard went outside and Tammy could see his moon shadow crossing back and forth across the crude doorway.

She straightened the blankets on the pallet and spread the deer skins over them and the stinking bear hide, and again she lay on the cold sand floor and took off her clothes and she forced herself to fold them neatly, though it seemed like an absurdity to do so.

Under the animal hides she shivered with the cold. Eventually she drifted off to sleep and later, perhaps only moments later or maybe hours, she woke and the fire's embers were cold and dark and the only light in the chamber was the moon's meek offering and she felt his naked body behind her and he curled around her like a living blanket and she felt his heart beat in time with her own.

12

From the cave overlooking the sandy wash that its sole human inhabitant had named Nahal-Joseph-Smith, to the tent at the highest flat spot in Dharma Camp, the marquee in which Tammy Cohen waited, alone, holding a glass of water, wearing dirty, ill-fitting clothes, still bruised and bandaged, still shocked and outraged, was but five miles as the crow flies but it was more than thirty miles afoot.

Tammy was still disappointed in herself for having so easily succumbed to the base flattery of a simple invitation from the White House. No matter how she ranted and railed about the president's hubris and willful blindness, no matter how many times she had said both privately and publicly that it was the Martinez administration that would be remembered for loading humanity on a bus bound direct for hell, she still did not hesitate in driving herself through the night to be at the beck and call of that selfsame president.

Maybe she's not yet lost to reason. Perhaps it's not too late. Maybe the president wants me in the audience because despite all that was said before she's going to take my recommendations.

Tammy sat, one leg crossed over the other, and bobbed her top foot like a nervous job applicant who had forgotten to shower or change into clean clothes before the big interview. She reminded herself that she was closer to being a prisoner than she was to being a job applicant and yet her palms sweat and her heart jumped in its cage.

She and Leonard had walked for two days, sleeping only in the heat of the day, eating little, speaking only when necessary, all of their energy focused on the next step. They were figures in a maze whose walls rose to the heavens and whose sandy floor seemed to have the fires of hell boiling just below its surface.

Tammy sat on a cylindrical eighteen-inch-high cushion. A bolster covered in ethnic print. The seat stood in contrast to its circumstances. She had seen enough of the world to know that its tasseled design was Persian and while the chair was perhaps misplaced in the American wilderness, it was perfectly at home in the marquee in which it found itself, and Tammy thought that the seat seemed to imply that it had always been in some tent or another, in some desert or another, silently insisting that its sitters uncurl their backs, as if to remind them that sitting up was the very least history demanded of them.

The tent's interior was spare but surprisingly thought out. A small neat bed, no more than four inches off the ground, was dressed in crisp white sheets, hospital corners that the housekeeper at the Ritz Carlton would have been proud of, a carpet that so far as she could tell was Turkish in origin. A large, redwood desk, that appeared to be hewn from the heart of a single ancient tree, held court in the center of the chamber. Tucked into the gap on its business end, the head of a standard leather office chair could be seen, the type that might have been purchased at Crate and Barrel or Restoration Hardware or Staples. Tammy could not help but to think that the chairs themselves met across the ancient wooden desk and did not need inhabitants at all to be at odds with one another. It was possible, Tammy thought, that the chairs were negotiating the fate of the world.

Tammy could see through the tent's open flap the midday doings of Dharma Camp. A small, busy place in a cottonwood choked draw, up the unimportant side canyon of an unimportant side canyon. Dwellings were being built, a water catchment system put into place, terraces, some as small as a square foot, were being turned and fertilized and planted. Burdens of: food, wood, water, tools and dirt were being moved up and down the path by wheelbarrow and armload and makeshift sked. The workers seemed to carry their goods willingly and some even with pleasure. From their stance alone, Tammy could tell that these workers were no slaves, that there was not a conscript among them. From what her small view afforded, Dharma Camp appeared to Tammy to be some sort of utopian experiment, inheritor of the communes and the kibbutzim of the past. This unlikely village in this unlikely place seemed to be thriving on the idea of collectivism, just at the same moment that our cities full of individuals were burning.

Tammy also considered the possibility that it was all a show, common enough. It could have been an immersive theatrical experience in which the performers had forgotten that the reality they had constructed so meticulously was nothing but an illusion nested inside another reality, a reality that may in fact be nested inside yet another. Russian Dolls, built not of wood but of nostalgia for a past whose hardships had been forgotten, but whose charms easily transcended the barrier of time. Tammy had the feeling that she had woken up in the middle of a Ren Fair. That any minute now some "wench" barely contained in a sexy red velvet bodice was going to come into the tent and offer her a cup of honey mead.

While Tammy sat on the strange cushion and looked out the open flap, a woman entered the tent unseen and unheard through a tab ninety degrees to the side of the main opening. It seemed to Tammy that in one instant she was alone but in the next there was another woman standing in the tent with her, and it was as if that woman had always been there. Tammy stood and for a long time they regarded one another like boxers just after the initial bell, but before either had landed a blow. The younger woman had shoulder-length brown hair in loose curls. She wore a simple clean dress of blue cotton, a costume of adulthood that might be worn by a child. Her face expressed both the vigor of youth and the wisdom of age.

—Would you do me a favor?

—I guess.

—Would you close the front flap so we won't be disturbed?

—Who are you?

—If you can get the door, I'm sure there's no question I won't be willing to answer.

Tammy stood and went to the doorway and found a silver hasp at the end of a thick hemp rope. She opened it and let the heavy canvas fall across the threshold, changing the space from public to private, from light-filled to dim. As her eyes adjusted, Tammy found that that tent was quite pleasant, as if they were characters in a sepia tone photograph taken in some distant and simpler past.

—So?

—I'm Malcolm.

—*You're Malcolm?*

—Yes.

—Huh. Your mama give you that name?

—No, she insisted on calling me Vanessa.

—And who is Malcolm?

—A kind of unofficial, elected official.

—You were elected?

—Right. I stand corrected. Unofficial, unelected official.

Tammy took a step toward her interlocutor and her eyes were close to those bottomless wells of blue. Despite her heart bashing itself against her breast bone, she found her voice:

—Fuck you.

—Right, okay, cup of tea?

—Tea?

—I have English Breakfast and I can also make you chai if you'd like.

—I had friends who died at Bright Angel.

—I am so sorry for your loss.

—You're fucking sorry?

—Yes, I understand why you would be angry, but I promise you the bombing had nothing at all to do with me. I neither planned it, paid for it, carried it out nor condone it.

—Yet here we are, so you must've had something to do with it.

—I knew it was going to happen, but there wasn't anything I could do about it.

—If you knew ahead of time, you could've warned people. You could've stopped it.

—That's funny. I've read your work. You think it's all a matter of resources and environment. One big correction, Mother Earth's Revenge: you don't see that our generation's struggle is the same as any generation's struggle; people, resources and power. The rest is just background.

—Who did it then?

—Does it matter?

—My ears are still fucking ringing!

—Might have something for that. Again, would you like a cup of tea?

—Do all those people out there call you Malcolm?

—No. It's complicated, but when they see me they call me Sakti. To them I am simply the yoga teacher.

—The yoga teacher?

—Yes, we've been practicing since we were children.

—We?

—Like I said, it's complicated.

—So all these people are following a person they've never seen before?

—Yes.

—And who the hell do they think Malcolm is?

—More powerful for being able to rule from the shadows, I guess.

—And a man.

—The patriarchy doesn't die easily, but it does have its uses.

—What a sham.

—Okay, well, I'm having a cup of tea.

She shuffled to a side table behind the desk and turned on an electric kettle.

—You have electricity?

—Solar.

—Where'd you get the tea?

—We sent an envoy to England to see if we could open formal relations, but they didn't come back with much. I imagine it might be different now. Anyway he's a dear man and he brought me some tea. I've learned to live without milk, but I have hope for the future.

The younger woman opened a drawer and came up with two cups, and from a square metal tin, she scooped a twig-like substance into two metal balls, and they waited silently until the water boiled, and they waited for the tea to steep and Tammy was reminded of the former president of the United States, now dead, most likely murdered by the woman in front of her, and she remembered sharing tea in the president's office and for a brief moment the young woman before her and President Sonia Martinez were the same woman, and just for an instant Tammy was unsure as to where she sat and with whom.

The young woman took the metal ball out of the water and let the water drain from it and placed the ball on a small dish on her desk and she set the cup down in front of Tammy and adjusted the handle so it was facing her guest.

The tea was as good as anything Tammy ever imagined could exist.

—It's quite an honor to have a scientist of your caliber here with us.

—Is it?

—Yes.

—I almost fucking died.

—And yet, there is a great gap between almost and dead, isn't there?

—What am I doing here?

—Having a cup of tea.

—And then?

—And then we'll see.

—You know, I wasn't looking for a job.

—No?

—No.

—Maybe a job was looking for you.

They sat for a long while in the dim tent, drinking tea, looking at one another and also looking away, each in her own private orb of thought. Tammy Cohen thought about Ted Weiner, the last person she spoke to before Bright Angel Lodge was reduced to splinters. Tammy knew that the iron pillar that blocked her view of the president also saved her life, and she knew that it was the woman across from her that made sure that it was Tammy, and no other, who was sat behind that pillar.

—Why me?

—Do you know what's happened in the month since Bright Angel?

—No.

—Would you like to?

—I suppose you'll tell me either way.

—California is at open war with Nevada and Arizona. The Federal Government has abandoned the region entirely to its own devices. This war's not going to have any winners, believe me.

—What do you want with me?

—For now, nothing. We have yoga at four, or if you'd prefer Ivan has tai chi at sunrise and sunset on the other side of the camp.

—You put my life at risk and then went to great pains to save it, all so that I could go to yoga at four?

—I'm glad to see you have plenty of fight left, you're gonna need it. At the bottom of the hill, if you want it, there's a yurt with your name on it.

And the young woman with blue eyes stood and then left through the same side flap from which she'd entered, silently, with neither preamble nor salutation, and after she had gone, Tammy sat alone with her thoughts. Eventually she rose and left the tent and walked on to the main path.

She entered the flow of people ascending and descending. People either smiled at her or did not particularly notice her, but none made her feel as if she were a stranger. She asked a young man who was sat at the side of the path sorting through a barrel of shelled corn with great concentration:

—Where are the yurts?

—Are you Tammy Cohen ?

—How did you know that?

—We've been expecting you.

—What do you mean?

—It was in the newsletter.

—What?

—Yeah, on the board in front of the co-op, every few days they post the doings. So anyway, your digs are down by Devil's Creek.

—Devil's Creek?

—Well, there's no creek there now, but a couple of good rains and… boom.

—Where is it?

—Make a left at the co-op. You can't miss it.

The co-op was a country store without a till or attendant. Goods were taken and others left behind: baskets of corn and wheat, bushels of asparagus, spring onions, beans, a barrel of dried brook trout. People gathered in the front of the rough wooden structure, and all the people that she met were kind to her and smiled at her, and more than one asked if she needed anything, and indeed there was a handwritten missive outside of the store. Articles of news: the changing weather, a change of time for the knitting class, a bighorn sheep cheese-making seminar, and sure enough, a brief article about the impending arrival of an important scientist. The article had some of Tammy's biography and although some of it was wrong, most of it was at least factually correct. Raised in West Texas, educated at Stanford, winner of the National Medal of Science, nominated for the Nobel Prize. The article left out her service to the Martinez Administration, or exile from the same, or her presence at the Bright Angel bombing, or her rescue from the same, or even that such a world-altering event had occurred, and Tammy wondered if all the friendly people she met knew anything at all about the mass murder of the American leadership.

Please, make her feel welcome!

She found the yurt number four, and as promised, it had her name on it, stitched in needlepoint as if to imply that her stay would be permanent. Inside, she found a bed, and on top of its blankets, new clothes: heavyweight wool pants and three thick sweaters, all hand woven. Colors which she had, in the past, favored. She found a ceramic water cooler and a box of food: dried brook trout, wild asparagus, corn and beans. She sat down heavily on the bed and the bed was softer than she expected it to be. She lay back and tears filled her eyes and she wept quietly until she slept.

She dreamt of warning Ted that the building was going to explode, and also of her mother and their home in El Paso, and of President Martinez, whom she idolized before she despised, and the beach in Bali before it slipped under the sea, and in her dream the leaders of the world listened to her and prepared their populations for the changes that were coming. When she woke, the sun had arced across the sky and she changed into her new clothes and came out of the yurt with her name etched on it in curly purple script, and she asked a passerby what time it was, and he told her that the sun would hit the edge of the canyon in about an hour and she made her way to the center of the encampment and there she saw there were no fewer than thirty people gathered doing yoga at the direction of the woman she knew to be Malcolm, the woman whose mother knew her as Vanessa, and whom the people of Dharma knew as Sakti.

They started with Pranayama and then moved to Chair Pose and then Sakti twisted her arms up into Eagle Pose and then Standing Head to Knee, and then to Bow and Stick and Triangle and Tree and then the Wind Removing Pose and Cobra and Half Tortoise and Rabbit and the Spine Twisting and Blowing Poses, and the sun passed beyond the western wall of the canyon and pain radiated from her spine and through her legs and out of her bare feet and it soaked into the dry ground below her. They did all the poses again as the temperature dropped. The second time they passed through the sequence, Tammy lost herself in the ancient wisdom of her own body and her body's pain was beyond feeling until it was nothing at all, and her mind's chatter slowed, and for a moment she stopped weighing the pros and cons of running or staying, and when she said *Namaste* she was with them, not one among many but part of a whole, complete and inseparable.

As she was walking slowly back to her yurt, she felt a presence keeping step with her. She looked to her right and there he was, and she knew that Leonard would try to help her no matter what she decided.

—Did you meet Malcolm?

—Yes.

—And?

—Have you ever met him?

—No, not yet.

—I see.

—What did you think?

—I couldn't really tell you.

He walked her to her door and wished her goodnight, and she went in and lit the beeswax candle on the table and she ate dried fish, and she thought about her little stone house nestled in the Chisos mountains and she wondered if she would ever see it again.

Months passed in the way that months sometimes do. Her wounds healed. She regained her strength. She went to Sakti's yoga class twice every day on the large sand bar left behind by what was once called Hoosgow Creek, which had long since ceased to run, and she placed herself in the front of the class and often she and the teacher, who was more than she appeared to be, looked directly at one another and theirs became a sort of long, silent negotiation, and it became clear to those who payed attention that there was something between the yoga teacher and the mysterious scientist and many assumed that something was sexual, though it was not.

Every few mornings she would wake up to a box of food that had been delivered in the night. Potatoes, leeks, beans, dried fish. She made a few friends in the camp, mostly women but some men. She ate with them and cooked with them and went on long hikes in the desert with them. Casually at first and then with growing formality, she helped her friends with projects. Simple things. She changed the angle of a greenhouse, adjusted a drip irrigation system, gave a friend advice regarding the erratic behavior of a lover.

Eventually she took on larger projects. She could not help herself. Knowledge was not anything if not utilized, and knowledge had lodged itself within her body both by education and experimentation. Tammy Cohen was first and foremost a scientist, and she used her expertise in the fields of botany and hydrology and geology to help the community.

Southern Utah was hotter and dryer every year, and plants and animals were dying at a rate never seen before in the Holocene Era, and yet, she found within that hot sheet of death pockets where life thrived. She managed to find water where before there was none, unearthed springs long since driven underground and made a garden in every patch of shade. Over time, her contributions changed the clothes that people wore, the hours in which they worked, the way they thought of plants and other animals, and water and sun. Ideas that she once presented to the president of the United States to be instituted on a grand scale, she instituted herself on a small scale, and she saw a community thrive around her. Tammy Cohen was unable to save the world, but one day as she helped her neighbor Patricia plant a small fruit-bearing bush by using water distilled from an ancient barrel cactus, Tammy thought that perhaps with one neighbor helped, the world entire might be saved.

Leonard would be gone for a week or more at a time, and then he would spend the nights he was in camp in her bed. On those nights they fucked and fucked and fucked, and no words were said and no arrangements were made and he was not an Indian or a Marine or a traitor to his country, nor was she an important scientist or a prize winner or a public figure or a whisperer with a million riders aboard. She was not her father's daughter, nor her mother's greatest pride and they fucked until they were exhausted and sore. They had tumbled through the universe untethered by time and unbound from their physical beings.

Over time, Tammy would learn through the whispers of her friends, that Dharma Camp was loosely affiliated with as many as ten camps of similar size. They traded between one another, swapped blankets for grain, and animal protein for fish, water purifiers for old bottles of wine, solar panels for whiskey, charcoal for animal dung. There were those among the denizens of Dharma camp who harbored fantasies of living in the Old West, and for them, reality rose up to meet their steps.

As the days turned to months, Tammy discovered herself. For the first time, she was part of a community, and within that community she held a place of security and status and sometimes whole strings of days might go by and she would forget that she was not really in Dharma camp of her own accord. Sometimes she wondered what the point of bringing her to this place was, and also, often, she ceased to wonder at all. It was when her resistance was at its weakest point, it was after she felt truly at home, with friends, purpose, a lover, a physical practice and a spiritual discipline... it was after she delivered her first baby because she was the closest thing to a medical doctor the camp had, and it was after her friend Anais died for want of insulin. It was after Anais was mourned by the community and her body burned in a ritual pyre and Tammy and Anais's other girlfriends danced all night around the fire and chanted and sang and burned their clothes that, when they were naked and exultant and under a perfect dome of stars, each knew that they would never be alone again, for they had seen beyond the veil of the world.

It was after the temperature had dropped and snow blanketed the ground, it was after the time that Tammy had forgotten who she once was, that she woke up to a handwritten note pinned to the door of her yurt.

Malcolm would like to see you. Sunset in his tent. Please come unseen and alone.

There was a glass of water waiting for her on the Redwood desk. After a time, Vanessa came in and asked that the flap be closed. Tammy closed the flap and they were alone and instantly plunged into darkness. After a moment, Vanessa lit a candle and they both sat down.

—Cup of tea?

—Yes, please.

And when the water was boiled and the tea steeped and was served and had been consumed in its entirety:

—Do you know how long you've been here?

—Sixteen months, five days and nine hours.

—And are you ready to leave?

—Depends on where I'm going.

—And what if I told you that this community, and for that matter the other communities within the network are relying on you, your mind, your will and your indomitable spirit to save us from a fate, that but for your efforts, is all but assured?

—That seems like an awful lot to put on a person.

—And yet it has always been here waiting for you.

—What has always been waiting for me?

—You believed in her, didn't you?

—Who?

—Sonia Martinez.

—Why would that possibly matter?

—You wanted to save the world, give us a chance at restarting. You had ideas, didn't you?

—All that's over now.

—You're wrong. *All that* is just getting started.

—Find somebody else.

—Have you made friends here?

—What do you want?

—You can see that our resources are dwindling. Do you think that Shandra and Tanya and Joy and Estelle and Chris, and Xylon and Cedar and Daniel and Alicia and Sasha and Rachel are going to be here in a year? I mean you might survive, but do you think they will?

—Maybe it'll fucking rain.

—Of course it will, eventually, but you know that's not going to be enough.

—There's nothing I can do about that now. There never really was.

—There is something you can do to try and save your friends.

—Why don't you just tell me what you want me to do, and I'll decide if I want to do it or not.

13

MAY 1ˢᵀ, 2049

They tried to keep parallel to the road, not within sight of it but just beyond. This was the challenge of their daily lives. There was a constant battle that raged along the decaying and IED blasted pavements. The road was the fight's medium, its diamond, its pitch, its ring. A place for the remnants of the sentimental conservative movement and that of the high-minded liberal party to once and for all fight it out for the soul of America, and the fact that the country for which they fought no longer existed exerted little pressure on the hearts of the combatants if it had ever really pressed them at all. The labels had faded though the symbols remained: donkeys and elephants, swastikas and crosses, six-pointed stars and pentagrams, male and female, and team logos that far outlasted their storied franchises. South Beach and Chavez Ravine had long since closed for business, one now home to a weekly slave market and the other empty and quiet and irradiated beyond the hope of baseball within the half-life of plutonium, and yet Giants and Dodgers fought still, traded dominance week by bloody week, just as they always had—and the gods for whom these warriors fought, for whom they would lay down their lives, gods whose ink covered their backs and arms and legs and necks remained hidden and silent and safe in their havens, real or imagined. Leonard and Tammy kept to the fringe and watched the fight through binoculars, ran when the tattooed beasts were engaged and hid when they patrolled for their enemy.

—What's happening now?

Leonard lowered the cracked binoculars and looked at her curled into the dry ditch they'd followed as it meandered vaguely west to east.

—From what I can tell they're interrogating the poor bastards.

—Which poor bastards are those?

—The Dodgers they caught flat-footed. It looks like it's gonna be bad.

—You a sympathizer?

—When they're done asking questions I guess they're gonna rape them, her at least, and then kill 'em both.

—Yeah, Jesus. How long's that gonna take?

—Damn, when'd you get so cold-blooded?

—Is there something we can do about it?

—No.

—If it had gone the other way, would the Dodgers rape and kill the Giants?

—Definitely.

—Well then, it's the world they choose to live in, but I been sitting in this ditch for two damn hours and my back hurts and I'm hot and sunburnt and so if they are gonna do some raping and killing they could at least get on with it.

—What if it was you they were raping?

—Do you have some kinda point here, Leonard?

—My point is... naw just passing the time I guess. Maybe try and sleep and we'll make our miles at night.

—K.

—K.

He lay down next to her in the ditch and curled himself around her as best as the rocky ground would allow, not sleeping but not awake either, and after a time they heard the woman's screams and despite Tammy's earlier show of callousness and bravado Leonard felt her body tense and shudder at the thought of her fellow woman's pain, and then a short while later they heard three shots and an explosion and then the oxygen suck of a car on fire, and then the roar of engines and the throaty growl of glass pack mufflers and the squeal of tires. She clutched at him as it seemed that the Giants were coming directly to rape and kill them next but the road curved north and the bangers dopplered away until they diminished to nothing at all and then they only heard the wind and the baking earth and they lay still as stones, afraid to move.

It had been three weeks and about one hundred and twenty miles since they had left Dharma Camp. They had a grand sendoff complete with a sweat lodge and smudging ceremony, both of which Leonard openly mocked, and they had butchered one of the remaining bighorn and half of its meat had been dried and put in Tammy and Leonard's packs, and the other half was shared out between the gathered company. Ninety-four sinners. And while no one ate more than a bite of the meat, it was enough for it to feel like a celebration. Though Tammy had been there for more than a year, she looked around the flat sandy plane of Hoosegow Creek and saw how skinny and ragged they all were and she knew for the first time just how desperate her undertaking was. They would all starve to death in the case of her failure and even if she were to make it all the way there and all the way back Tammy had her doubts about ever seeing any of the souls of Dharma Camp again.

Climbing out of the canyon and onto White Mesa took five days. They got lost or found themselves cliffed-out over and over again. They were not carrying technical equipment, though it was available to them, and they were both proficient in its use. They would have been forced to leave the gear at the Canyon's rim. They had decided that leaving behind such a valuable kit was a waste the community could ill afford. Twice they were within sight of the rim and yet were forced back to the bottom of the canyon because the last one hundred feet of their chosen route was too exposed. It was as if the canyon itself was telling them not to even attempt the long journey. More than once, Tammy got the feeling that if it was not for her Leonard would have made the climb alone, but Tammy also realized that it was her that needed to make it to the north of the world and that without her Leonard had no need to make the assent at all. On the evening of the fifth day they managed to find a passable route to the rim.

They made a cold camp on the mesa, and slept pressed against one another for warmth. In two days they found themselves stuffed into the vertical folds of a sandstone outcropping looking over what was once simply call I-70 but had since taken the name of Refugee Lane for the type of traffic it carried. From their vantage it looked like some kind of apocalyptic holiday parade. Overburdened vehicles of every type headed to some location other than their homes, yet bringing as much of home as they could carry. From where

Tammy and Leonard watched, there was no way to know the desperation that filled each vehicle's interior. They could not see each driver's face watching the line of opposing traffic and wondering why so many people would choose to drive in the direction of the hell that they themselves had just fled. Each driver wondered if they were not driving from somewhere bad to somewhere worse. What Tammy and Leonard had no way of knowing was that they were looking at the remnant of the elite population that still had goods tantamount to a tank of gas. It may have been nonperishable food, it may have been guns, or munitions. In many cases it was sex, or a child or a mother sold into slavery. Desperation can be measured in the calculations people are willing to make. Sacrifices, that a month previous, or even a week before would have been unthinkable become the coin of the realm. Even after such profound sacrifices, most would abandon their junk-laden cars at the side of the road and succumb to death wandering the desert on foot.

On the right day at the right time, thousands of refugees could be seen walking south toward the Mexican border wall, on the other side of which it was rumored that warlords had managed to create pockets of prosperity similar to that of the old United States. Rumors that there were those who still lived like the caesars of Rome. So there were those who traveled south in the hope that they would simply be recognized as natural citizens of such prosperity, that they were favored by

God, that ease and wealth were simply their birthright, that they need only present themselves so that they might resume their privileged existence.

Tammy and Leonard's first fourteen days of walking would see them to the ghost town of Fort Garland at the southern end of the Rockies. The snowcapped peaks of Blanca and Mount Linsey looked down and saw nothing out of the ordinary in the meaningless human migration that took place at their feet. Storefronts and broken traffic lights, telephone wires, shattered glass and swirling eddies of radioactive dust were all that was left at the once busy corner of Miranda and Sixth. The Council had tried to preserve the Old West feel of the town, and what two years previous had looked like a cheerful facsimile of a frontier settlement had taken on the grim mien of the real thing.

They passed a gem shop with its charms still on display in the windows: diamonds, garnets and moonstones, hackmanite and magnetite, all with their prices proudly displayed, but the gems themselves patiently waiting for the building around them to dissolve, so that they might return to the darkness and comforting pressure of the Earth itself.

—My grandpa used to be into this kind of thing.

—What kind of thing?

—Minerals. He had all kinds of geodes and crystals and whatever, all kinds. He had this bookcase in the sitting room that he displayed them on.

—What happened to 'em?

—The minerals? Who knows?

—And him?

—Louis? He lived a long decent life and died of the bad heart he was born with.

—Huh. Do you remember him?

—Barely. I remember that he was tall and kind, and made eggs with Matzah in them.

—Jewish Migas.

—Sure. He had a pacemaker that was just under the skin of his chest, and though I never saw it move or anything, I always thought of it as some kind of second heart.

The next door they passed had been a convenience store, still open twenty-four hours but now left unattended. Its shelves were stripped bare. Not a crumb remained, not a Twinkie not a Hoho not a chimichanga, not a hot wing not a toothbrush not a magazine, not a tube of sun cream nor a bottle of ibuprofen. No cheap sunglasses graced the empty racks; not a tampon or a single ballpoint pen was left. All of those items had been deemed indispensable or at least tradable in the post United States economy. Hundred-dollar bills could be seen blowing down the streets, each one with its own smear of shit on both sides, a graphic reminder that even in hard times Americans took some joy in an act of irony, however, in God, the American could clearly no longer trust. Tammy stood on the sidewalk looking at the storefronts and Leonard scanned the other side of the street for movement.

—Where'd they all go?

—I don't know. If I had to guess I'd say they all bailed when they shut off the taps.

—The taps?

—Water, electricity, gas—the shit people believe they can't live without, but really

lots of people been living without 'em all along. Plenty of sad fucks never saw a Volker, or an Angius or even a goddam toaster, so they ain't missing that shit now, but these fuckers…

And he gestured broadly to the population of Fort Garland in absentia.

— …they don't know how to live without those things. My guess is there are plenty of them that actually can't, and I guess there are a fair few that maybe can but don't want to. Been living inside the damn Holoverse so long they can't see living anywhere else.

—And who's they?

171

—What do you mean?

—You said *they* turned off the taps. Who's they?

—Whoever's in charge now. Ever since the Mayflower some white eye or another been running the shit, why should it be different now?

Per Malcolm's instructions: Tammy and Leonard walked south along route sixty-four and they caught a glimpse of the cleft in the earth that the Rio Grande had made its home for two million years and more. They could not see the bottom of the canyon but they did not need to in order to know that only a dry riverbed remained. They walked south. Hours passed and they said nothing at all. When Leonard spoke, he spoke as if they had been talking all along.

—Tell me more about Ellen then.

—Ellen. I wouldn't know where to start.

—Start at the beginning.

—Which beginning?

—You said she was born in the DC suburbs....

—Really? That beginning?

—We got nothing but time.

—She was born in the DC suburbs, her father worked for the FBI, her mother was a nurse.

—Wait a minute. The mineral collector was a G-man?

—More Like a J man.

—What?

At the time they didn't let Jews become FBI agents. After a few years of getting passed over, he quit the bureau and started selling life insurance. After a few more years they moved to Jersey and so far as I know they lived on her salary.

—How'd that go?

—I got the feeling that it didn't really go very well, but, I know he lived to be pretty old and then he died. In that sense I guess it went fine. Ellen flew to the East Coast to bury him and came back all within the same weekend, and if she was sad I didn't really notice because I was a kid then and it was not really mine to notice those things.

—Oh yeah? What was yours to notice?

—Ryan Seacrest's top forty countdown on my JBL and working on my tan. Thirty minutes a side like buttered toast. It's hard to believe now. I would lay there and let the sun cook my skin and I would call it work. I even had a sense of achievement if I managed to get a noticeable shade darker, without burning and peeling of course.

Leonard shook his head slowly.

—White people.

They walked a silent mile and then he asked her, like no time had passed at all:

—Do you remember any of the songs?

They walked for two more miles and the fallow ground spread out before them. The Costilla Peaks rose to the east as the Rio Grande Gorge fell into the west.

They bore silent witness as Gaia took back what had been hers all along, and they walked past harvesting machines and plows sinking into the earth, and sometimes the remains of a house or a country church, whose adobe was melting back into the ground. They were silent and Tammy tried to put herself in the backyard of her childhood. She could see the sad magnolia tree and the lawn that was mostly dirt with a couple patches of grass, and the concrete pad, and the round metal table and metal chairs that were rusting and had cushions tied to them that had been half-eaten by the weather and bugs. There were the concrete steps that led into the small kitchen and she could hear the neighbor's dog that never seemed to stop barking, and the white sun that burned a hole in the sky, and she remembered a vague feeling of angst filling her chest. A favorite song rose or slipped on the charts and Tammy's spirits rose and slipped with it. She had convinced herself that it mattered, that the fate of the world was somehow tied to the countdown. It was sold in exactly that way and she took it for nothing less. A logical gap to be sure, and yet as she walked through the ruined landscape and the airwaves were freed of pop music or any other invisible signal, the gap did not seem so great. When pop music died, the country was soon to follow.

Finally, one came to her, and why that one she would never know. It was one of the hundreds that she had listened to and sung along with and felt to the bottom of her adolescent soul for the real human emotions it had expressed. These glorious songs told of love and loss and spoke of the exuberance and joy of being alive. She sang what she could remember:

—All the hot Miami nights…

Of a barrio, Barrio

He was living in the shadows huh

But he's got that fire though…

Fire in his heart that's made of something more….

Leonard looked at Tammy and his eyes were full of surprise and amazement.

—That was lodged inside of you?

—Yeah, I guess so. I wonder what it will do now that it's free.

—Who knows?

—What were you singing along to circa 2018?

—Cradle prolly. I was on the rez. We didn't have a computer or nothing. But my cousin had a radio and we used to listen to a station out of Albuquerque and pretend that we were thugs.

—Well, go ahead.

—What?

—I sang for you.

—Naw, fuck that.

But then after a moment he stopped walking and he closed his eyes. The pause was long enough that Tammy was about to break the silence, when Leonard struck a pose, arms crossed like an old school rapper.

—*Just like eys staring out a broken soul.*

Walking down this lonesome road

And trying to find his way home

I am just trying to find my way home…

—I remember that

—Yeah, Cradle on the radio and vagina on the brain.

—How old were you?

—Bout fifteen.

—Bit young for vagina brain, don't you think?

—Maybe. Maybe I was thinking of the X-Men or dreaming up ways to make a rocket out of tied together firecrackers so I could go to space and get off the damn rez. I don't know. Really, I was just waiting for the sun to go down so I could go back to my own damn house.

—You couldn't go into your house in the daytime?

—Naw, my old man said that boys were supposed to be outside during the day, but really he was a junkie piece of shit and I guess he needed the house so he could shoot up and nod off in peace.

—What about your mom?

—She was at work. Worked at this horrible fucking warehouse where they'd bring old dairy cows to be ground up and sold for dog food. The place reeked of death, and she always had a cigarette lit and she always smelled like dead cows and tobacco. It was a weird place. After that she go to this bar and come home late and drunk. To her I was always asleep. To me she was always at work. Weeks went by and I didn't see her at all and when I did, I wished I didn't.

—What happened to them?

—She disappeared, maybe she still out there whoring it up somewhere, who knows?

—And your father?

—Well, he got off the horse, and for a while was off of everything, but last I saw him he was pretty strung out on fentanyl, said some doctor gave it to him cause he twisted his ankle at work. It most likely killed him, but I don't know that for sure. I was in Syria and Pakistan and Iraq, wherever the shit was really. When I did finally come home I didn't look for them and I didn't find them neither. I looked for my grandparents, even though I knew they were dead a long time already. I tried to find out everything I could about them.

—Like what?

—Where they lived, what they did, who their friends were…anything.

—Why?

—I had this idea that they were the last real Apaches in my line, and I had some notion that maybe I could pick up where they left off.

—And?

—Well, the truth is slippery I s'pose. He wasn't a heroin addict but I guess he had his bouts with the booze. Lived out there on this little patch in Eastern Arizona. He had this old truck and would drive into Show Low pretty often to stop by the bar, or buy supplies. People liked him, called him Chuck even though that wasn't his name. This old man I met claimed that he got the name because when he got drunk he used to move across the bar Chuck Berry style, you know that whole leg flopping in front number.

—How'd he make his living?

—Swinging a chainsaw I think. He'd go into the mountains on the rez and cut down trees and then sell the wood to the white people.

They walked in silence and the hours passed and the landscape did not change at all and the sun seemed not to move westward in the sky. Eventually they came even with a free-standing cinder cone to their west.

—Is that it?

—Yeah, I think so.

—Were supposed to hike to the top of that?

—I guess. We could skip it if you want, but we did walk all the way down here so…

—Why not? We climbed on the crazy train a long time ago. We may as well see where it goes.

In two hours, they stood at the base of San Antonio Mountain. They made camp in a dry arroyo and built a small fire, hiding its light in a natural sandstone grotto and they ate what meager rations they had, and they felt the Earth pulling on their bodies as if insisting that they go no further on their absurd errand. When the fire's embers died they could see the

Milky Way etched in sharp relief across the New Mexico sky and for a moment they were cured of pretension and false importance and knew that the success or failure of their efforts would yield largely the same result and thus they were freed of obscene responsibility. They both slept well for the first time since leaving Dharma Camp.

14

MAY 2ND, 2049

They rose in the dark, with dawn not even a rumor in the east, and they ate three bites of dried sheep, and chewed slowly and Tammy was so stripped of excess that she could feel the meat's stored energy move into her and begin to burn. An ancient transfer of wealth, from sun to grass, from sheep to woman. She knew that she would have to scale the mountain in front of her before the fuel tank hit empty or they would have wasted a day's rations to go only halfway. They shouldered their packs and began the climb.

They followed an old fire-road and by two they had reached the summit of San Antonio Mountain, much lower than the Costilla Peaks to their east or Blanca to their north. San Antonio was a once active volcano, now no more than a sharp tit on the flat plain that stretched between the Southern Rockies and the Colorado Plateau. The ascent took them from an undulating scoria of basalt to a gimp forest of gnarled juniper and then up into a scorched copse of Douglas fir skeletons, ravaged first by bark beetle then by fire; a forest of the dammed whose blackened sentinels pointed toward the clear sky as if in mass accusation. While they saw no living thing in that highland, there were signs of elk or deer or mountain goat or some other pellet-shitting animal, and Tammy saw Leonard check his carbine, in the first and only sign she had ever had that there may be bullets lodged inside the rifle he carried.

When they reached the peak, they found three abandoned outbuildings and a small solar-powered array of weather monitoring equipment. They stood staring blankly and short of breath in front of a device that looked like a robot that had been starved to death and now had its skinny arms bent at the elbow, raised in surrender. Tammy opened the rubber sealed lid that formed the creature's chest cavity and a screen on the inside came to life.

Wind: east-south-east, 10 Mph

Dew: .60 degrees

Pressure ↓ 1013 millibars

Precipitation: 24 hrs= 0 inches, 1 week= 0 inches, one mth=0 inches, YTD rainfall= 0 inches.

—Do you think there is anyone on the receiving end of this information?

—Aliens maybe…

The voice came from behind them, thin and effeminate and full of glee and mischief and with the second pronounced syllable Leonard had already spun and had the rifle trained on the gut of the speaker.

—…or perhaps Gaia herself, checking on the numbers to make sure her revenge is going just as planned. It's not very useful, however, there is something about how it's gathered that is some comfort. A relic from the time of connectedness, I guess.

The speaker was a small man, standing less than five-and-a-half feet above the ground, sharp blue eyes, a pre-fall smile, white straight teeth, his hands and face soft and moisturized and well cared for, and he stood before the road-worn travelers in what appeared to be a hand-tailored suit.

Everything about his dress and demeanor was at odds with the landscape, as if the travelers saw not only his visage, but that he himself was standing in some glass tower of some still thriving metropolis, in some unknown part of the world, or perhaps off planet altogether, someplace where human progress had not been stopped, but instead had pivoted past obstacles and impediments spinning forever toward mankind's mastery of the universe itself.

—I assume that you are Tammy Cohen, the famed ecologist, and so you must be Leonard Shorty, the Navy Seal sent by "God" to deliver her.

—Who the fuck are you?

—My name is Andy. I am the caretaker here. I've been expecting you.

—How?

—Vanessa told me you were coming.

—Who the fuck told you what?

—I believe you call her Malcolm.

—Her?

—She sent out a runner about six months ago. Mouthy Irishman. Kept going on about Faulkner and Melville. Asked me to keep an eye out. I have to admit that given the nature of your errand I expected you a bit sooner.

Tammy took a step behind Leonard.

—Why should we trust you?

—I don't know, but he has the gun, so.

And he showed them his soft palms, not only as a gesture of assurance, but also of immediate and unconditional surrender. A gesture they would see again.

—Why are you dressed that way?

—What way?

—The fucken suit, holmes. Last I checked, Goldman Sachs has closed shop.

—Damn, no wonder I never get my check.

Neither Leonard nor Tammy chuckled at their host's attempt at levity. He spoke as if they were old friends who had not seen one another in a long time.

—I don't know. I always wore a suit, even as a teenager, although I guess I had to then. We all had to wear suits. Eventually you get used to it and then before long it's who you are.

And he turned from Leonard to Tammy and his gaze was both direct and calming, not a challenge but an invitation.

— Maybe that was the whole point of the suit. It was shaping who we were from outside in. Jesus… I have to think about that, maybe it is time to update my wardrobe. Do you think some sort of hooded robe might be more in keeping?

—How many people live here?

—Complicated question. Or a kimono?

—It ain't that complicated.

—Alive that you can talk to? Just me and my wife, Olivia, and our daughter, Juniper.

—What about alive that I can't talk to?

—Listen friend, you're asking for information I don't feel quite comfortable in giving, so if you'd like to shoot me, go ahead I guess.

Leonard looked at Tammy, who raised her shoulders and lowered them. Finally, she spoke.

—You a sports fan?

—No.

—Religious?

—No.

—You eat meat?

—I used to.

—And now?

—Well, there's still some elk up here but I guess I'm not very good at hunting them.

He turned to Leonard and made a vague gesture toward the gun Leonard still had trained on his belly.

—Hey, how about you? You any good at hunting?

—I've bagged a few.

—Maybe after we all have some lunch or tomorrow or whatever, we could try our hand. I'd be willing to share whatever we got.

—I see where I come in, and the elk if there really are any, but I'm still struggling to see why I should give a damn thing to you.

—Well, theoretically you're on Red Axe property, and well, right now, I am kinda Red Axe, so they're my elk I guess. But, you know, whatever, you don't want to go hunting with me, no problem. You want to go hunting by yourself, what can I do to stop you?

Tammy wanted to change the subject before their welcome disappeared.

—So what's for lunch then?

—Protein cultured in vats, vegetables grown under lights.

—What powers the lights?

—Geothermal, all you can eat. Listen, I would love to sit up here and commiserate about the strange circumstance we all find ourselves in since the world ended, but in all honesty it took you longer to get from the base than anyone expected, and Olivia was planning lunch for one o'clock, and she gets pissy if everyone's not at the table at the expected time. It's just one of those things about being married, I guess. So, we really should get down there. Admittedly, more for my sake than for yours.

Andy walked toward the smallest of the three sheet-metal outbuildings and the curiously suited man entered without hand gesture or head tilt, leaving Tammy and Leonard alone to decide their fate between them.

—I don't know, the whole thing seems fucked.

—She wanted us to come here for some reason.

—She?

—Yeah.

—She?

—Yes. Does it make some sort of difference here?

—It's a long damn walk for secrets, particularly important ones.

—So noted.

—Hey lady, I got other things I could be doing.

—Sakti.

—Jesus. Fuck.

Tammy took a deep breath and walked head down toward the door of the shed. On the threshold, she turned back.

—I'm sorry. I wanted to tell you, I also thought that maybe you knew and it was something we just weren't talking about out of respect or something, or caution, like maybe we were being followed, or I don't know. It won't happen again, I promise.

Leonard gave Tammy no indication of his thoughts or intentions and after a moment she lowered her eyes and followed Andy into the shed.

Leonard stood alone under the vast dome of the sky and began the long process of revising everything he thought he knew of the world. He thought about what it would be like to walk down the mountain and make his way south and west to the rez, to his family, or if not his family his family's land so he could make his stand, whatever that stand may be, and he took the full seven seconds to make his decision and that decision was like all that had come before it and all that would follow: final and binding.

The inside of the shed smelled of dust and recently disturbed chemicals. It was dimly lit. The single window was mostly blocked by junk piled on a work table. The shed had at one time been a man's sanctuary, a place for his hands to do while his mind wandered. It was a kind of portrait. It told of interests and ambitions, youthful fantasies that persisted into old age, loneliness and also aloneness. It told of a man's thrift and his tendency to see a piece of garbage for its usefulness.

An old office chair held court in the center of the room, its covering material long since replaced by layer upon layer of tape. Old skis hung from the walls, their bindings progressed from hemp rope to titanium, hand tools covered in layers of dust, cans of paint turned to stone, a plastic bucket of rusty nails and a large spring that might have at one time been a part of an automobile or some other type of industrial conveyance, a pair of coiled extension cords, one with a simple light fixture attached, the other splitting into strands; a sagging bookshelf that held a dozen manuals for machines long since disappeared from the Earth, a book on bee keeping, a catalogue of plumbing fixtures, a guide to wind energy, a farm to table cookbook, a complete collection of *Calvin and Hobbes*, cardboard boxes in various states of dry rot; computer cables, connections and adaptors, magazines; girls, cars, music and gossip, jars of chemicals; paint thinner, astringent, bleach, lye, WD-40, lamp oil, rags, adhesives; simple white paste, Gorilla, silicon, caulking, two-part epoxy, all fossilized, a tangle of spaghetti wires bound beyond the hope of disentanglement, and on and on. The minutiae of a man's life filled the small metal chamber, stayed only temporarily from following the man himself into the dust.

—What is this place?

—Just what you see. We found it this way when Red Axe bought the land in ` 24. Whosever's shed it was most likely died in the teens, but we've worked hard at maintaining it just as it was.

—Why?

—A lot of reasons I suppose. Sometimes I think of it as a monument to a stranger and while I never met him or saw a picture of him, there is something about his things that always fills me with awe.

—Oh.

—Though really, we keep the shed intact for cover.

—Cover?

—Yeah.

—This place has been found more than a hundred times since the elevator went in but not once did anyone bother to look past the junk. Just more junk in a world of junk, nothing to see.

Leonard had been looking through a box of vintage magazines: *Jugs*, *MILF Catcher*, *Asian Fever*, *Club*.

—The elevator?

Andy reached under the table and he appeared to be concentrating on some unseen task, using the tips of his fingers to see some switch and, after a moment, the hiss of pressure released sounded and the back wall of the shed moved aside and then smoothly dropped below sight to reveal a gleaming brushed stainless steel door.

—What the fuck?

—Did you really think we all returned to the time of the caveman?

So incongruous was the sight of that gleaming metal door surrounded by garbage that its vertical black aperture seemed to be a crack in reality itself. Andy pushed the glowing purple button that would have been comfortable in a Berlin nightclub circa 2025 and the door opened and the velvet grey interior revealed itself and Andy bowed slightly and swept his upturned palm across his body suggesting that his guests should enter first, and although Tammy did not hesitate, Leonard made sure that he was the last to enter.

—Music?

—Really?

Tammy'd had music playing in her truck the morning of the Bright Angel bombing, and she wondered how long ago that was. A month, a year, ten? She had come to accept that she would never hear recorded music again. Of all things, why would they let that go?

—Yes. Hell yes.

—Requests?

—Like what?

—Almost anything.

—Yesterday we were talking about Cinthia Pérez. Do you remember Cinthia Pérez?

—I'm afraid I don't, but that's no matter. We'll check.

After a short pause they heard it: D minor, A, B flat.

—Seem familiar?

Smooth, rich piano chords. The doors closed and by the end of the first phrase the elevator had begun its descent. From the small window in the door they could see the brushed steel shaft passing with increasing speed as the small falling chamber sung to its passengers in a voice that once belonged to a famous Cuban American teenager, now only a fading memory.

— *Hey said he from the corner huh..*

And Tammy closed her eyes and was returned to her nine-year-old self and she felt the warm California sun on her skin.

And the bass came in and it was the sound of her father's voice yelling at the news on TV.

And the trumpets rose to meet the voices in the choir, and they were her school friends and her school enemies and she could see that there was no real discernable difference between them. The song played and they fell into the throat of the volcano and she mouthed the words over and over again.

Of a barrio, Barrio

He was living in the shadows huh

But he's got that fire though…

—That's her!

Leonard looked directly at Tammy.

—Well now we know what Cinthia Pérez 'been doing.

The elevator doors opened into a room of rough plank wood, walls, floor and ceiling clad in the same grey as if worn smooth by time.

—Where are we?

—Just the antechamber. When Trevor made it, he wanted it to provide a material juxtaposition to the experience of the elevator, as if to imply that time exists all at once, that everything that ever was, or will be, is here now.

—Why?

—Maybe one day you'll get to ask him.

Andy went on to explain that the wood had come from a barn that had withstood the Colorado elements for a hundred years and more before the economics of cattle ranching gave into reality.

—Architects always think their work means more than other people's. The rest of the compound has a more stone and metal kind of feel.

—How big is the compound?

—Our living chambers, and the lab, and the catacombs. The developed section of the magma chamber is less than an acre, all told.

—And the undeveloped section?

—We have yet to find the edges of it.

—What the fuck are the catacombs?

—I can show them to you after lunch if you'd like, but right now, come on let's go meet Olivia and Juniper.

They followed him through the weathered wood room, into a hallway of polished concrete. He opened a simple pressed wood door and they were in an apartment like any that might have been found in the upper reaches of Park Avenue in the year of nineteen hundred and seventy-five. They were greeted by the warm sound of a laugh track. A young blonde woman sat on a single cushion sofa smiling with her legs tucked into a pleated navy dress, her eyes glued to a color TV housed in an outsized wooden cabinet.

—What are you watching?

—*Welcome Back, Kotter.*

—Really? Where'd you get it?

—China, apparently. They also have a mid-century America unit.

—Did you steal it?

—Well, no more than they did.

—Okay, and...

—Well, it's not without merit. It's about teenagers who think that they won't ever grow old.

—Okay, and....

—Well, these particular teenagers did grow old, a couple of them even died of old age, but on the other hand this show was filmed more than seventy years ago and here they are, still teenagers, and so I guess they were, in some sense at least, right.

Leonard got the impression that this sort of Socratic discourse was a show put on for their benefit.

—I see your point. I would like to introduce you to some friends of ours.

Juniper stood up, uncurling her long legs, and she smiled warmly and smoothed her dress and extended a hand to Tammy and then Leonard in turn.

Juniper is studying post-war America.

—You must be Dr. Cohen.

Tammy shook her hand.

—And Mr. Shorty.

Leonard nodded. Andy walked over to the large box and switched it off shrinking its image to a single dot of light in the middle of the screen.

—Where's your mother?

—She's in the kitchen, putting seventies lunch on seventies plates.

—Okay, shall we join her then?

Juniper led them through the well-appointed apartment, shag white carpet, soft black leather sofas, a chrome arc pole lamp stretching from a heavy base in the corner to the center of the living room, leaving a round pool of yellow light on the floor below.

In the kitchen, Olivia was just setting down china plates in the breakfast nook for lunch.

—Hi.

—Hi, oh hi.

Unlike her daughter, her clothes were not immediately placeable in time. Eighteen hundred or twenty-thirties, her garb could only be described as androgenic and practical and she too put her hand out to greet her guest. Her grip was firm, her hands calloused, her gaze direct. In that gaze was an invitation but also a warning.

—I'm glad you made it. We were starting to wonder.

—Nice to meet you.

—Should we skip to lunch and go back to the intros maybe after?

And having come from a breakfast of three bites of dried sheep tendon, they were now sitting on Tonette chairs around a Saarinen table and passing heaping plates and pressing napkins into laps and a false sun came through the windows and it was warm on their faces and birds flew past and the faint sound of car horns could be heard from the traffic far below and they could see into other apartments and they saw the lives of others, families eating other lunches, a writer at his desk, a baby asleep in its crib. Though they all knew that none of it was real, it was not long before reality was hard to remember. This world was but a facsimile of one that was ending in floods and drought and fire and riots. The illusion was inviting and gave the real world stiff competition in the minds of the lunchers and so they ate their tuna salads and oxtail soup and roast beef sandwiches in silence because to speak was to risk breaking the illusion. Talk could only lead to someone pointing out that it was not real and so they all willingly colluded and all that they heard was the scrape of silver on china, the slurp of soup, the intermittent drip from the faucet in the kitchen and the pleasant hum of the city below. When Andy was finished and he thought that his guests were ready to move on, he wiped the corners of his mouth.

—So…

—So.

—I'm ready to answer any questions you might have and provide any assistance I can for your upcoming trip.

Leonard did not put down his fork but his fingers curled around it and it was revealed for the silver-plated weapon that was its true nature.

—Let's start with where the fuck we are?

—This is San Antonio Mountain. We are the caretakers here.

—What's here?

—Twelve hundred and forty-three persons are in the hibernation chambers.

—For how long?

—Well, most have been in two years, but they will be there for a long time I suspect. Long as it takes.

—Long as what takes?

—The restoration of some kind of order, and a level of prosperity and possibility similar to that which existed when they went in.

—You telling me that even the complete breakdown of society is not going to mean the end of the rich white fuckers whose greed brought the whole thing on in the first place?

—Well, among the twelve hundred souls stored here I can guarantee there are going to be a few that the community as a whole would prefer not to wake up next to, but there are also some of the greatest minds we've ever known and I propose that even the least among them is brave.

—Why's that?

—Would you bet your life now for a possible life in the future?

Tammy placed her knife and fork parallel to one another at the four o'clock position on her plate and she placed her hand gently on Leonard's thigh and the slight pressure of her touch carried its wordless message. Leonard uncurled his fingers and released the fork in his hand and placed it on the table next to his plate.

—What were you before you were the caretaker here?

—I was an ethicist.

—A what?

—An expert on right and wrong.

—Fucking white people. This was something you got paid for?

—Not that it much matters now but yes, I was paid well but more than that it led me to here, so I guess being an ethicist worked out okay despite my father's apprehensions.

Leonard turned to Olivia who stood and began to gather the dishes.

—And you?

—I was the Chief of Surgery at Johns Hopkins.

—And now?

—This month I'm a housewife, circa 1975.

—And before that?

—We were studying the Dust Bowl.

—Okay, and after this?

—Juniper is gunning for the late 20's Paris. I have been lobbying for Babylon around 1600 BC.

—How far can you go?

—In space, just the apartment. In time… as far back as the Big Bang.

There they were. Racks rising from below the floor to beyond the ceiling, they were attended by machines, scanned daily from head to toe to make sure that they were receiving the correct nutrients, oxygen and hydration. Their bodies were exercised, they were exposed to slow cell replacement therapies. If they stayed asleep more than ten years, the ones who went in blind could thread a needle and the deaf could listen to Mozart. The longer the better. Slow magic. The processes were automatic, all Andy had to do was check in on them.

—Easiest job I ever had. No boss, lifetime appointment, great benefits.

—And who are they?

All kinds really. I mean all kinds of people with ten billion dollars to spare, so you know, there's a famous plastic surgeon, a couple of supreme court justices, a lot of tech billionaires, Bill Gates's grandson, the Alibaba guy who went to sleep at one hundred twenty-three but left instructions saying he did not want to be woken up until he could wake up as a ten-year-old girl. Ex-presidents and insurance magnates, a couple of old Hollywood types, the guy who invented plastaskin, and in one case we have a man who is repeated three times because he bought spots for himself and two clones. Even we don't know which one is the original.

—What happens when they wake up and they all claim to be him?

—Maybe they all are him and he can just be three places at once. Who knows?

Andy walked across the polished concrete floor that was the color of blood and sat at a banged-up steel desk in the corner. From the largest of the three drawers he produced an oversized leather-bound volume. He pulled all four of his fingers toward himself, beckoning his guests to cross the room. Tammy was no match for her curiosity and for the second time that day she left Leonard standing alone.

Andy had opened the great volume to a page in the middle. The leaves were thin, the print small and each page bore a name and a square containing pictures and text which filled the rest of the page. Tim Walker. In the pictures he seemed happy. A snap of him atop Kilimanjaro. A drone selfie of him standing on a thin spit of land surrounded in pale blue water. An image, presumably Tim, flying off a cliff on skis. A picture of him in a suit leaning against the Merrill Lynch bull, a smile on his face.

The pictures told of a happy and active life and Tammy wondered who curated them. During the years of social media, she'd learned to ask herself what the pictures were there to hide. What were the missing pictures? The text told of his birth in Oakland and his raising on the central coast of California. It described a motorcycle accident he had when he was young, and the time he spent in a coma. In a later paragraph he talked about his brother whom he claimed to love above all others and how that brother had died of a sudden embolism. He talked about how he hoped that during the period of sleep he would be able to find his brother so he might say all the things he never had.

In his closing paragraph he talked about what he hoped to wake up to and by implication what he hoped to sleep through.

Tammy looked up from the book.

—May I read another?

—You can read them all if you want.

She gripped a raft of pages from the left-hand side and flipped them over. Bess Glorioso.

Tammy read silently, skimming her finger across the page quickly.

Bess was an heiress but worked as a stage manager on Broadway. Had no kids, loved dogs and her husband whom she is hoping she will wake up next to so they can continue their long conversation regarding Shakespeare and his intentions. She says she will miss New York, not the New York of twenty-forty but the New York of the twenties when the theaters were always full and the streets were brimming with life. She hopes the war is over by the time she wakes up and that the Dems have won. She says: FUCK BARON TRUMP in all caps.

—Have you read them all?

—Yeah, it took me six months.

Tammy turned to Leonard.

—Come on, pick one.

—No thanks.

—Come on. It'll give us something to talk about on the road. Just one. A randomer.

He did not move, and then after precisely seven seconds, he crossed the room and looked at the book and flipped it to the first page. He did not look at the photographs. If he had, he would have seen that they were all watercolors of the same woman. One just her hair, another her lips, her eyes, her walking on the beach, swimming in a sea of blood.

He took a moment and then read aloud, his voice echoing off of the floor and the wall of glass that separated him from the sleeping billionaires in front of him.

Juanjo Abeyta. I used to stand at the corner of Alvarado and Sunset and sell my mother's tamales…

—If you are only going to read one, I would not read that one.

—Why?

—Just trust me.

—I don't fucking trust you.

—Fair enough. I would still pick a different one.

—I used to stand at the corner of Alvarado and Sunset and sell my mother's tamales from a cooler. Then when I was a little older I used to set up a camping stove on a card table outside a dance club and when the pillheads would pour into the streets at 4 AM I'd sell 'em huitlacoche quesadillas. Then I had a shack that sold burgers and when those became illegal I sold jeat-filled *pupusas* from a converted burger stand at the corner of Hillhurst and Hollywood and from that I started a fast-food empire. That story's pretty easy to find so I'm not going to use any more of my little space here to tell it. Maybe the story will survive whatever's coming and if it doesn't, well, so be it. Suffice it to say I went to sleep a rich man, who knows what I will wake up to, if I wake up at all.

I want to talk about Liana, whom I will never see again, who was the smartest person I ever met, the kindest, the easiest in her skin, the most beautiful, the wisest and funniest. Liana who could fold a cloth napkin into a swan while delivering her thesis on the prevalence of anti-vax culture among the world's wealthy. Liana, who could multiply any two four digit numbers in her head, whose thick auburn hair smelled of vervain, whose emerald green eyes lit up at the talk of skiing or rock climbing or kayaking or just a walk in Griffith Park at sunset. Liana, who knew her Coppola from her Tarantino, her Lynch from her Stone, her Murakami from her Ishiguro. Liana who carried both breath mints and tabs of ecstasy in her handbag and would give you either, without warning or hesitation, accompanied by the same irrepressible smile.

We met at Maggie Clark's fiftieth birthday party. She had dressed down when all the hangers-on had dressed up, and would pull the reverse trick a week later at Frank Smith's famed "old Hollywood" Luau. We spent that first night hiking by headlamp up to the high micro-springs behind the Hollywood sign, secret pools plumbed for one but that could fit two, if those two were very close to one another. As she dressed and her clothes clung to her wet body, I asked her to marry me, and she laughed as if I were joking. I asked her again the next day over hush puppies at Rosco's Chicken and Waffles, and the next and the next. And while she never said no, it was six months before she said yes. I had already purchased my space in the catacombs and I was in the process of securing hers when the tattooed beasts breached the wall of our city... and then our compound.

We were running, hands clasped, steps away from the room I called Valhalla, when we were overwhelmed by the savages. Twenty years' worth of food, nine hundred tins of foie gras and not a single tube of jeat. We faced a time without sunlight, but what we were to get in exchange was more than fair trade: a collection of film that might have rivaled that of Kolamiranki's or Scorsese's, a print library that would take ten lifetimes to read, the best food money could buy, a wine cave three thousand bottles deep, refrigeration, electricity and a VR room with its endless permutations that, while not real, would provide more than enough entertainment and education to see us through. It was all within reach. I remember the wet grass on the soles of my bare feet and the softness of her palm against my own. We were going to make it. We were in sight of the iron gates and my fingers were inches from the pin pad when they appeared from nowhere: two of them, then four, then eight, then maybe a hundred. Who knows? Within reach. Close is the same as a million light years away. We got close. We were almost gods, almost immortal, but we failed to scale the last mountain, failed to jump the last hurdle, failed to break through the atmosphere. We failed to cross the damn backyard. I thought that if I gave them everything, the house, the cars, the vast store of food, they would let us go but I was wrong. Liana was raped until she was dead. All minus stone will be replaced by depravity and the net and its promise of a united humanity hand in hand at the far end of the universe is no more than a cautionary tale, our very own Tower of Babble.

I lived by luck, good or bad. A rival gang appeared on the tail of the first. The enemy of your enemy is your friend. Shock and awe. Overwhelming force. And I heard the cries of a dying tattooed warrior lament the theft of what was "rightfully" his, and I remember thinking how fast the illusion of ownership takes hold of the human mind. I slipped out unnoticed and stumbled nine hundred miles across the desert.

The first steps away from the Pacific were perhaps similar to our last in the other direction. Manifest Destiny was also brutal in reverse. Whatever love or faith I had in humanity was leached away by the time I reached the Rocky Mountains. The fools that thought that this land was a gift from some god or another could never have faced the Mojave with their illusions intact. No loving god could exist in concordance with such a place.

I wanted to keep living, not because I care whether society is rebuilt or not, or whether we as a species survive or not. I only want to remember her. I want to spend long years remembering her.

I wonder if I will dream of my once-green lawn running with blood. Maybe I will dream of Liana. God I hope so.

For a time all three were as silent as stones and their thoughts were private and unreadable to one another and so they would never really know how far apart they really were. It was Leonard who finally spoke:

—Dude's a fool.

—Why?

—Let's say he dreams of his woman, and then he gets woken up. Dumbass loses her all over again.

—He must have done the math.

—Yeah, I guess.

Tammy walked up to a child suspended on her rack. She looked as if she was wrapped in the most satisfying sleep.

—Do they actually dream?

—It's hard to say. They have peaks and valleys in their brain activity but there is no way for us to say those peaks and valleys represent dreams. The idea was that they would simply be suspended until such time that they could resume their lives.

—Why them?

—No reason, no good reason. They had dollars when dollars still meant something.

—But they don't anymore, so…

—I gave my word.

—A deal's a deal?

—Once a dollar's not worth anything, all you have is your word. Maybe it's all we ever had. Besides, if I did not have this, what would I do with myself?

Tammy turned and widened her stance and her eyes bore into Andy. She demanded the truth.

—Why are we here?

—In a fundamental sense, I don't think I could answer that.

—Malcolm wanted us to come here, made us walk pretty far out of our way and it's not like we got a lot of time to spare, so I want to know why.

—She's part of this project from its inception. Her work and mine are the same.

Leonard spun on his heels.

—The bitch wrote about revolution and restarting America and fundamental principles but it was all bullshit. In the end she was just carrying water for a bunch of rich fuckers asleep in a cave. Is that what we're to fucking understand here?

—Look, you want to have an argument with her go ahead. You know where she is.

Again, Leonard pointed his gun at Andy's chest.

—Fuck you.

—Go ahead, but quit threatening me with your toy. I'm afraid of a lot of things, but death is just not one of them.

Tammy stepped between them.

—Look, we got a long walk ahead of us. And Leonard is just frustrated because he feels like important information is being kept from him. You could understand that right?

—Yes, absolutely.

—Good. Leonard please, the gun's not helping…. Thank you. Andy, why *are* we here, really?

—I can offer you a place here. You and the billionaires, sleeping soundly till the storm passes. A chance to restart your life.

—What?

—Go to the Seed Bank, get what we need, come back and go to sleep. Let other people take care of their part. When you wake up maybe the world will have been restarted. That's our offer.

—Why didn't she make me that proposal back at Dharma camp?

—I don't know, but if I had to guess, I'd say she wanted to know if you would be willing to do it simply because it's the right thing to do, and then once she saw that you were…

Leonard could hold his tongue no more.

—The Yoga Bitch didn't tell you at Dharma Camp because we had to be well away from there before we knew any of this even existed. Imagine the fucking chaos that would erupt there if they knew that they were really just doing the grunt work while the same fuckers who broke the damn place the first time were sleeping it off.

—Now that she's seen that you were willing to do it for nothing, she's offering you much more than nothing. I think it's a pretty good deal.

Tammy sat down in the only chair.

—And if we fail?

—Well, bluntly, if you fail, we all fail, but you are certainly no worse off for having tried.

—What if, instead of waking up to Disneyworld, it's just one big Mojave or you never wake up but you don't die either and you just have bad dreams forever?

—Well, eventually the sun envelops the earth so there is no forever.

—What if we don't want it?

—Then you don't take it. What can I do?

—Nothing.

—Nothing, Andy agreed. Nothing at all.

15

They hardly spoke at all on their way down the mountain and their march north across the sage back to Fort Garland was marked by an unnamed tension between them. Tammy took advantage of the silence to think about Juniper.

After dinner, which was an ersatz meatloaf and gravy with string beans, followed by ersatz Jell-O in a fruit mold, they retired to the living room and Juniper played Beethoven on the piano. While not perfect she was not bad. When that was finished, she asked if either Tammy or Leonard was interested in a game of chess. Leonard declined but Tammy said that she wouldn't mind playing. She was beaten quickly and Juniper claimed to have gotten lucky. The second and third times she toppled Tammy's king she made no such claim. For the fourth game, Leonard stood behind Tammy and made disapproving grunts whenever she touched a piece and finally Tammy handed the board over, and Leonard and Juniper played to a draw twice, and Leonard finally won on their third game and his eyes shone in a way that was completely new to Tammy.

—You're a player, there is no doubt about that. I managed to distract you with my queen so you wouldn't see the bishop lurking on the opposite corner.

They played again in the morning and Leonard lost but he did not seem to mind.

Over a breakfast of ersatz poached eggs and pancakes, with the city far below coming to life with its false morning business, the travelers and the family talked about the journey ahead.

Andy stood up and paced back and forth.

—You must avoid the road as much as possible. It will, of course, be tempting because of the relative ease of walking that it offers, or even the chance of motorized transport. Don't give in to the temptation. The road will see you killed. I can give you twenty pounds of V-cell each, and two pounds of supplements. Any more than that and you are using more energy in the carrying than you can replace in the eating. If you're careful and disciplined you should be able to pass the better part of your land trip with only a few supplements. Obviously, you will need to reprovision when you get to

Damascus. With any luck, Pat will have your boat procured and provisioned by then.

Juniper was taking in the conversation with growing alarm.

—Couldn't you just stay here for another couple of days? You're the only flesh and blood people I've seen in two years, except my parents.

—But you see people in your class every day.

—Yeah but it's not the same. Real people. Real, living, breathing people.

Olivia took Juniper's hand.

—We feel you bug, and we know that the situation is hard, but right now everyone's situation's hard. It won't always be this way.

—Could I at least walk them down the mountain?

Andy shook his head.

—No. It's too dangerous. Tammy and Leonard will be back and we can all go exploring the outside together. Just... now is not that time.

Juniper lowered her eyes and they could all see that she was doing her best not to let the tears that had built up against the dam of her lids spill over.

—I'm sorry. I know that what you are doing is really important, and I... I just hope you come back.

At Andy's suggestion, they crossed the Rockies at La Veta pass, hiking up the old narrow gage. It was not the fastest and certainly not the easiest way over the continental divide, but it was the way in which they would have the least exposure to the war that raged along the highways. The rail grade saw some foot traffic during the warmer seasons but close to none during the snowy months. It was late in the spring and the snow had receded to the higher elevations. They believed that there would be few, if any, with whom they would need to parlay in those desolate mountains.

It was a warm spring day when they left the ghost town of Fort Garland for the second time. They ascended through the Rio Grande Volcanic Basin and up through the same fire-ravaged forests, only this time the flame's victims were ponderosa, some twenty feet in diameter, some reaching better than one hundred and fifty feet; Ponderosa with stubborn green boughs near their ragged tops, as if to claim that they had lived through this blight and that they would persist through the next. These trees had seen the Sioux's rout of the Cheyenne, and the Apaches rout of the Sioux and the

Conquistador's complete and indiscriminate conquest of the natives regardless of tribe, only to themselves decline slowly and irrevocably at the hands of stronger, more lasting empires. The ponderosa saw the wagon trains full of Eastern delusion, and then the beaver trade and the bear hunters, the cattle ranchers, the hippies and the survivalists, the utopians and the gun freaks, the marijuana growers and the software engineers, all gone now. With their living branches, these trees, which smelled of burnt vanilla, raised a green middle finger to that which was beyond their ken.

With three thousand feet climbed, the temperature had steadily dropped and near the top of the pass it snowed. The ground, the air, the peaks above and the valleys below were carpeted in the same white and for a time the world was fair and unspoiled. The same as it had ever been. And though Tammy and Leonard knew exactly what rot lay beneath the blanket of crystals, the snow lied directly to their hearts and as they walked it crunched under their boots and they forgot all that they knew, and their fears evaporated and their spirits were unexpectedly buoyed. Tammy thought that she could've stayed in those mountains for a million years and not tired of that sound and the feeling of snow lightly falling on the hood of her canvas jacket, but no sooner had she realized her profound enjoyment of the present than the pace of the snow increased, and the wind moved from caressing to cutting, and it occurred to her just how alone they were, and where they were, and perhaps because they had overestimated the danger that their fellow man posed on the much lower and snow-free highway, they had committed the crime of underestimating the danger that the wounded earth herself could still bring to bear. The punishment for such a crime was, and always had been, death. The peaks were like looming and angry giants and what moments before seemed like a reprieve from the harsh endgame of man gave way to nature's indiscriminate brutality. Visibility reduced to near zero, and their pace slowed and they began to look nervously for the sun's print in the sky and as the snow swirled around them, challenging them to walk in a simple straight line, they focused their attention on the ground so as not to lose the train grade which was their only sure path out of the Rockies. They placed all of their attention on their feet, on the next step, and the next and the next.

For Leonard it was a smell, some thread of rot that twisted through the high mountain air. The sticky sweet smell of decomposing flesh found his nose through all of that snow and wind and confusion. Like an old time letter. *Neither snow nor rain nor heat nor gloom of night stays these couriers from the swift completion of their appointed rounds.* A letter from his actual life.

It was a low howling that caused Tammy to look up, not the howling of an animal but more the open-throated death rattle of a colossus nearly slain.

They stood gaping at the chipped brick maw of a tunnel's opening, dark against the white mountains and the white sky and the white ground so as to seem like a vertical pool of spilled black paint on a newly gessoed canvas.

—Fuck.

—Did you know about this?

—Nah.

—Anything could be in there.

—I tell you what, something's in there, and that something is dead.

—How are we fixed for fire?

—We have a few matches but if we use them today we may regret it tomorrow.

—I don't want to go in there.

—I get it but…

—We could make a fire here, and get warm and wait for the storm to clear and then go over the top.

—Everything's wet. We'd have to sleep here…

The economy that failed after Bright Angel was the economy of faith. Value had been assigned to paper by mass agreement. Enough people declared something to be true and so it was. In this way, the appearance of truth had long since eclipsed truth itself. The ancient inventors of money had confidence in their idea, had reason to believe, thought it just might take, because the concept of faith had already worked so well with the invention of the gods.

America existed, and her dollar existed, and her power was as real as that of any empire that had come before it or any that would come after, but near the summit of La Veta pass at the crisis of a spring storm that would drop more snow in a single hour than any winter event had that year or in the three years previous—then, at that moment, only the economy of calories was real. Energy burned versus energy needed. No matter their fear, no matter the cold, no matter the stench of rot that exhaled from that tunnel like the devil's breath, they knew it would cost them too much to spend the night in the mountains. They had made an error in climbing so high during any month save July, and so fixed their resolve not to compound that error.

As the tunnel curved deeper into the mountain, the blackness closed in around them until there were no seams of light at all, and time and space were decoupled from one another and the universe itself unraveled around them. They walked on. The reek came at them in waves. The crunch of gravel was all that they heard and their exposed skin was numbed by the steady cold wind which blew at them. They moved forward by feel of the wood ties beneath their feet and the gently curving cold metal of the rails against the sides of their boots. They did not speak of anything, not of Dharma Camp, not of the sleeping billionaires of San Antonio Mountain nor their lives before the explosion. In the silence and darkness the world outside of themselves was replaced by the world within, and though their hands remained tightly clasped and they kept stride with one another, their paths diverged wildly.

In her mind, Tammy replaced the past that she remembered with a past that could have been, and she followed that past into a future that included the salvation of humankind. Tammy picked a point in her memory and began her divergence from there.

She waited alone in the president's outer office. The president's secretary sat behind his desk, typing on his computer. He had smiled at Tammy and his smile was instantly disarming and welcoming and Tammy thought that this man had been born just for this purpose, for just that smile. He offered her a drink, which she declined, and he assured her that the president would only be a few more minutes and so Tammy settled into the high-backed chair that looked as though it had sat in the president's outer office since the Lincoln administration.

Tammy had reached the halls of power, not by being well placed at birth, not by going to the right preschool and matriculating to the right elementary, leading to Harvard or

Yale or Princeton, not by being well connected in life, not through the SATs, not through letters of recommendation, the right internship, nor the will of the Freemasons. She achieved her position in life by always being correct in public, and she was sure she was correct because she plied all of her intelligence, education and will on disproving her own theories before they ever made it through her lips or found their way to the page. She excelled at being wrong in private so that she might be right in public.

The habits which led to her stratospheric elevation would also lead to her eventual isolation. She chose being correct over being loved and, even as she sat in the presidential antechamber, she wondered if she had made the correct choices.

Tammy had worn her most formal business outfit and had even put on lipstick and eyeliner, and while she did not look or feel like the Tammy she knew, she told herself over and over again that the clothes and the lipstick and the eyeliner were just things she wore in order to survive in the ecosystem that she found herself in, not unlike a spacesuit or diving mask, both of which she had worn without hesitation during the circumstances which had called for them.

—She's ready to see you now.

It was as if the message came from the Oval Office directly into his mind and Tammy wondered if such a thing were possible.

—Okay.

—Are you ready?

—As I'll ever be.

—She puts her pants on just like you do.

And he walked soundlessly across the famous blue carpet and opened the door. A door like any other.

—Tammy Cohen, Head of the United States Geological Survey...

The president was sat at her desk writing something. She had looked up and nodded to the secretary who turned his broad face directly at Tammy and offered what reassurance a smile could contain, and then he stepped back into his own office, closing the door behind him. President Martinez kept writing and Tammy stood, suddenly aware of her hands flopping around in front of her and her toes pointed inward.

—I apologize. It is my step-mother-in-law's ninetieth birthday and my wife is not even going to remember to call, let alone write a note.

The Oval Office was as grand and staid as Tammy imagined it would be, like a room at the center of the world, turning its face ever so slowly while the world whipped and disintegrated around it. The woman that sat behind the large oak desk at its center was known to be small and yet she was not dwarfed by the great room itself. She filled it. Tammy wondered if this was true of President Martinez's first day in office or if what she saw was not so much the woman she stood in awe of but a projection of her power.

—I read your report and your recommendation.

—I'm honored.

—You strayed a little far from your purview there, didn't you?

—Yes, ma'am perhaps I did but…

—But what?

—This is an extreme moment in Man's life on the planet and so it is a moment that calls for extreme action from all of us, even me.

—Do you realize that if I did what you're suggesting there'd be an armed insurrection?

It was at this point in the conversation when Tammy's mind allowed her to stray from the past that occurred and drift toward the past that she longed for. Instead of stuttering and apologizing and backtracking, she stood firm and spoke truth to power for she had known the math and knew that she had nothing at all to lose.

—There will be an armed insurrection no matter what you do Madam President, so that cannot be the question. The question is whether you will act or react. The difference is as profound as the outcomes.

—Go on.

—If you shut down the southwestern states now… Turn off the taps, move everyone out no matter what that means, be it guns or money, carrots or sticks, honey or vinegar. Act now, Madam President, and we may survive as a nation. If you fail to, I believe we will crumble under the weight of the drought and famine that is to come.

Sonya Martinez looked directly at Tammy, and this time Tammy did not shrivel under power's gaze. She continued.

—I believe if you look at the individual constitutions of each of the drought-affected states, you will see that their governments are dutybound to fight the other states for the lives of their citizens, so either way…The Federal Government must exercise power while it still has it…

—Would you like a cup of tea?

—If you're having one, Ma'am.

The president forced a smile and pushed a button on her desk and Tammy assumed that somewhere in the bowels of the White House a small panic had begun.

—Let us suppose I were to do as you recommend and force the evacuation of California and Arizona, Nevada, New Mexico, Utah and Western Colorado. How long would we have to, as you say, let these areas rest?

—Not forever.

—No? Give me a number.

—They say that the first two-hundred-year-old woman has already been born. I think we can move back into the Southwest within her lifetime, so a single generation.

—Two hundred years.

—Maybe even less.

—What you're talking about might be impossible.

—The Manhattan Project was impossible and yet it was done.

In a universe without boundaries, she went on to convince the president of the United States to take extreme action in order to protect and preserve. This time it was not after the fact, this time it was not too late, and the scenario played out in her mind and it went backward to the Big Bang and forward to the same and perhaps there were still famines and droughts and riots and wars. Fire still consumed the land but the fires subsided over time and the population of the world was reduced gently, and sense and conservation and common cause won out over greed and corruption and graft, and how real the creation of this universe was it is not possible to say as there was no one outside of its creator to judge its solidity, not unlike the darkness in which she slowly walked.

Leonard also looked within, and he found a thing complete though it were a thing of a different nature entirely. A gift of the darkness perhaps. It was not an alternate world, nor was it a story told in words or even images, but it was something that existed in the memory of his cells. A thing repeated in minutia over and over again, thirty trillion times within his own body. Somehow, within that horizontal well of darkness, he knew the complete story. A tale of hardship and woe, to be sure, but also of wonder and harmony. In the long arc of the universe... some part of Leonard, some part of his very flesh, the part of him which was not just him but all of those that came before him, the part of him that is immortal, that part had been in this tunnel before, but pushing west instead of east. Slowly. Brutally. Inch by inch. One swing of the pickaxe at a time. Shovel in hand, lit by a flickering whale-oil lamp, whip to his back, himself no different than the miners hunting minerals in those very same mountains on that same day. This man, not Leonard, but pieces of Leonard, had spent long years in this very tunnel, laboring, somewhere between indentured servitude and slavery, tunneling in desperation so that the iron horse might someday carry the white man forever westward. That though this man, not Leonard but *not not Leonard,* loathed to spend his sweat and indeed his very life on a thing that would aid in the destruction of his whole world, his cells rejoiced at their unexpected return to that well of sorrow, not because they longed to reveal themselves to their carrier, but more that that carrier should be the unexpected beneficiary of his own ancient and sad labor. Without that path through the mountain, Leonard and Tammy would have been unable to cross the alpine barrier which had taken the lives of so many travelers before them. Leonard felt unaccountable warmth and joy in that impenetrable blackness. He felt a return to himself that he could not account for, and though he could not know the details of the story, he knew the broad facts of it. Leonard had never really considered the phrase "he knew it in his bones" and if he had he would likely have dismissed it as some kind of new-fangled spiritualist idiocy, yet as he walked along the tracks with Tammy Cohen's hand pressed tight against his own, he knew that he had been in that tunnel before. He knew it in his bones.

Then came the barrier. How long they had been walking in that darkness, lost within themselves, it was not possible to say, as they had no way of marking time. Thirty minutes, or ten million years. The stench had become thicker, and eventually it would become so dense as to have a physical form. Their toes found the base of the wall, and they stretched their arms in front of them, like Gloucester at the edge of his precipice, and cold flesh met their searching hands. They took three steps back.

—What the fuck?

—I don't know.

Leonard rummaged in his pack until he found his matches and he struck one and the light flared and the wall before them looked back at them with one hundred lifeless eyes. As the light faded, they saw them stacked ceiling to floor, human bodies stretched out and fixed like so many bricks. The flame lasted less than a minute yet its afterglow would be burned behind their eyes, diminishing but always present, there like a silent companion, with them until the hour of their own deaths.

—We can't go back.

—No.

The wall of flesh and bone in front of them was easier to scale than the other walls that had come before. It was like ascending a ladder in comparison to the micro ridges on which they hung their lives in Red Breast Canyon. Human hair provided firm handholds, and the gaps between feet and heads were easy places to find purchase and the holes of eyes and noses and mouths let them find their way up in the dark and in this way they ascended the wall of bodies.

When they reached the top of the wall, they pushed on the uppermost bodies until they gave in to gravity and as they did, a bright red light burst into the darkness and they found the world remade around them in blood. Leonard and Tammy squeezed over the top of the barrier and started down, bathed in that deep red light. The descent was much harder than the way up, as they were forced to reckon with the crimsoned faces of the dead, hair not grass, real eyes and mouths that they were forced to invade with their fingers. Death masks of horrible countenance. There were old men and young women, children and babies, and bodies that appeared to have expired in their prime. When at last their feet reached the train grade again, the sun set behind them and the valley to their east was bathed in the blood of Christ for which those mountains are aptly named. They walked down the train grade as night fell and their way was lit by a waxing gibbous moon and the darkness of night was in no way comparable to the dark of the day that they had passed through. They did not speak but their hands remained clasped and they kept stride with one another, their souls now forever bound.

16

MAY5TH 2049

They saw her walking toward them first through the field glasses. She had the face of an old woman, but the gait of a much younger one. She lifted her hand in greeting and Tammy lifted her own in reply, and they passed an hour reducing the distance between them until there was none at all. By the time their paths met, it was as if they had been involved in a long discussion.

—… but where are you going?

—Taos.

—Why would you go there?

—It's where I'm from.

—You won't make it past the mountains.

—Probably not, we'll see….

They shared a meal together, her food and theirs, and she was as skeptical of their prospects of survival as they were of hers.

—If you really want to know what America has become or maybe what it always was, you need look no further than the twin stadiums of Kansas City. Visit them both of a Friday night and then decide whether your errand is worth the trouble. I used to want the world to be a better place too, but now I just want to go home and lay down in the hammock under the willow tree and look through the leaves at the sky and take what pleasure is there to be taken and then maybe go.

—Go where?

—Somewhere else.

There were politenesses exchanged and pleasantries given and received and wishes for luck sincerely offered and then they parted ways, each on the inverse of the other's path and when Tammy looked over her shoulder a second time the old lady was gone as if she had never been at all.

—We need to go to Kansas City.

—No. Fuck no.

—There's something I need to see there.

—Oh yeah, you think this a good time for sightseeing?

—No. But we still have to go.

Their days blended with one another and they made tens of miles with each sunset and when a fortnight had passed they found themselves at the edge of a metropolis.

Leonard did not voice his opposition again, though Tammy could see it in his stance. They crossed the filthy remnant of the Missouri River and in a grotto on its bank they hid their packs and walked north beneath a tangle of underpasses and for a moment, freed from the weight of their burdens, they tread lightly and they did not know themselves and their spirits floated and they made no prints in the dust and there was no record of their presence.

People were everywhere. Dirty and ragged. They saw no man, woman or child who was not armed, or at least who did not appear to be so. Eventually they found themselves at the edge of a vast tent city that seemed to stretch beyond the horizon, and in the center of that sea of tents rose the twin stadiums, side by side, and it seemed to the travelers that the tents were the immature offspring of the same, some of whom would be bleached and tattered to nothing, but a few of whom would grow hard shells and rise up to be great stadiums themselves.

Between the tents, footpaths had formed and grown into roads and people walked or biked in both directions with an incredible sense of order, people signaled their intent, waited their turn at crossroads, and showed other walkers courtesy at every turn. When Tammy and Leonard joined that highway of pedestrians, Tammy saw the common will for a society based in rules and laws. In the very same actions ,Leonard saw the workings of a diseased hivemind on full display. Nascent fascism. Men who wished deeply to be a part of a machine, no matter how tiny or insignificant a part.

After hours of walking in concert with the thousands of other humans, they came at last to the split. Some people went into the big rectangular stadium that once housed the Kansas City Chiefs to their left and some into the rounded home of the Royals to their right.

Tammy and Leonard stood downstream of the split at the crossroads and watched people go their separate ways, most silently, although by no means all of them. There were couples who walked together and split apart at the last moment with a wave or a blown kiss.

Both types of people looked mad for something but those going right seemed more at peace while those going left seemed to bristle with some kind of perverse anticipation.

—Well?

—Let's see what's happening in this one and then we can go to the other.

—Does it work like that?

—We ain't been told otherwise.

They went right, following a hushed crowd into the baseball stadium. They followed an orderly line up the concrete stairs until they were near the top. From where they sat they could see the slight difference in the color of the ground between the infield and the out. A great fire had been lit in front of a reflective metal dome. The stands were full. Thirty thousand people waited on the verge of something.

Eventually, a small pale woman, no more than twenty-five years of age, in a diaphanous gown with eyes so clear they could be seen reflecting the fire from the top of the stands, stepped onto the small wooden stage in the middle of the infield. She spoke and her voice was soft yet clear and amplified.

It was not very sunny these last days so I don't know if the microphone is going to last until the end. You may get the opportunity to really listen tonight. We could all hear a pebble fall on home plate if we could just shut down the noise in our heads and listen not just with our ears but also with our souls. However, while this microphone works let's not waste time. The Bible teaches us that waste is a sin. I see no reason why that would not include time. In fact, when I think about it, I'm not sure if there is really any other kind of waste.

Now, I want everyone to close their eyes and take the hand of the person next to them and feel it. Go ahead.

And she waited.

Do you feel the life within that person, the warmth of the blood flowing through their hands as it travels back to their hearts… that living man, that living woman, do you think that the goddess is something other than that? I do not mean the man himself, or the woman, but the life within them. People say that the goddess is everywhere. Well I'm not sure I ever believed that, but I understand the sentiment behind it, the desire. We been through a lot haven't we, we Kansans? I'm not just talking about the last few years. I mean the whole thing from the buffalo to the Dust Bowl, and beyond that. Womankind has been struggling to find herself and indeed find the goddess on this soil since she set foot on it. There was the War Between the States and we were in the middle of it. We were considered the Far West until we weren't. Finally, we were just the middle they ignored. Flyover country. So much the better, I say. The American gods, the false shiny gods, tried to gang up and slay her, with sharp staves of lust they attacked her, not just lust for the flesh, lust for wealth, lust to be entertained, lust to laugh at nothing and to cry at the same, and even lust to feel joy and we became so encased in that lust, so distracted by the baubles of wealth. I think you know what I'm talking about here, new cars and better handhelds and goggles and haptics. Do you remember the new cars, and goggles and the haptics? How about the televisions? They got bigger and bigger and brighter and brighter until they could not get bigger nor brighter, and then they escaped their frames altogether and we were so awed by their magic that we failed to see they had turned our homes into prisons we could not escape from. We were enslaved by a story, a *story in which we were the protagonists, **we** were the superheroes, the geniuses who bent the world to their will. A story in which we were the masters and when we became truly convinced that the story was really our story, the chains were almost unbreakable, and we were unable to escape from our pornography. We were wasting away in those VR chambers while our wealth, right down to our life force, was being sucked from us.... But the goddess remembered us. Our mother never forgot us. She loved us, loved us far more than we loved ourselves. She killed off those false gods with a snap of her fingers, so that we might come back to ourselves, so we could turn away from sin and from wealth and lust and entertainment and she made room in our hearts and our heads, and it is up to us to decide what to fill our heads and our hearts with. I intend to fill mine with the Holy One, and hope you do the same. I want to fill my head, my heart and indeed my soul with her. I know there are lots of nooks and crannies in a soul and yet, with time I will find them all, pry them open and let the good news in. I think I can. I hope I can. Let's bow our heads and pray. Let no man shuffle his feet or clear his throat, let no woman rustle her skirts, but let us pray in silence.*

The stadium, that was for almost a century the home of the storied Kansas City Royals was as quiet as the center of the earth. When the silent moment had passed and a nervousness and rustling had begun, the blue-eyed woman went to speak into the microphone but it was gone. She banged it against her palm and then she smiled up at the crowd and shrugged and she gestured behind her and a young boy, four years old, maybe five, was brought forward. He had the same face as she, the same eyes. He took her hand and led him to the middle of the stage. She whispered in his ear and he nodded and she took three steps back and then crouched down like a catcher waiting for the agreed-upon pitch to arrive. The stadium was as silent as the ruins of Atlantis. The child closed his eyes, waited a moment and then opened his mouth and sang and if his was not the voice of an angel than the angels had been silent all along.

—*Amazing grace! How sweet the sound*

That saved a wretch like me.

And then he was joined by those standing on the field, just at the edge of the stage.

I once was lost, but now am found,

Was blind, but now I see.

And they in turn were joined by the rows behind them, and the boy's song spread through the stadium like fire through dry brush.

— *'Twas grace that taught my heart to fear,*

And grace my fears relieved.

How precious did that grace appear

The hour I first believed.

Through many dangers, toils and snares

I have already come

'Tis grace hath brought me safe thus far

And grace will lead me home.

The Lord has promised good to me

His word my hope secures

He will my shield and portion be,

As long as life endures.

Yea, when this flesh and heart shall fail,

and mortal life shall cease,

*I shall possess within **the veil**,*

A life of joy and peace.

When we've been there ten thousand years

Bright shining as the sun,

We've no less days to sing God's praise

Than when we've first begun.

And when the song was sung they began to hear the kettledrums from the stadium across the parking lot, and they knew that the executions had begun, and that they would continue for hours, perhaps until the dawn if there were criminals enough to hang and to choke and to disembowel.

The majority of that crowd, thirty-five thousand strong, would stay in the baseball stadium for more hymns and blessings both personal and general, and then they would walk home and try to ignore the sounds coming from that other stadium, and they would try to ignore the fact that it was because of those sounds that they could walk home in relative safety. And there were those in the crowd, few, but more than none, who had in the sober morning chosen the goddess of light but in the darkness of night felt the pull of the other side. Justice. Perhaps there were answers to be found in justice.

Slowly, sheepishly, as if to sneak away and not be seen by their neighbors, there was movement for the exits. Tammy and Leonard walked with a steady stream of the justice curious the two hundred yards across the parking lot.

As they walked atop the lake of concrete, they could hear the call and response of the Old Man's amplified voice, and the collective voice of the crowd seventy thousand strong,

—Guilty!

—Do you want blood?

—By the gallon!

—Do you demand justice!

—Nothing but!

—Will anything less keep you safe in your homes?

—No!

—If you want to keep the devil at bay you have to make an example of his demons.

—Justice! Justice! Justice!

Leonard and Tammy were accompanied by no fewer than one hundred curious souls from that other stadium. They walked into the dim concrete corridors opening onto the bright arena, lit by evenly placed fires in cast-iron bowls at the edge of the field. They entered the stadium to find anger's distillate in every form: light bright enough to blind, noise loud enough to deafen, the rank stench and black smoke of raw diesel-fueled fire, and the palpable insanity of the mob, their attention focused like fifty thousand lasers at the edge of the small stage in the center of the football field.

—Well, what should we do with him then?

—Burn him!

—Hang him!

—Rip him apart with the trucks!

And the Old Man stood at the center of the stage, small and misshapen, his back hunched, his teeth sharp and wide-spaced, his eyes black and cruel, and on his splotched pate were patches of fur that seemed to have their own will and purpose.

As if by instinct, he turned when the latecomers entered the stadium, and he smiled.

—Ahh… right on time, a few refugees from the holy arena across the way. Come in, come in, we saved a few seats for you up near the front. Come across the field, please, we welcome you with open hearts and open minds.

And he placed his palms together and he bowed.

And the hundred made their way across the field and they looked up and saw that the stands were heaving, and that the crowd looked down with unvarnished lust and it was hard to say that they would not be fallen upon and torn to shreds.

—Do not fear my friends, if you've done no wrong you have nothing to fear from us. We are just like you, we only want to live in peace.

As they walked close to the stage they saw him, his black eyes reflecting no light back and his smile a mere crack of pain. Though his words were of inclusion and comfort, his stance held neither, and every soul among the hundred walkers questioned their decision to cross the lot, and in this way Tammy learned that though visiting both stadiums was not prohibited, it was also not without cost.

Just as the Old Man had claimed, there was a section of seats that were saved at the fifty-yard line, once reserved for elite season ticket holders. The gate was opened by a giant, naked to the waist, and they were let in, and the newcomers sat and settled uncomfortably.

—Now where were we? Ahh yes, we were about to sentence this rapist to his fate.

And the Old Man raised his face to the crowd.

—I heard *hang him*, I heard that we should fire up the old trucks and rip him limb from limb. I heard that we should burn him…. Anyone else?

A myriad of voices was heard shouting out the names of arcane executions from firing squad to crucifixion. The Old Man smiled.

—I have an idea. Let's let this savage breathe a few more minutes while we have a little fun. Let's do something new. A treat. We are here in a great and famous football stadium and yet we have not seen an honest game of football here for so long.

The crowd's approval of this idea was ecstatic.

Tearing through paper banners at either end of the field came the teams, helmeted and padded, wearing unmarked practice uniforms, and at the sight of these gladiators the crowd erupted further with a mix of joy and venom and nostalgia.

—Yes, back in the bad old days they used to use this great game to sell us cars and dish soap, and potato chips, and pills for erectile dysfunction. The great game was merely filler for the ads and each one of them told us that we were not as good as we could be, that we did not love our children enough, or fuck our wives good enough, reminding us that we were not as young as we used to be or as strong as we could be, and we put up with it all, allowed ourselves to be abused both in body and mind all because we loved this game so much. We loved to see the clash of titans and know that a game could only have one victor. Here, I bring you the game again, this time without the ads, without the guilt, without the theft of your very life. Not only will the game be played without the bother of commercial interruption, but it will be played in the name of justice. Let them play football with his head!

And the crowd verged on insanity jumping up and down and screaming. There could be seen men pumping their fists in the air, and other men jumping over railings to get closer to the game that they dreamed of being at the center of since childhood. Men were seen fighting, gun-fire erupted at random intervals, and couples appeared to fuck in the open air.

The Old Man growled up at the stands.

—Welcome home Kansas City! Welcome home!

Linesmen came out in their full black and white regalia, some caring field-down markers and some armed only with whistles.

The teams met at the fifty, and a coin was tossed, and the greys won and both teams walked back toward their respective end-zones. A guillotine was wheeled out and affixed to the blue thirty-yard line.

—Quiet now! Quiet! Shut up! Now who is doing the kicking for the blues?

One gladiator lifted his hand.

—When the blade comes down you should have an instant before the head falls. Do you think you can get a foot on it right off the blade?

—Yes, I think I can.

—Well, it'd be real good if you could. My understanding is that the decapitated head retains consciousness for a couple of seconds after being cut off, and it would be real good if you give this rapist one last look at the crowd here to celebrate his demise as he goes.

—I'll try my best, sir.

—Well, there's not much more you can do than that.

The Old Man lifted a finger and from all sides of the stadium the kettledrums began their thunderous roll and the fires were fed and they blazed brighter and black smoke rose from the great iron pots. The accused was brought onto the field, made to look small at six foot by the gigantic bare-chested men at each of his elbows.

When they came even with the guillotine's frame, the brutes forced the condemned man to kneel on the back side and they pushed his head down through the wooden locks.

—Now, I have a special treat for you tonight. None other than this man's accuser shall pull the cord that releases the blade and starts this game.

From the side of the stage they brought out a young girl, no more than ten, barefoot in a flower print dress. She walked holding the hand of a man that one assumed to be her father. When they came even with the defensive line, one of the giant bare-chested men handed the little girl the rope. It was clear that she was ready to collapse from fear.

The voice came from the stage.

—Angela? That is your name, yes?

She nodded.

—Is there anything you have to say to this man?

She shook her head.

—You want to spit in his face, or kick him or whatever you'd like?

Again, she shook her head.

—Well then, you may pull the cord and end this vile man's existence on the Earth.

For a long moment she was frozen in place at the center of that arena full of blood lust and expectation, and her father put his hand over hers on the rope and he helped her pull the cord until a loud click was heard and the blade released, and it fell with astounding speed. The man's head was separated from his body as if they had never been united. As it fell toward the ground the kicker's waiting foot reared back and caught the man on his cheek and the severed head flew high into the air, spinning slowly, trailing spirals of blood, as it arced toward the opposing team waiting on the opposite thirty-yard line. What the rapist actually saw it is not possible for any man to say, nor could it even be said assuredly that he was a rapist, but what he would have seen was nothing less than man's endgame on earth. Two million years of history, progress and failure, trial and error, advance and retreat. Packed onto a five-acre slope surrounding a one-hundred-and-twenty-yard field was what was left of the American spirit, stripped of all excess and illusion. He would have seen our passion and our blind furor, our hunger to live and squeeze from life every ounce of joy and excitement and, like always, that joy and excitement had to be paid for. The hunger fed itself on the living flesh of other humans. The rapist's last glimpse of the world might have been a gift. He might have seen his debt brought to even. If he had taken from a child in lust, well, then he paid in blood.

When the head was caught by one of the opposing running backs, he held it up by its hair and the face appeared to snarl and the running back growled as the defense came pouring across the field ready to kill to regain possession of that which had at one time been sentient, but was now no more than a marker of opportunity. The teams clashed with the customary noise and brutality of the game. The vindicated were cleared from the field by the linesmen and the game continued for a full hour of inches given and inches taken. Calls were made and disputed by players and coaches alike, and the fans seemed to pick sides based on the people nearest them and in a short time the two sides of the stadium were divided between grey and blue and Tammy was not sure that a deadly riot between the team's fans would not erupt. Tammy looked at Leonard for the first time since they had entered the stadium and she saw writ clear in his stone-like visage the scars that war had left on him. She put her hand on his but she received no response.

The head which could not spiral like a regular football was instead tossed by the hair, and the receivers were splattered in blood and every time a tackle was made the head crushed a little and eventually it gave way and the skull broke into a hundred pieces and what was left of the man's reason was no more than a stain on a grey jersey.

The field was cleared, and more sentences were handed down. A woman was behanded for stealing an apple. A child was whipped by the Old Man himself for peeping into the baths on women's day. A man was pulled apart by monster trucks for killing his brother in a dispute over tent space. The executions would continue until dawn. How justice was settled on and by whom it was settled was opaque, but of its sanctity there was not a single questioner. If the condemned had a defense it was not heard from on that night. Tammy and Leonard found their way through the bloodthirsty crowd into the dim corridors of the stadium and then the parking lot and they walked slowly through the tent city on their way back to the Missouri River.

17

MAY 18TH, 2049

Leaving Kansas City, or what only a year previous had been Kansas City, they located the riverbed in the dark and found their packs and shouldered them, and the weight of the packs pressed their feet into the sand and rooted them to the earth.

They walked along the river until they came to the train tracks and the sun rose and then arced through the sky and they took note of its path and made sure that they were walking in its opposite direction. It seemed to Tammy that since she opened her eyes in Leonard's cave, the world had changed so much as to be almost unrecognizable, but the sun still moved through the sky from east to west and storms still moved across the land west to east.

Every once and again Leonard would look at the compass and mutter, but they kept to the tracks, and the sun set and they walked on in the gloaming until they found a stand of dead trees and they tried to sleep, but could not for fear of strangers. They whispered about the things that they had seen in Kansas City, and Tammy was surprised to learn that Leonard found the piousness of the baseball diamond more disturbing than the savagery of the football stadium.

In the days to come they met an increasing number of refugees walking along the tracks. Some were mad with hunger and others with loneliness. Despair was universal. Leonard met all comers with the same silent nod, his large rifle trained on them until they were gone from sight.

They left the tracks and simply followed the compass and though their path overland was slower it allowed them to more easily avoid people. Sometimes they fucked, and though their sex was neither urgent nor passionate, there was comfort in it and it served to bring them closer to one another, not just while they were fucking but when they were walking and most in need of the assurance of companionship. They tried to avoid human settlement as much as they could, and yet by the time they would reach the Atlantic they would see rampant cannibalism and colonies of slaves on the march, propelled by lash or cattle prod or rifle. They saw mass executions and open air torture chambers which seemed to serve no purpose save the infliction of pain, as if human cries were a bankable currency in the world to come. Mass rapes. They saw the indiscriminate killing of children, and human sacrifice in the name of Jesus, Allah, Quetzalcoatl and in the name of gods they had never heard of. They walked across the burning landscape and took in the acrid smoke of its fallowing until their skin was the same color as the ashen plane. Leonard became sure that they had become invisible, and so they walked unhidden in the light of day down the middle of the interstate and they were completely ignored by the sports fans, ronin and highwaymen that seemed to have inherited the remains of America's final civil war.

The sun rose and they walked toward it and it set to their backs. They saw firsthand the ruin of a once powerful nation. Once they had exhausted their biographies and their parents' biographies and their parents' parents', back and back, once they had told one another their fantasies, revealed their ambitions, told of their greatest sorrows and their moments of grand success and failure they walked silently side by side and let the days pass over their heads and the miles beneath their feet. Theirs was an arranged marriage, but a marriage nonetheless. By and by they knew one another. Not the rumor of one another, not the theory. No profile was posted and liked. Nobody swiped left or right. They were not friends, and there was no trail of emojis that led to a sea of hearts. No resumes were exchanged. No dowry paid. No connections were made. No lands were exchanged. No treaties signed. No kingdoms were joined. They were not bound in the eyes of God or anyone else. All of those were just stories. Justifications.

They were married by time and distance, by footsore, by common sadness, by shared love of country and disgust for the same. They were married by the human need for touch, by biological imperative. They were married by fear and by loneliness. They were married by shared sorrow and optimism in the face of overwhelming odds, by dogged determination and by distrust. Time and distance would reveal that they were married by the common urge toward continuance, by the will toward immortality no matter how at odds that will was with the fact of temporality that lay so openly before them. Months passed. They made three stops on their way east. At each stop they found that they were expected, and that they were expected sooner than they had arrived. Pat had been there and he left an impression both of himself and of Leonard who came to every hamlet as a kind of Indian messiah. They had been waiting for him, though none knew why, and they were none the wiser when he left.

They arrived to the western edge of the Blueridge mountains during the month of October. Isolation was easier to come by, though the miles passed even slower than they had before. They passed through dry calciferous forests of oak and maple, blue spruce and fir, and the grey inland sea that they had crossed in order to arrive at the foot of those mountains gave way to color that would not be suppressed. While the red and purple and gold, filled Tammy with renewed courage and strength, they made Leonard long for death. He wished to lie down and die before the last leaves fell.

What kind of fool would leave such a forest once he had entered it?

But they kept on. The nights were colder and they slept curled into one another taking what heat and comfort the other could offer, while still refusing to melt into a single being.

The road to Damascus took them fifty miles south of the most direct route to the sea, and they considered skipping it altogether, but they were ten whole days short of provisions from simply being able to walk to the coast. The idea of starving to death, steps away from their intended goal did not appeal to them. Before they left Dharma Camp they were told that Damascus was a must-make stop, and that assertion was repeated at San Antonio Mountain, but the things they had seen on the great plains, the bodies, the starvation, and the unchecked savagery of the human animal had finally altered their ability to simply follow orders.

What manner of command supersedes the sight of a child slowly roasting on a spit, eyes open, fingers curled. After that, how do any man's bidding?

Leonard argued that they could stretch their remaining V-cell and probably arrive to the sea alive. Tammy did not disagree, yet somehow they balked.

They stood at the crossroads. One path leading east, up and over the mountains and to the sea and the other generally south around the bottom of Mount Rodgers.

—Well?

—It's looking like it gets pretty cold up there. Maybe they might have some better coats for us in Damascus.

—And what if Damascus is like Peytona, and is just another place that once was?

—Well then, we added a hundred miles to a two-thousand-mile walk. In the long run it's not that bad.

—Why are we doing this? Any of this?

—What else are we going to do?

The trail took them past two settlements, but they visited neither as both were proceeded by the smell of smoked meat, and they knew but were ashamed to admit that the smell threatened their resolve and stood counter to their purpose. Like all strong aromas, the aroma of cooking meat endowed the human spirit with the ability to travel backward in time. Swine, slow-cooked in its own juices, never hotter than 225 degrees, never cooked less than ten hours.

The pig is as genetically close to the human animal as any to have evolved from the single-celled common foremother, yet Tammy was able to make the distinction and her revulsion was instant. A pig had no family, was mourned by none, was raised to be meat, and thus was fair game, but to Leonard, the pig and the long pig, so named by Polynesian cannibals, whose cooking aroma wove its way through the hollow, were different only in that a nearly defunct society had once arrogantly claimed them to be so. Leonard had time to commit the mental heresy of wondering how different the meat really was.

They returned to walking at night and hiding during the day. They were almost to their fourth dawn, walking south with the sun due to rise from their left when no less than twenty red dots appeared on their bodies like a conclave of half-inch luminescent aliens. A few of the dots wavered in their positions, some wildly, exposing the nervousness of the shooter on the other end of the scope, but there were other points of red light that appeared on their breasts steady as logos sewn over their hearts—Polo, Izod, Pointe Rouge—somewhere in those dark woods were soldiers ready to fill them with lead and report back to their commanders that orders had been followed and carried out.

—Jesus.

They both lifted their arms in the air.

Tammy cleared her throat and realized that she had not spoken aloud in days and for a moment she wondered if she even had the capacity to do so.

—I am Tammy Cohen and this is Leonard Shorty. We come from Dharma Camp by way of San Antonio Mountain.

It is my firm belief that we've been expected. We bring warm greetings from Malcolm of Red Axe, as well as Andy and his wife Olivia.

The dots wavered slightly. They stood stock still and waited.

They heard the crunch of gravel closing in on them. From out of the predawn darkness came a face so familiar that both Tammy and Leonard were struck dumb and stood mouths agape. She stopped a foot from them, impossible, smiling and luminous.

—Vanessa?

—Sakti?

But the familiar face just smiled at them.

—Stand down. Seriously, these are friends of ours and they've walked a long way and this is certainly no way to greet them.

All of the dots fell away and the three stood in silence, she smiling at their confusion, and they genuinely confused.

—How did you get here before us?

—By being here all along.

—What?

—I'm glad you made it. We expected you sooner and the worry was starting to eat at people.

—What people?

—Well, me, particularly.

—What fucking people?

Tammy put a hand on Leonard's shoulder and she felt the tension running through his body.

Vanessa or Sakti or whoever she was, showed her empty palms to Leonard in a gesture that exactly matched Andy's atop San Antonio Mountain one thousand six hundred miles to the west.

—Are you angry?

He did not answer her but his gaze was murderous and direct.

—Do you feel you've been deceived? Made to do something which was not in your interest, or the interest of the community as a whole?

—Fuck you, lady.

—Then why are you still here? Why did you not go back to your reservation or Afghanistan or up to your little rock hut up on Ash Creek in Salt River Canyon, *like a womb in the Great Mother,* or wherever it was that you were last happy and make your stand there, just as you had always been threatening to do?

Any question as to her identity was removed from Leonard's mind. He had whispered those things in confidence to one person and one person only, and he had used those exact same words, and while Leonard and Sakti's moment as lovers and even as friends had long since passed, leaving behind little nostalgia, it struck him hard to have those same words made cheap and returned to him in this new context. Tammy was far less sure.

Their interlocutor's eyes shone with the joy of having deployed power with confidence.

—Listen, you've walked a long way and through some tough territory. You must be exhausted and there is plenty of time for explanations. Let's go in and have a cup of tea and some food.

She turned and walked toward the brightening east and Leonard noted that her ass had neither spread nor fallen in the years since he had curled himself around it.

The three walked in silence for a mile, maybe more, and Tammy stole glances at the woman who was so shockingly familiar to her. They had silently done yoga together hundreds of times. In that physical practice Tammy was the apprentice and the other the master. Tammy had sought her approval, they had negotiated, had tea, agreed, and disagreed. They were neither friends nor enemies, yet here Tammy was unquestionably doing her will. They came to a high gently curving limestone wall topped with ugly nests of barbed wire.

—What the fuck?

—The walls of Damascus were always going to be high and strong.

—The walls of Damascus?

—Here in the heart of America, who would have thought that it would have returned to this?

She smiled and leaned back against the wall. She closed her eyes, drew a breath and was gone. For a moment Tammy and Leonard stood alone. Tammy Laughed.

—She walked through the damn wall.

Leonard put his hands up to the wall, and felt the limestone firm against his palms. He closed his eyes. By instinct or by coincidence or just by fatigue he relaxed, resting his forehead against the limestone, and then he too was gone.

Tammy waited alone. Shocked, thrilled, frightened. It was her first moment alone since leaving Utah. She was tempted to run away. She could turn from whatever errand she had been compelled to complete and she knew that she would not be pursued. They would let her go. She knew that her presence in that place had to be voluntary.

—Anything can happen day, huh?

She too put her hands flat against the limestone wall.

They found themselves inside a large, dimly lit room. Black walls, black floors and black ceilings. Later, when Leonard had long hours to do nothing but lie on his thin bunk and think and remember, his mind would close in on the fact that the strange room's light appeared to be source less, non-directional and impossible.

On the far wall was a five by two metal engraving of a tree. Vanessa or whoever she was, was busying herself with some paperwork standing at a desk near where she would have entered the room. A rotund man, no less than seventy-years-old, sat at his own desk and looked up at them from over his spectacles and smiled.

—Hiya, welcome to Damascus.

She looked up from her papers and introduced the man at the desk as if nothing strange had happened. As if they had not just walked through a limestone wall.

—This is Richard. Richard this is Leonard and Tammy.

—I've heard so much about you.

—That's funny cuz we don't know a damn thing about you.

—Right. Richard here is in charge of security at the Ashville gate. I imagine he is going to ask you to leave your weapon.

—Not a chance fuckstick.

—Sorry pal, but the rules are the rules.

Their negotiation went on for some time, but in the end Leonard walked into Damascus with his carbine slung over his shoulder, just has it had been for almost two thousand miles.

They were disturbed by many of the things that they saw in the country, and had lost the capacity for shock, but dawn breaking over the walled American settlement of Damascus penetrated the thick skin of their dulled senses.

The sight of the long green tracts of grass and the orderly playgrounds for children, gleaming blue metal slides two stories high, and manicured hedges and the live oaks and willows, bright spots of purple where jacaranda bloomed and magnolia trees with deep red flowers as big as a man's hand, and the rhythmic *chick chick chack* of sprinklers slowly turning their faces. The American Damascus beggared their minds and called into question the reality of all that they had seen and even whether they were living or dead.

—Come on, let's go to the commissary, we're a little early for the hot breakfast but we can get started on cereal and toast and by the time the toast is buttered the rest should be ready.

They walked to the center of the compound on color rich walkways. Some sections were muraled and told stories that went from light through dark and back to light again. Other sections were intricately tiled. Mosaic patterns: flowers, mountains and mandalic designs which brought together the free imagination of children and the steady hand of a master. A long section of the sidewalk was built of thick glass which covered the palest of travertine water, and after a moment of walking, bright schools of tropical fish rose from unseen depths to meet their steps.

—They think they're going to get fed, although Jorge is the only one allowed to feed them and I don't believe he does so for another couple of hours yet.

On either side of the aquarium sidewalk grew a tangled garden of roses, tended, but on the edge of wild, a rose garden to rival any that Tammy had seen, including that of The People's House—a rose garden in which Tammy had spent long hours contemplating the fate of man and her own potential role within that fate. She could not help but feel that this garden with its vast tangle of thorns and hidden blooms was an answer to that other, now surely abandoned. This was a garden somehow more in harmony with nature.

The commissary was staffed by sleepy-looking teens in simple white uniforms. The dining area was covered in a dome of glass. As they sat, tables were being wiped down and chairs unstacked. A few of the teens revealed some surprise at the presence of pre-opening visitors though none complained and a table was quickly made ready for them, and they were served breakfast:

Muesli and bananas, fresh milk and coffee, smoked trout and streaky bacon and delicate buttery croissants with fresh gooseberry jam, and while it confounded the imagination as to how it could be, none of the food carried the metallic taste which gave away the V-cell beneath the appearance of post apian collapse food. It seemed to them that they were eating actual food. Food from their childhoods.

Tammy and Leonard did not look at each other or the perplexing woman who was their host, and when they had finished their breakfasts the woman knocked on the table and smiled her wide, crooked grin.

—So, welcome to the kingdom.

—The kingdom?

—There isn't actually a king but people started calling it that and I guess it stuck.

—You like it better than Dharma Camp?

—I don't know, I've never had the pleasure of going to Dharma Camp.

—Sakti, I don't like being fucked with so…

—Mr. Shorty, I consider you a hero and perhaps the very hope of our nation. I would never fuck with you. I believe what we have here is a case of mistaken identity and while it was not intentional I suppose I saw the confusion, and did nothing to disabuse you of that confusion. That was an error, and so I apologize. I assure you I am neither Ruth or Vanessa but I am well- aware of them both.

Tammy looked up from her poached eggs.

—So who are you, then?

—My name is Virginia, although my friends call me Ginnie.

—Okay Virginia, how is it that you look just like Vanessa?

—I'm sure you could guess.

—We walked a long way for riddles.

—What can I answer for you? I will be as clear as I can be.

—Fine. Let's start with why we're here?

—Well, you did walk quite far out of your way, and of your own accord, however when your journey was conceived, which was during that time before, when all of this was merely speculation, the conjecture was that you would probably need some rest and comfort after what promised to be a long and uncomfortable journey, and of course, it was calculated that you would need to reprovision. Most importantly, you are here so that you can see firsthand why it is you're going at all. We wanted you to see just what is at stake.

—And what is at stake?

—Peace and prosperity. Instead of six enclaves of peace and prosperity, in a continent of desperation and mayhem we can bring America back, a light to nations, the hope of the world.

—You want to make America great again, huh?

—No, great for the first time. Not an America built on the backs of slaves and theft but an America built on sustainable agriculture, gender equality, racial equality, and above all fairness.

—And you think a handful of seeds from Mesopotamia is gonna do the trick, huh?

—Yes, and so do you or you would not have walked this long way.

Tammy looked up into the face of the woman who had captured her, killed her friends and most likely broken the world.

—You've added five days and one hundred miles to our journey and I want to know why.

—Twenty more pounds of V-cell. And we didn't want to send you all the way to the coast if there wasn't going to be something there waiting for you.

—And?

—Pat has secured and provisioned your boat and he's here and looking forward to seeing you. He'll give you the exact details of where your boat is.

—Pat's here?

—You can find him in his classroom in twenty minutes.

—What does he teach?

—Humanities, I think.

The school halls were covered in the artwork of children: pictures of trees and birds and animals of every stripe, from tigers to elephants, and Leonard could not help but to think that those animals were all gone now, erased from the Earth.

All that was left of them were photographs. The children's illustrations could have only been based on photos. Leonard could not help but to think that it was cruel to show them photos of beings they would never get to see in real life, but then he remembered being a boy and endlessly drawing pictures of dinosaurs. They too were long gone.

This was not like the dingy halls of his childhood school, which was hardly a school at all, but a place that Indian children went to get out of their parents' way so mom and dad could go to work or stay home and shoot up in peace.

Leonard found Pat's class, slipped into the back and sat in an empty desk and watched the proceedings. Pat was a man he scarcely knew but for some reason thought about a lot.

This is what he imagined school off the rez was like. A well-read and kind teacher stood in front of a calm and well-groomed group of students imparting ancient wisdom.

He remembered school as a place where he learned only brute survival and strategic alliance. Leonard watched Pat hold forth and give himself to his students completely, and he felt a pang of jealousy but he also recognized that the school he was given did in fact prepare him for the reality he would receive, and as he watched he wondered what world these students were being prepared for.

They were discussing *The Odyssey*.

—...and why would Calypso be wanting to keep Odysseus on her island for so long?

For Leonard to hear that round Irish accent again placed his mind not on the nymph's island of Ogygia, but in Leonard's old Search and Rescue Suburban, where they had waited to play their part in the demise of Western Man.

A student raised his hand and it was apparent to Leonard that Pat wished it had been one of the other students, any other student.

—Edgar...

—Dick.

—Dick?

—Definitely. Calypso wanted some dick.

—You mean to say she wanted sex?

—That's what I mean, boss.

—Okay, so this is a very common assumption. Let's go ahead and open it up a bit and see if there's anything to it. So... she's immortal, so if she wants dick, as you so eloquently expressed, it seems to me like there might be easier ways of getting it....

A bell rang. Not a bell to make a person jump, but one to gently let the students know that the time to move to the next class had come. Pat finished his sentence and assigned the night's reading and wished them luck and congratulated them on their good fortune.

This was met with grumbling by a few, acknowledgment by some, and derision by others. Leonard watched the students shuffle out of the class; teenagers, well-fed, well-watered, shiny and new. The apocalypse had come, but it seemed that it had not come for everyone and Leonard knew that even he was a latecomer to it, that for some, for many, it was centuries old already. Ask an Apache ghost when the end of the world was, and any worth his salt would tell you that the end came with the conquistador in their year of 1620.

Pat walked over and sat down on the desktop next to Leonard.

—Jaysus, I see ya sitting there and was sure I was having some kinda SBD flashback.

—Where the hell'd you go?

—Fishing just like we talked about.

—You didn't come back with no fish, fucker.

—No mate, that I did not. But I swear on all that is holy that I tried me damnedest to.

—Really?

—See I go down to Tamarind Creek and it was bone dry like, not even a dirty old trickle, and so I tried to get to that other one you told me about, and then it fucking snowed like and I was freezing me tits off, and I couldn't see fuck all like, everything was the same white and I got completely lost, and snow blind, and stupid from the hunger and mental from the cold, you shoulda seen me I was wandering around like I was the demon lovechild of Earnest Shackleton and Holy Moses.

—Okay.

—Well by the time I realized where the hell I was I was practically back at Dharma so I figured I would go there and supply up and get right back to you.

—Well, that sure as shit didn't happen.

—I know it, mate, and I've felt plenty bad about it and had a lot of miles of walking to think about it and how I mighta done it different. But when I got back to Dharma didn't I get summoned straight away into the management tent at the top of the hill, and I am thinking that yer one Claire's gonna burst on in and start giving it all that for me coming back to the camp with no scientist or Indian in tow or nothing, but Claire's nowhere to be found, but instead it's the Yoga Lady and doesn't it turn out that she's the one who's been in charge of the whole circus all along?

—Yeah I know.

—Fecking shocking like. Anyway yer one starts saying that I'm not going back to you but am to go on ahead to my next thing like, and I says hold on Missus Bendy I am not abandoning the only big fecking Indian friend I have, but by and by she convinces me that it's really quite the opposite, that I'm really looking out for you, that really I am the advanced party, and I got to go get things set up so you and yer one can go on her really super important top-secret mission. And I'm there thinking that my life is turned into some kinda mashup between James Bond and the Flintstones.

—Nobody said nothing about seeing you back in Dharma. I went out looking for you three goddam times. Was pretty sure you died.

—Because nobody saw me, mate. Missus Bendy had me hiking out that afternoon, like it was urgent. Yer one gave me whatever she thought I needed and told me to fuck off across the whole bleeding country so I could find you some kinda seaworthy craft.

—What does that mean?

—A sailboat.

—And did you?

—Jaysus, Mary and Holy Saint Joseph did I wha? The old Hunter '33's been sitting there waiting for you in a warehouse in Virginia Beach for the better part of a year. A real beauty, if I don't say so meself. After it was set and secure and full of stodge enough to get you round the world and back I sat around there a couple of weeks and then I came back here. That was the deal I made with Miss Bendy's mean twin sister, anyway.

—Yeah, what's the deal with that?

—Fecking bananas like, and isn't yer one the spit of the other and check this out but I been hearing from credible sources about a third.

—A third what?

Pat raised an eyebrow and waited for Leonard's slight nod.

— Yep. Ruth. And from what I understand she makes the other two seem meek like, and actually yer one's the chief of the whole damn thing.

—Where's she?

—Well you remember the late twenties when they put up the wall in Chicago, and told the black people that they could kill each other all they wanted on the other side. Well, apparently on the other side of that wall, that's where herself and her followers are making their stand. And if Jahia is to be believed and I got every reason to believe her like, it's the best place on earth.

—Who's Jahia?

—The sun and the moon, mate. If you can stick a few days, I'll introduce ya.

—Right. Seems like you went fishing after all.

—Sure, I mean in a lot of ways Damascus is everything I thought I stood against, but well it's also everything I ever wanted, so....

— Okay, but, where are we? What the hell is this place? How does this work so well when the rest of everything doesn't work at all?

—Well, ya remember when we sat there up on that ridge in your old hi-ace and we heard that boom and didn't we really know that that was what we were waiting for?

—Yeah, I guess.

—Well, there is no way to look at this place and San Antonio Mountain, and South Side and not see that this whole smoke was planned long before Bright Angel even happened. Clean water comes right out of the ground here. We have our own sources of energy, food production and a fuckoff store of printer material. We could damn near print anything, from houses to cling-film. We have a well-fed army of jackbooted cunts to keep us safe from the cannibals. This here compound is as secure as any walled city throughout the history of walled cities, which is most of history in the end, isn't it?

—So it's all the same cabal, huh?

—I think so. But it's too late now for any self-righteous feelings on the matter my man. You ain't gonna beat 'em so you might as well join 'em.

—Why?

—Well surviving is right nice for one thing. But I don't know, maybe seeing the start of humanity 2.0 is a thing too. Aren't you that bit curious, anyway?

—And who gets to choose?

—Choose what?

—Who survives and who doesn't, who is inside the compound, and who the fuck is out.

—I don't know, not me that's for sure, but we're in the compound, and that's a fact borne out by the reality of us sitting right here talking, so, we were obviously chosen.

—Was I chosen to be in the compound or to just be the compound's red nigger?

—Couldn't we all ask the same thing, or some version of it?

—Will I ever get to sit in your classroom and learn about Odysseus and Calypso?

—You might not, but your child might.

—I don't have no children.

—And yet the possibility is not at all closed to you.

Tammy lay in the hot bath that was drawn and waiting for her when she came into the cottage. Sea salt and lavender oil spread through the water and she closed her eyes and felt the layers of grime lift off of her skin. If a bath was not a feeling she'd missed it was only because she had no hope of ever having one again. She fell asleep, and when she woke the water was dark and cool so she drained the tub, and rinsed off the ring of grime and refilled the tub, and let herself float just inches above the ceramic floor. She thought that the key to luxury was not wealth at all, but the deprivation and then restoration of the same. She knew where she was. She knew that there was a direct connection between wealth and poverty, and the depth of one told an accurate story about the breadth of the other. It was no different now than it ever had been. That they were made to walk across the country was no accident. She dried herself off and put on the light linen pants and top that had been left for her. When she came out of the bathroom Virginia was there waiting for her.

—How was your bath?

—How many of you are there?

—You mean how many people live here in Damascus?

—No, how many clones?

 —Three.

—Who's the third?

—Why?

—Because at the very least I'd like to know who I work for.

—Her name is Ruth and you no more work for her than she does for you.

—Is that it?

—That I know of. There could be others.

—Why should I be a part of any of this?

—You're not a prisoner.

—What the hell is Red Axe anyway?

 —I think they borrowed it from the bible.

—Meaning what?

—To me? Only that we are not afraid.

—Yeah but who thought this whole thing up?

—Does it really matter?

—Yes.

—Well it was a collaboration, but, well, Judith was certainly one of the collaborators.

—Okay, what was the plan?

—Just to start over in a better way, that's all.

—Who are you to say what is a better way?

—Look, maybe this attempt at society ends up in the exact same place as the last, maybe it's even worse, but one thing I think we can admit is that the path the world was on was only that of human extinction, and given that that was the situation it seems like any plan, any plan at all, has got to be better than none, and seeing that there was no mechanism for the world to make sensible decisions, unilateral action seemed like the best thing going. Do you disagree?

They were silent for a long time.

—Tea?

—Sure.

—English breakfast?

—From England?

—No, from our greenhouse. It's not perfect but it's the closest thing we have.

Virginia boiled an electric kettle and scalded a ceramic blue and white teapot with an intricate floral design.

—My father brought it back from Vietnam as a gift for my mother in 1968. I was born the next year.

—You're very well-preserved for seventy-some.

—Well, Judith, the woman from whom I am cloned, the woman with whom I share one hundred percent of my DNA, she was born in 1969.

—Why did Judith decide to clone herself?

—Who knows? Because she could. She was not ready to grow old and thought she'd start over. Maybe she liked the idea of replicating herself but did not much care for men. I really don't know.

—And where is Judith now?

—There's a pretty good argument to say she's right in front of you.

—Again.

—Again.

—Or what about Vanessa and Ruth, what are they to you?

—They are me.

—Jesus, do you all ever get together?

—We have.

—And what's that like?

—It is a feeling of return, of wholeness. That is all I can say.

—And who's in charge?

—Nobody. We wanted to end patriarchy, not replicate it.

—So what the hell are me and Leonard doing here?

—So far as I know you are on your way to the north of the world so you can get some seeds and come back. A pretty important mission if you ask me. Maybe the most important.

—Why should I do anything for you?

—Oh you shouldn't. You shouldn't do anything for me, or even for humanity or anything like that. You should do it for you, because salvaging what we can from this mess is perfectly in keeping with what you were doing.

They drank the rest of their tea in silence and Tammy went through the mental exercise of weighing the pros and cons of continuing. By the time she had narrowed her options to one, their cups were dry and the sun cut slantwise across the top of the walled city of Damascus.

—We'll need fifty pounds of V-cell, ten pounds of that tea and an escort to the sea.

18

JANUARY 3RD, 2050

Leonard stood on the foredeck with the sextant held up to his right eye, and he slid the index arm across the curved plane of the graduated arc and so measured the angle of the sun above the horizon. He did this at noon or what he believed to be noon. He used this information to plot their course. Tammy had no choice but to trust in his knowledge and his tools and his methodology, as she had none of those things of her own in which to place her trust, or alternatively with which to voice her doubt, and if they sailed north into icy oblivion or over the pole and south and into the sun itself she could have no real effect. She felt helpless and at the mercy of forces greater than herself: the vast sea, the angry planet, time, history, the stars and sun and moon wheeling overhead. To be small among the large is to see the gods for who they really are: infinite and uncaring. Tammy was not used to feeling helpless and swore to herself that if her head ever stopped spinning and her stomach sopped donating its contents to the sea she would learn the theory and practice of celestial navigation so that she might share some agency in their heading and some responsibility in the case of their getting lost at sea. Their destination was rumor at best.

Tammy had been sitting in her usual spot in the companionway. On the stairs leading from the cockpit down to the cabin, her legs were in the boat's belly but her eyes were fixed on the slanted line of the horizon. To go beyond the splashguard was to be wet and cold but to go down into the cabin was to be ill, to have one's stomach churn and one's head wheel, to be so sick as to have one's soul probe for the escape hatch and so she sat there neither out nor in and was there for the best part of three days. She saw the edge of the known world recede behind her. What they were doing was insane, verging on suicidal, but maybe sanity itself had slipped its moorings. What was once mad was now simply de rigueur.

Leonard had been trained for this. Somewhere in the halls of the Naval Command Center in Maryland some admiral thought that celestial navigation ought to be a thing every sailor knew how to do. The fact that it had not been used as a real method of navigation for almost one hundred years was of no consequence. It was the bedrock. It did not require the ping of satellites or land-based electricity or ship-based sonar or even dead reckoning, but only a limited knowledge of the celestial bodies and their movements in the heavens. He remembered having to take the course and he remembered the general sentiment that was held about it. Leonard and his fellow cadets thought they were being made fun of, that they were being given busywork in order to fill the time until their bodies would be needed for cannon fodder.

They took sun shots from the bell tower on Mahan Hall. They found Polis' from the top of Dan's rock. They triangulated the arc of the sun and that of the moon and from this scant information knew where on the great Earth they placed their feet. To understand celestial navigation is to understand that we truly stand on the shoulders of giants. Since before Jesus walked the Earth we knew how to do it. It's true the white man destroyed this planet with his insatiable appetite, with his love of all things electric, with his fascination with gizmos and his need to talk at his fellows at all hours, despite having little or nothing to say. With his inborn greed and outsized ambition he stripped the Earth of her vitality, but before he did, his curiosity took his mind to the very edge of the universe. He dismantled time itself, saw the power inside of a single atom, built fast ships which could cross the sea, first by slave, then by wind, then by fire and then by fusion. Months, to weeks, to days. Planes to cross the sky faster than the speed of sound and spaceships to cross the galaxy within a hair's breadth of the speed of light.

Leonard took a sun shot at noon, and then pored over charts and tables for a quarter of an hour and then made adjustments to the tiller's shock cord and trimmed the sails to adjust for the changes he made in their course and he then made himself a cup of tea on the gimbaled stove. He asked if Tammy wanted one but she declined saying she was unsure her stomach could "countenance such a thing" although Leonard got the feeling that that was just an excuse. He wondered if she did not decline the tea because she felt like she did not deserve it.

—Are we on course, Captain?

—I think so.

—What if you're wrong?

—Then we'll be lost at sea.

—Right. Okay.

—I'm not wrong.

—I believe you.

—We'll get you there.

—How long do you think?

—Depends on if the winds hold up. Four months at a minimum but probably longer. We'll hit the Feldge sooner or later and there is really no telling how long it'll take to cross or even if we can cross.

285

—The what?

—Dead latitudes. It was small when I was in school, but the rumor was that the warmer water was feeding it and that it was growing.

—What if we can't?

—I don't know. We starve to death I guess.

—Do you think that's gonna happen?

—No.

—Okay, so what now?

—I don't know. Save your strength, no matter what you're gonna need it.

The months of walking gave way to the months of sitting. They had real tea, and ate V-cell, raw and without supplements because their tongues could no longer be fooled anyway. They read the books Pat had left them, each with a stamp proudly claiming that the book was the property of Virginia Beach Public Library; like a dog claiming to be its master's keeper. Each title was considered for its length and its content. Leonard thought of his friend in the ruins of the library, picking books and he could almost hear Pat's soft brogue delivering lectures and he felt invisibly guided through the thickets of fiction.

They read and read, and over four months eight thousand miles passed beneath their bright hull. The longer the yarn the shorter the length of the world they'd left to cross when the reader looked up. *War and Peace, Shikasta, Anna Karenina, Infinite Jest, iQ84, Gone with the Wind, East of Eden, The Iliad, To the Lighthouse, One Hundred Years of Solitude, Don Quixote, The Blood Meridian, The King James Bible, Les Misérables, Beloved, Light in August, Sense and Sensibility, Ulysses, Underworld,* The complete works of William Shakespeare, *Moby-Dick* and the *Lord of the Rings* were on the top shelf. There were three shelves below. They read, mostly to themselves but sometimes aloud, and while the world contracted to the size of their small vessel, it also expanded to include the better part of recorded time and the experience of hundreds of others flowed into their own and those experiences became inseparable from theirs. For company they had no less than Areliano Buendia, and Frodo Baggins, and Elinor Dashwood, Seth and Denver and the Kid and Cossette and Abraham and Isaac, Achilles and Jesus Christ and if the world had become empty of people it had also become full of the chatter of characters.

They played chess. The first three hundred games Tammy lost by blunder, a bishop lurking in the corner that she did not see, a knight timely sprung for a three-way fork, a queen lost from the failure to think about the other player's malicious intent. Then, the next three hundred games she lost by weaker strategy. Poor tactics. On her seven-hundred-and-sixty-fifth game, she won, and she felt joy that she did not expect and she danced and sang and howled at the endless night from the deck of their small boat.

Tammy lost the next twenty-three games, then she won three in a row, and after that either one of them might win or lose any contest and the stakes invisibly rose toward the level of war, on which the game was based. They progressed north at seven knots an hour and the horrors of America and their long walk across it fell from their souls like scales from their eyes. They spent the nighttime hours curled up together in the small fore cabin. They fucked often, sometimes for seconds sometimes for hours. When the sun finally rose and the days grew bright and warmer than they had expected, they spent whole days naked. They read out loud to one another. They sang songs that they could remember and made up others. Pat had left them a harmonica and they both gave their honest efforts at learning to play but in the end they had to admit that they made better music without it and so overboard it went.

The wind was steady off their port side and it pushed them with an intensity to match their purpose, and try as they might, for a time, for those blessed months, they could not help but feel that some force greater than themselves, that some higher power was behind them, encouraging them, that some god or another was lending them aid. Then, the winds diminished in strength and one day they rose to find the sails luffing noisily against the stays and the sea like a silver mirror reflecting the clear blue skies. That day they swam in the frigid North Atlantic and they sunbathed on the deck and Tammy was heartened by her sun shot which revealed that they still made progress north by current alone. Days passed and with no landmarks to break the horizon they had the impression of stillness. Their world had long since been reduced, but now it was truly condensed to two, and there, naked, on the deck of the Hunter '33 Tammy mused aloud.

—Maybe we're the new Adam and Eve.

In the days to come the wind did not return but they rose each day to thickening trash. Each day the garbage would increase in volume: a million water bottles, milk jugs, Barbie dolls missing limbs, or just the head of a doll, or a doll shockingly whole but somehow still defiled, flower pots and picture frames, lawn chairs and umbrella skeletons, sunglasses, plates and cups, sachets that once held everything from apple sauce to shampoo, congregated and moved as one and challenged Leonard to say that they had no sentience at all, as how could they have formed a school in which to travel without first having had the will to do so?

Plastic in the molds of fruit long since eaten, whose species and even genus were disappeared from the Earth entirely for lack of insects to propagate them. Plastic which at one time encased other plastic, and remote controls and cellphone covers and landlines and fax machines and 2d printers and 3d printers and traffic cones, and crowd barriers, dog toys, and a billion drinking straws, used only once to suck up sugarwater poison and then discarded to roam the seas for a million years, and compact discs that had no players to read their zeros and ones, coffee containers, a boxer's mouthpiece, ten thousand fishing nets though the fish were long since gone and the fishermen too, a cook's colander, a man's comb and a woman's hairbrush, toys and toys and toys, dollhouses and racecar tracks, and whole miniature kitchens for children to harmlessly pretend to be a mom or a dad in, but mostly it was just bits, pieces of plastic that had broken down closer to its base form yet by no means were broken down; bits, as unnatural as apes on the moon.

They found themselves surrounded by a myriad of weirdly shaped objects all of which seemed to be making their way to some sort of plastic conclave. Tammy and Leonard entertained themselves by identifying individual pieces of plastic within the forming island of trash and then telling tales of that specific piece of plastic's origin and history…

A doll, once the beloved plaything of a girl named Margaret. When she had the doll she was in second grade. She had ambitions to be an astronaut or alternatively a doctor or perhaps a marine biologist but she died in the great Missouri flood of `25 along with ten thousand other souls who were washed out to sea.

A chair that used to belong to Sadie Phillips who dragged it out of her apartment nearly every day to sit with her friends, who themselves had dragged their own plastic chairs to the sidewalk so that they could sit and talk about better and worse times while around them the Bronx transformed itself from an unredeemable ghetto to an unaffordable zip code.

A red poker chip that was the bottommost in a stack of them represented the moment when Tim Murphy's luck changed and with just this one chip and a full house, wealth began its inevitable migration back to him. Three hands later he held a heart flush. Tim invested his winnings in a startup called Xanothis and lived out his life drinking champagne and snorting cocaine as the world fell to pieces around him, however, it was also the same chip on the very same night that started Latisha Washington's journey from homeowner to renter to homeless, where she died on the streets of Los Angeles in the great heatwave of `32.

There was the facemask of a sleep apnea machine and Leonard told the story of how an old married couple's sex life was reinvigorated by the addition of the machine to their bedroom. Both Doris and Morris thought that their time in the sack was long since over but with the introduction of nighttime oxygen and the added potential of futuristic role playing games the couple rediscovered their bodies. They had a few great months of sexual play before it all became too much for the old woman's heart and she died, although Leonard noted that she died happy and Morris followed Doris into death, waiting only a week in order to set straight their affairs and then he traded the oxygen machine for a plastic bag and he too died with a smile on his lips.

A pregnancy test with its positive result burned into its window. Tammy told how the embryo represented on that stick went on to be none other than Monica Ganzie, who would not only invent the all immersive haptic VR suit, which all but replaced the VR chamber, but she also invented the antidote to the suit's dark magic; a real-world therapy which was slowly returning a large segment of the population to the more difficult reality of reality which led to a wave of psychotic breaks and rape on wholesale scale, and real suicides and real murders—Monica Ganzie, like a million other souls, ceased to be during the great siege of New York in 2042.

Tammy and Leonard's game went on and on, and though none of the stories were the true stories they were as good, as they represented the world as fairly and as accurately as those other narratives, which in any case had no tellers but only poor plastic remnants with which to stave off nonexistence.

Tammy and Leonard found themselves trapped in plastic's heartland and as the days wore on the game began to lose its appeal and what had started out as a spontaneous celebration of humanity turned into an elegy for the same. Finally, they woke to the sound of an object thumping against the side of the Hunter `33. Leonard got up to investigate and he found nothing shy of a demon that had parted the mists of time to come and collect its promised tithe. A hideous object there to remind him of his past folly, of his mortality, and of the mortality of others. There it was. The same colors, black and red. Seeing it he felt instantly sick, and a past that he was sure he had banished came back at him, undiminished for its long absence.

—What the fuck…

He pulled the miniature yet oversized plastic ninja motorcycle out of the water and laid it at his feet and let the seawater drain from it. A ninja made for a toddler to push with his legs, while presumably his mouth made the high-pitched whine of the crotch rocket he sat astride. A toy for a child molded in the shape of a toy for a man, cast to fulfill the same fantasy of flight. Leonard was reminded of the pretty girl with the red bandana and the bruises down her arms. He did not really know her. Her name he'd only learn after her death. Was she attracted to the Apache or the Kawasaki? It did not matter to him, not in the least, not on that day. She curled herself around him and pressed her pert breasts against his back, and hugged him tight as they navigated the sharp turns of Mogillon Canyon. He spent his entire enrollment bonus on the down payment, and for the first time in his life he felt both wanted and free. One-hundred-and-seventy miles per hour on the flats between Tempe and the highlands, and eighty-five through the mountain pass between Show Low and Globe. Nothing compared to that, and nothing ever would. The melding of man and machine was never more complete or more real. Not even a fighter jet responded to a man's body in the way a crotch rocket did; one wrong turn of the head, a muscle spasm, a twitch of the finger, and death would come and find the rider and tear him from his bike and rip him limb from limb on the merciless concrete.

A blind corner, a stalled Mazda, a patch of salt left over from the plowing season....

Leonard walked away bruised and wide-eyed, but the girl whose name he would later learn was Beth would not walk away at all, her neck broken, her red bandana shredded to ribbons, her unhelmeted head smashed on the blacktop. Leonard went to her funeral and the girl's mother, red-eyed and wild with grief, beat on his chest with her clenched fist but then folded herself into him and cried and cried and whispered in his ear that it was not his fault, that Beth had always been marked by death, that she longed for it and had called out for it since she was just a child, but death, patient and precise, met her at the designated placed and at the appointed hour.

Twenty-four-and-a-half years later, Leonard sat on the deck of the Hunter '33 with the child's plastic balance bike at his feet and he wept. He wept for Beth and for himself and for the dying world which had briefly been the wonder of the universe.

Tammy came up from below with a cup of tea for him and she curled herself around him and she pressed her pert breasts into his back and she held him and she did not ask any questions and he offered no explanations.

When it seemed that Tammy and Leonard were doomed to become part of the trash, more rubbish in a sea of rubbish, a light breeze rose to their stern and Tammy unfurled the genoa and then the spinnaker and Leonard had to stand at the bow and use the jib arm to fend off the debris that they had become entrapped in, and in seven days of hard labor they found the edge of the Great North Atlantic Garbage Patch and were again on their way to Svalbard and the seeds that humanity had left there for times just such as these.

For seven days the wind was at their backs and they forgot the despair that had settled over them and they felt the smallest kindling of hope within their tired souls. Just after noon on the seventh day, the clouds which had been streaming past them began to coalesce. The skies darkened and great rolling waves started to lift and drop them, gently at first but then with increasing aggression. When the drenching rain began they dropped their sails and rode bare poled up and down the backs of giants which seemed to come at them from every direction and at every angle. They were bandied about like a toy in a mad child's bath. They felt the mast slam into the ocean's roiling surface, and more than once it seemed that the boat would turtle completely, her mast pointed straight down, her inhabitants surely drowning, but then the water released them and they catapulted in the opposite direction and were thrown about the cabin like ragdolls, and the wind howled and played the braded iron stays like some kind of satanic lyre calling up demons from the ocean's dark, and the boat creaked and groaned and threatened to break apart and leave them to cling to bits of shredded fiberglass. They wished they had a god to pray to but they did not. There would be no one to call for help and they buried themselves among the tubes of nutrients, charts, and loose chessmen; queen, knight, bishop and castle all reduced to pawns before gods, and Tammy and Leonard clung to one another and cried and yelled and sang at the top of their voices and buried their heads into the comfort of the other's breast and the dark sleepless hours crept by but in the morning the storm had passed and the sea was flat. The Hunter '33 was a mess though it was not damaged profoundly, and at noon Tammy calculated that they had only been blown fifty miles off course. In the grand scheme of things it was not so bad, and they were embarrassed for their tears and their cries, but by 5 PM they had set a new course and sails were hoisted, and again they made progress toward the north of the world and humanity's best hope of survival.

With the wind at their backs they read and played chess and fucked sometimes and made love others. They sang and the days turned into weeks, and they paid the cost of the time they spent idle in the Feldge as their supplies dwindled and the sea gave them only garbage and nothing at all to eat, and they grew thin. They cut up the tubes of V-cell and licked the remnants from their metal peels and worry ate at their minds and salt ate at their skins and they ceased to sleep more than a couple of fitful minutes at a time, and the sun did loops in the sky, but never appeared to sink below the horizon. They believed their conversations had become more lucid, clear-eyed and real, but if they had been overheard by others they would have been as unintelligible as babbling toddlers or grunting macaques.

When the hope of ever seeing land again was at its most distant and its possibility had become unimportant they found themselves within sight of the snow-covered cliffs of Sor Spitzbergen. The stars had led them to the Island of Svalbard. The only problem being that they were on the wrong side of the island and neither the wind nor the currents favored their sailing to their intended destination. After a brief celebration, it struck them that they would still have thirty hard miles to trek up glaciers and over snow-covered mountains. The most treacherous part of their journey still lay before them.

6/21/50

Dear Friends,

It's been a hard June here at Dharma. There is no way to spin the deaths of Jim, Laura, Tomas, Sage, and especially Baby Percy as anything but devastating. As our number continues to shrink I am sure some of you, maybe all of you, are considering your chances topside. I can only say that I wish you luck and strength and I assure you that you have all of my love and support as you go. I only ask that you protect those of us who remain with your silence. We are in your hands and our survival depends on your discretion. I am staying here. For those of you who still have perseverance left to see this through, well, these next hard months will require that we bring to bear all that we are, that we reach down within and find our last hidden reservoirs of strength. Have Faith in the Restoration as foretold by Judith and some of us will live to see it come to pass, and though I hope that it is all of us, that we do not give one more of Dharma's brave souls to the dry death that dogs our steps and clouds our minds. I fear that we will. It will not be all of us at that first Thanksgiving table. I may not be there myself. After all, Moses never stepped foot in the promised land but he led his people to its gates, and three thousand years later we still tell his story.

Maybe it is just a story, but perhaps it is a useful one. Friends, I promise you this: Split Tree Canyon can bloom again, it can be verdant, green and teeming with life.

Steel yourselves for the hot dry months to come, strengthen your resolve. Our salvation is closer at hand than you think.

Love,

Vanessa

III

19

JULY 4TH, 2050

Of all his cities, of his New York, and London and of his Paris and Tokyo, Adam loved his Lyon best of all. He loved its mix of order and disorder. He loved how the hill that works, with its silk factories, and their two-story windows built to accommodate the giant looms of the 19th century, looked west like supplicants across the Saône to the fairytale basilica on the hill that prays. He liked the orangy-red color of the retaining walls, first built by Romans. He loved the cobblestone alleyways and the wide orderly boulevards. He loved the galloping statue of Louis XIV on the Plaza Belcour. He had even picked a building at the heart of the Croix Ruse on the top floor of which was "his" apartment with its roof deck, complete with a pool and garden. He had other apartments which he loved—his apartment on 59th Street in Manhattan overlooking Central Park, aflame with eternal autumn, and his apartment in the Hinokicho Tower, surrounded in cherry blossoms, forever in bloom, with its views of Midtown on the left and Tokyo Bay on the right—but it was his apartment in the fourth arrondissement of Lyon that he felt was his true home, that was where he sent his mind to sit in the sun and rest.

—Subah Bakhai. App ka din acha guzaray. Me Adam hooh. Aap say mil ker khushl hui.

He was repeating simple Urdu phrases and building his new city when he heard the alarm.

Male, female, male, female, present continuous, past perfect, future simple. He aped the guttural intonations of his long-dead teachers while his hands placed the driftwood towers into the foundations he had prepared for them. This city was different from the others. This one was not a city based on the three-dimensional holograms that Iris produced of the actual cities in their prime. This city was not built of carbon fiber polymer, but completely of objects that he had hunted during the long summer days on Rasmussen Beach. It was not a city based on some other, it was not the collective product of a million minds spanning ten generations. It was a city based in some other order entirely. It was the product of one man's mind, and that which the sea brought him. Natural driftwood or glass bottles were his greatest prizes, but there were also metal straws and parts of cars and ships and planes and even

302

spacecraft, iron railings and reams of barbed wire and while there was plenty of plastic to be found on Rasmussen Beach he did not use it to build his Babylon. This was not a material judgment, as he was never taught to favor one material over another. It was only his aim to build a thing that would still be standing long after his other cities had melted back into the earth. He wanted to build a city from which he could watch the sun crash into the Earth.

From the day after their parent's sudden departure, Iris guided Adam's every action until she no longer needed to.

Pour the milk into the bowl, tie your shoes, mop the floor, clean up your room. *We are not savages after all*, she would say imitating the stern tones their mother once used. The mental work of survival was led by Iris. She decided what they grew and when, the timing of seed germination and planting and harvesting. She saw to the production of V-cell, and seed replacement, cloning and hybridizing. She dictated when Adam rose, when he went to sleep, what he ate, what he watched and what he read. She saw to the education of his mind and the careful strengthening of his body.

His fitness routine was as rigorous as that of any Olympic athlete's, and his study schedule would rival that of any scholar. She pushed the limits of what a young human mind and body could intake, process and retain. She designed his diet to the molecule by analyzing his waste and making adjustments accordingly. Eventually, not a single empty calorie found its way past his lips.

Jessper had embedded emergency protocols into Iris's code, just in case. Iris had been tasked with Adam's survival in the unlikely event of his parents' absence and true to her programing no other considerations took precedence.

While Adam was reliant on Iris's vast knowledge, Iris needed Adam's fingers and Adam's thumbs and the large muscles of his arms and his legs. What his five-year-old body could not accommodate simply did not get done. They survived, and after twelve years they thrived, and while they were impoverished in some areas, they were rich in others. In his ten-acre warehouse of GPUs Jessper had left behind almost every film ever made, every book ever written, every photo of importance ever taken and what took a million years to create was theirs to dive into, to whatever depth they were capable of sounding.

Iris had no capacity for loneliness and Adam had long since absorbed loneliness into his daily state. Loneliness was the color of his eyes.

Adam wondered if he were not the digital and she the organic. He felt that he was getting smaller while she always found ways to grow larger. He studied and studied and yet as the world he knew grew, it only ever implied the size of the universe he did not. He knew he would never catch her. The pretense of their being the same "age" was dropped the day their parents did not turn up to enforce it. She started life with more knowledge than he would ever have and like any sibling he knew in his heart that equity was a lie passed from parents to children in order to avoid speaking hard truths.

Your sister is just smarter than you are.

Words never said, though many a brother knew them to be true.

Adam took in whole civilizational histories and complex mathematical equations and physical theories that looked deeply into the universe inside of an atom and he understood the implications those theories made about the vast space beyond them. He learned languages, though he knew most to be already dead, never to be spoken again, sounds that would never be used to communicate wants and needs, desires or dreams.

Adam considered the spiritual practices and traditions. He contemplated the life of Jesus and also of Abraham and Mohammed. He whirled like a dervish, tied himself into knots like a yogi, sat stalk still for a fortnight and more so that he could try to know what Siddhartha meant by "If you are quiet enough, you will hear the flow of the universe."

He read and read, from Thomas Aquinas to Marcus Aurelius to Margaret Atwood to Doris Lessing. Iris, on the other hand, had long since consumed the vast store of bits left behind by their common father and had begun trying to manifest herself physically. What started with steam and light moved through smoke and flame. She had even talked her brother through building a robotic body, but it was too cold and mechanical to express the vast being she knew herself to be. She found more and more ways of expressing herself. With a snowmobile, and ten thousand gallons of beet juice she was able to draw in the vast frozen fields behind their house, at first just portraits of her and Adam but then whole comic books writ large that told stories that even she did not know the origin of. Her brother would glance up from his texts, smile at his sister's efforts and then return to his own.

Time, temperature, lightness and dark, the vast sea and the wounded planet, all took on a countenance and scale unique to the observers, who sat alone at its far northern edge and waited, and waited. For what, they did not know.

There were times, always during the blackness of the long arctic night, when Adam knew that he was alone, truly alone, that his sister was not really a sister, but merely code and that he survived only by a cruel twist of fate. Adam banished these thoughts as he could not bear their weight, and while his aloneness squared with his logic it did not fit with his experience, and so he chose experience over logic and built his world upon its solid foundation. Thus, he spun his loneliness into aloneness, from straw to gold, and like Jesus and

Siddhartha before him, from his deep well of sadness sweet notes of harmony began to rise.

Adam was studying Urdu because the bank held grain deposits from the region where Urdu had once been spoken, and he had made it his mission to at least be able to have a quotidian conversation with any depositor should they come to the Seed Bank to make a withdrawal, no matter how unlikely the appearance of that depositor be.

When the alarm sounded, he stood up from his studies, and though it was the first time he had heard the noise, he did not panic. It was likely nothing. As he walked down the long hallway opening and closing the floodproof doors, he told himself stories that made sense, even if those stories were unlikely. He reminded himself that everything, existence included, was unlikely. His mind settled on an old fishing net blown in off the sea that had become caught on the drainage ditch fence, and an old buoy that was being blown over and over again against the metal door. He hatched other theories, some more fanciful if even less probable, a djinn, a genie, a tax collector, but what he opened the door to lay beyond his most outrageous hallway theories. Tammy Cohen stood in front of him, thin, weathered, filthy and luminous, and though she was exactly what and whom he had been waiting for, his mind balked at the sight of her. Adam could only imagine that she was an angel fallen to Earth, or perhaps a goddess come down from the heights of Olympus, or a refugee from beyond the gates of Valhalla.

They stood and looked at one another in the open doorway. When she spoke, he had to lean into her to make out the words. English, the same language that his long-departed parents had taught him, and while Adam understood the content of her words the context of them was impossible to grasp.

—You need to go get him, please, he'll die if you don't.

—Who?

—Him. Leonard. He fell, far I think but maybe he's still alive, I think he's still alive. Please, you have to try.

Adam had not seen a human being in the flesh in twelve years, and in his heart he never expected that he would again. He stood in the doorway and stared, unable to move. Finally, he heard Iris's voice behind him. She spoke to him in Urdu.

—Get her inside, get her some food and water and then we'll see about whomever it is she's talking about.

—Who's that?

—It's just Iris. Come inside.

—Why Urdu?

—I don't know.

—We need to get Leonard, please.

—Of course. We'll get him, just come inside.

—Is he gonna die?

—I don't know.

Leonard lay at the bottom of a talus slope at the edge of the dry lake of bones and watched a cold white sun burn a hole in a featureless sky. In a land without night, time cannot be counted, and if time is not a system of counting then it is nothing at all; hours, days, seconds, how is one to know? Tammy had the map, the compass, the watch and the sextant. With those tools she had learned to track their position across the earth's surface and from their second week under sail, navigation had become her responsibility and her obsession. Leonard knew that Tammy no longer needed him. Maybe, he thought, she never really had. She would have to make the last steps north by herself and then sail south and make the long walk west and Leonard knew that she was equal to the task, and he felt a tinge of pride in the thought that he had played a small part in that equalization.

The sun appeared over the ridge behind him for the second time since he lay in that same spot but it was impossible to say that it had gone around the world and returned. It was as likely that he had merely blinked and experienced it anew upon his eyes opening again. It seemed as if the sun merely doubled back on itself, proof that it was no more than a solar imposter; not a real sun, an illusion sun, a dream sun. Leonard tried to organize his mind. He wanted to get the order of things right. They had tied the Hunter '33 to old pilings on the south side of the island. They had calculated a two or possibly three day walk over what was left of the Larsbreen glacier. They had camped for one sun-filled night. For six hours on the wristwatch they tried to sleep, but fear and light and hunger kept them awake. They walked most of the next day, shuffling, stooped, weak with hunger and as silent as penitents in contemplation of a wrathful god. They passed over the flinty ground that the glacier's retreat had left behind. This was not the frozen Arctic of their childhood fantasies. Old Saint Nick's workshop had been relocated, if it had ever been here at all. No ice remained, just an immense and ancient plane of cold granitic scree. Stone as old as Earth itself, it too having traveled from the south of the globe to the north. They walked through the gigantic folds of Carboniferous and Permian strata, and though the ocean had imparted to them a sense of their bodies' scale in space, it was their final walk through the warped rock palaces of Sor Spitzbergen that drove home their life's brevity, their frailty and of the absolute hubris of their endeavor. A pair of fruit flies conspiring to rule the universe for eternity.

By and by, they came to a wide flat pan; sandy ground that may have at one time been an inland sea or a lake but had since dried and cracked and resembled a piece of the Mojave transported to the other side of the globe. Such geologic scramblings were common during the life of a planet, and where twenty years previous bearded seals still fished for cod and half-ton polar bears hunted those selfsame seals, and long tusked walrus battled one another for a shot at immortality, now only their bone frames remained and their sunbleached skulls with their hollow eyes and their long fangs looked up at the travelers in silent accusation. "You did this to us, *you* and no other." The walkers tried to quicken their pace so as to leave that inverted graveyard behind, but the faster they walked, the further the great northern bone pitch stretched and it seemed that they had traveled that long way only to make their skeletal contributions to the same.

They had water but they had long since run out of V-cell and had taken to scraping lichen from rocks, and licking the remnants of dry marrow from the sun-sucked bones that surrounded them.

They were frail in body and mind. When they came to the deepest bend in the canyon they turned west. They could skirt the jagged rocks of Hekla Hoak and twenty hard miles would have them within the shell of what had been the thriving boomtown of Longyearbyen.

They had climbed up more than six hundred vertical feet to a thick limestone vein that cut across the canyon wall and promised to provide them with a clearer path toward their destination. Their crawl up the rocks was a gamble, not only because of their caloric poverty, but because of the very real possibility that they were spending their finite energy to get to a position even more untenable than the one in which they found themselves. Yet, with a mile traveled along the intrusion, their wager seemed to be paying off as below the white vein lay a path of limestone talc, smooth and easy to traverse. As they walked their spirits were lifted, and again they felt as if they must be guided by a destiny that was beyond their will, and they wordlessly rejoiced, believing that the most unlikely of victories was within their grasp. Fools. Any true wayfarer knows that the most treacherous mile is the last. The mile in which tired arms let heavy shields drop, and bright smiles catch the attention of malevolent gods.

Tammy was thinking about a competition she had entered during her first year at Stanford in which the contestants were challenged to present new models of mass production that took into account exploding third-world populations and the changing global climate. Her model entailed vast floating islands of crops watered by closed system solar distillation. She didn't win. She thought that if she had it to do over again she would harness the ocean currents to power tremendous turbines that would be used to compress the continents of plastic garbage found in the ocean. She would compress the plastic into dense, yet perforated bricks. Bricks which she could then seed with Anthozoa, and with her magic bricks she would remake the coral reefs which the earth had lost.

Leonard was thinking about a sheepherder he had met in the mountains of Pakistan, and how they had smoked heroin together, and how the man told him in broken English with a smile to match, that any person who believed the story that he had been told about the nature of existence was open to the manipulation of the men who spun such tales. At least that is what Leonard took from what the man said, though it could have been that his intended message was the opposite. Leonard's mind was filled with the face of this sheepherder, who had these twenty years since been turned into irradiated carbon by Indian nuclear warheads. Leonard spoke out loud, his first such utterance since leaving their sleepless camp:

—Where are you now, sheepherder?

The ground simply disintegrated underneath him and Leonard tumbled for twenty-seven long and painful seconds.

All things begin in an instant and end in the same way.

If Tammy had been walking in front of Leonard, as so often was the case, it would have been her below and broken and he above and whole. Even as he tumbled he was thankful it was himself falling and not her. He flailed and clawed but weakened as he was no match for the maw which opened up to swallow him.

As he was scraped against the stone, he thought: *now I will never be able to tell her that I love her. Now I cannot tell her that she is the hope of the world.* As he fell, he contemplated the irony of so often being called the bravest, while he knew himself to be a coward. He had earned medals in service of his country. The Navy Cross for courage. The Bronze Star for heroism. The Purple Heart For love of country and self-sacrifice, and indeed Leonard had bravely faced down Syrian artillery and Russian fighter jets, and yet as he fell he knew that he had been afraid of Tammy Cohen's denying his love, of her calmly saying it would pass, of her quiet refusal to say "I love you too." He had had a million opportunities, five hundred days and more, but he took none of them. He could have told her at the end of a chess game, over a cup of tea, in the middle of one of the long silences which engulfed them for days and weeks, while she slept or better yet while she pretended to, after they fucked, or before they breakfasted. Anytime within the last eight thousand miles it would have been normal and natural and right to say the three little words. It was too late for bravery now.

He fell more than six hundred feet, at the bottom of which his body was bent at unnatural angles, all four of his limbs broken, a lung punctured and his skull fractured. The pain was blinding, all encompassing, a universe unto itself with vast stretches of nothing punctuated by cities of broken glass.

Leonard heard Tammy screaming his name, over and over again.

—Leonard! Leonard! Leonard! Len…

He tried, but he could not pull in the air he needed to call back to her. Their expedition was over. Leonard closed his eyes against the sun and the pain, and he felt the valley of bones pulling his small body into its large one.

In total blackness, Tammy returned to consciousness slowly. She had dreamt, if it could be called dreaming, only of impenetrable mass, of infinite density, of the instant before the Big Bang, and so her waking in darkness was a subtle shift in realities. She was nowhere/she was somewhere. Her first thought was simply, *where?* But the answer that came back was a response to a different question altogether.

Still Tammy Cohen.

As she woke, the light in the room began to increase slowly, as if her awakening had re-rendered the world. There was no window to the outside and so the light appeared to be without source. She could make out a small desk, a wooden chair, a 12" orange television, complete with rabbit ears and channel dials and tuning knob. Tammy wondered if she had woken up in her mother's childhood bedroom, or if she actually was her mother, Leah Cohen, and if Tammy Cohen was no more than a little girl's dream. Were such transcendental shifts possible? What if she were neither Tammy nor Leah but Grandma May, the long-suffering wife of the failed entrepreneur Louis Cohen, inventor of such things as: hotel key cards, intelligent call routing—for Cindy press one, for Julie press two— farmed chestnuts, and Indian casinos, and while all of those things came to pass, he profited from none of them as in each case he came upon the idea before the world was ready to hear it and someone else, someone with better timing, or more clout, someone without the stain of a Jewy last name brought each idea to bear. With each new idea he promised his wife a different vacation— Rome, Aruba, Thailand—and they were not empty promises, though they all went unfulfilled. May stood by Louis until his death, because despite his string of failures she believed in him until his last breath and beyond. One of his patents would catch, the widow thought, and she would die a rich woman just as he had always promised her. She died of the cigarettes she relied on for comfort through those long years. She died drowning in air, penniless and dependent on her daughter's generosity.

When Tammy Cohen, granddaughter of May Cohen, looked again, the room was full of light and she returned to her own aching body. Leonard. I have to get Leonard. She peeled back the printer-down comforter to see that she was dressed in cotton pajamas, cotton so soft it could have only come from the earth itself. What such pajamas would have fetched on the black market she could only guess.

There were lambskin slippers waiting for her, and though her cut and calloused feet cried out to wear them, she chose to proceed into the unknown, barefoot.

—Hello...

She started down a long corridor, white tile floors, walls of slate. Mounted on the wall was an axe, its handle dark veined walnut, it's head a deep red. The corridor opened up into a bright living room, fern-shaded soft leather couches and dark wood coffee tables. The south wall was dedicated to a large Andras Gurski print, a 99-cent store, ordered, colorful and apocalyptic. The western wall was dominated by three smaller paintings by Marc Chagall and Tammy seemed to know the shtetel portrayed within, and her mind went to an old story her grandfather once told about his own grandfather. It seemed to Tammy that Marc Chagall's painting had traveled a long way through time and space in order to lend her courage. It was just such a story.

She came to the kitchen, bright and airy. Great panes of glass rose twenty feet to a celling of sun-abused wood that faced the bright sea. The kitchen was separated from the living room by a counter with three stools parked underneath as if some family had breakfast in that very spot every morning before the school bus came to collect the children.

—Hello?.....Hello....Hello!.... Hello!...Fuck!

On the small kitchen table was a note: *Breakfast is in the refrigerator.*

The ticking wall clock claimed that it was 5:00, although AM or PM it was not possible for her to tell.

Tammy opened the refrigerator to find a large plate wrapped in plastic: rolls, each with a waiting pad of butter, muesli with oats and raisins and figs, fluffy dates, fresh pineapple, a small carved wood bowl full of yogurt, cooked bacon, scrambled eggs and sausage.

Tammy took the plate to the table and looked out at the expanse of sea surrounding the northernmost landmass in the world.

She found the milk protein in the refrigerator and poured the milk into her cereal. She spoke out loud.

—Now you've fucking done it, Cohen. You are alone and at the edge of the damn world, and for what?

—What should I have done instead?

She heard her own voice ask petulantly.

She did not realize, at least not right away, that the voice which she recognized as her own was not her voice as others heard it but as she herself heard it. The voice had her same timbre, rhythm and meter though it did not emanate from her own throat, nor even her mind.

—Anything. Fuck. Join the revolution or try to restart the government, or at least look for some way to fight on the side of right.

—Is that not what you're doing?

—Well, maybe, or maybe I am just doing errands for the same bastards that ruined the world in the first place. I've been manipulated.

—Manipulated by whom?

Her own voice asked.

—Well by…

…. and confusion fell on her like a drenching rain, and for a moment Tammy Cohen was lost, and everything she thought she knew of the world was washed away. She had fallen asleep sane and woken up mad. When did she lose control over the voice in her head? Were her thoughts her own? Were they ever?

She put her head on the table and screamed.

—FUCK! Who the fuck are you?

The voice changed, settling itself in the middle of the Atlantic circa 2030.

—My name is Iris.

—Why were you using my voice you fucking cunt?

—So as not to startle you. I see now that it had the opposite effect. I'm so sorry.

Tammy noticed a pair of footprints drawn in light on the dark-tile floor.

—You're a computer?

—I am a software-based intelligence.

—You're a computer.

—The word *computer* implies a thing limited by hardware.

—Okay, what does software-based intelligence mean then?

—If you have the time and patience, I am happy to try and explain it to you.

—Oh, you think my little human brain could take it?

—The constraint is not your mental capacity but your limited time.

—Ah I see, given an infinite amount time a monkey sat at a typewriter would eventually type Hamlet…

—Or any other variant.

—I've been around enough A.I.'s to know that your expanded capacity for data storage and retrieval does nothing to make up for your deficits in instinct or empathy.

—Perhaps there is not much profit in our arguing the finer points of sentience…

—Can you make me a cup of tea then… computer?

Tammy spit out the last word with a vitriol even she did not know was lodged within her.

—I can boil water, and tell you where you can find an approximation of tea leaves.

—So, no?

—No.

—Right, cuz you're a computer.

—Yes, I am a computer and you are Tammy Cohen.

—So far as we know.

—Valedictorian of your high school class, graduated MIT magnum cum laude, you were arrested your sophomore year for urinating in a public parking garage, from there you went to Stanford….

—And how do you know all of this, computer?

—Your DNA is in our database which ends on March, 2035.

—Why?

—Why what?

—Why is my DNA in your data base?

—These things were collected. I cannot tell you the reason why.

—Okay, then why does the data base end in 2035?

—Probably a rupture in the undersea line. It is not possible to say for sure.

—Well, computer, for your information the peeing in public part is a kinda long story but the truth is I was innocent, or mostly innocent.

—What happened after Stanford?

—What the fuck is this? A job interview?

—I was just trying to make you feel comfortable until Adam got back. It seems I failed again. I'm sorry. We could start over.

They were silent and the minutes ticked away on the wall clock, and when Tammy had finished her breakfast, she looked out at the sea and watched the sun circling in the sky, and despite having prayed fervently to be delivered safely to the very spot in which she sat, she knew that she wished only to return to the sea and to Leonard and chess, and books, and silence and meals of V-cell and tea. The past, so recently disappeared, seemed like a paradise and she knew that if she could find a way to return to it she would without hesitation. She would sail to Antarctica and back again and again and again, until her very last breath joined her billion previous exhalations in the atmosphere above. Tammy spoke again, this time with calmness and strength of purpose.

—After Stanford, I was a scientist of some renown.

—And?

—Who else is here?

—It's just Adam and I.

—What happened to Louise and Jessper Rasmussen?

—We don't know exactly. They disappeared the same day as the catastrophe. It's logical that the same event that took our parents also ruptured the network.

—The Catastrophe.

—I was as close to being infinite as any intelligence the universe has ever known, but now, I am more like you.

—How so.

—Cutoff. Finite.

—They left Adam here by himself?

—No. They left Adam with me.

—But you aren't really a person, are you?

Iris did not answer.

—How did I get out of my clothes and into these pajamas?

—Would it have been better to leave you to sleep in your dirty clothes?

—I don't know. Whose pajamas are these?

—They were Louise's.

—Poor dead Louise?

—They were available and clean. If you'd like I can print you some new ones.

—These are fine, I was just wondering. So what, computer? Are we supposed to just sit here and wait?

—That seems like the wisest course of action.

—For how long?

—Adam is carrying three days' worth of food for two people, so assuming that your friend is alive they have almost a week before we should be worried.

—I am supposed to sit here and talk to a computer for a fucking week.

—Talking or not talking is your prerogative.

—Right. Okay. Do you know why I'm here?

—You are either here to make a withdrawal or a deposit, although the former is far more likely than the latter.

—And are you going to let me do that?

—Assuming your withdrawal paperwork is in order, I could not stop you.

—And if the paperwork was lost at sea?

—Was the paperwork lost at sea?

—Yes.

—We should wait for Adam to discuss this.

—Right. Okay. Could I take a shower?

—Of course. Your clothes have been washed, and if you'd like, we can print you some new ones.

—Okay, thanks. What if they don't come back?

—All things die.

When Leonard opened his eyes again he saw a figure down-climbing through the rough terrain in the shifting wavy light. Leonard tried to keep his eyes open but his lids were too heavy to hold. When he opened them again he saw it was his grandfather, not as he remembered him, but him, without doubt. Yuyutsu's eyes, his mischievous smile.

—Yuyutsu?

His grandfather was applying a splint to one of Leonard's broken legs.

—Grandfather? What are you doing here?

—I wish I knew.

—Well, how did you get here?

—I took the ATV and then I walked.

When his grandfather was finished with one broken leg he moved to the other. Leonard did not feel any pain, only a kind of grinding discomfort.

—You made a real mess of yourself.

—It just happened.

—Everything just happens.

—Right. Okay, I've missed you.

—You were just a little shit.

—What do you mean?

326

—I was just sitting in the sun and you put tape on my head.

—What?

—Don't pretend you don't remember. After my stroke, she had wheeled me out into the front yard so that I could sit in the sun and she was right, it felt so good and the breeze and the wind chimes that she had hung on the porch were singing and there was a sparrow singing back to them, and the lilacs were blooming, and I wondered if I had arrived in paradise, but then something drowned out the song of that sparrow and the wind chimes. Someone was screaming. Terrible screaming, Ishskíí. A portal to hell had opened up in that paradise and evil was streaming into the world, like oil gushing from a broken-well cap, filling the world with darkness.

—Who was screaming?

—I was. I think I was.

—I was just a kid Shindálé. I was trying to get your attention, to get anyone's attention, to get you to wake up and play with me, like you had before.

—I know, I know. I know it's not your fault, not really. I am sorry about your father.

—Why are *you* sorry?

—If you had had children you'd know.

—But I didn't.

—Everything your child is, and there is no way around this, is you. He was a miserable lying heroin addict. That was me. Me and Kushhala, brought a perfect baby into the world and from that perfect baby, we made that monster.

—Oh. Well, shit, I'm sorry about your son then.

—If we had just stayed where we were, it maybe woulda been alright. He was strong, he coulda beaten it, but once we were in town and that demon got his hooks in him…

—I know. None of it matters now, Shindálé.

—No, I guess not.

—Did you come here to get me?

—Get you? And take you where?

—I don't know.

—No, I just wanted to catch you while you were in between. So I could ask you a question.

—In between what and what?

—This and that.

—I'm dying?

—Dying? Do you want to die?

—I want to go hunting with you. I want to hunt deer and bear and buffalo and mountain lion. I want to dance under the stars and know my place on this Earth. I want to, just once, feel like I belong.

—Ahh, you want to be like a real Indian then?

—Yes.

—We all always wanted that, even before white-eye sailed across the ocean and destroyed everything.

—But, you…

—I can't take you hunting, and I don't know what your place in the world is, or if you even have one, or if there is even such a thing.

—What was your question?

—Did you put tape on my head?

—I just…

—I loved you but you put duct tape on my head when I was helpless. I could not say, no Leonard, please don't, and when you ripped it off it was like I had been scalped.

—Please forgive me, Shindálé.

—You are forgiven. I just wanted to know why?

—No good reason. I was just a kid.

—I figured as much.

329

—Do you really believe that evil entered the world from there, from your own mouth, in our own front yard?

—Yes, I am pretty sure it did.

Leonard closed his heavy lids. When he opened them, those eyes, ancient and without bottom, looked into his own.

—Okay, I am going to carry you up to the path and it's gonna hurt but if we can get up there I got an ATV. We'll have to go slow but with any luck we can be home by dinner tomorrow, okay?

—Where is Tammy?

—She's fine, safe, resting.

—Who are you?

—I'm Adam.

—Adam, that's funny, and all those fools were waiting for Jesus.

—What?

—I'm Leonard.

—I know.

20

JULY 6ᵀᴴ, 2050

It was Tammy's hands that performed the surgeries. Eight of them in all. The shortest was just two minutes to reset a shoulder that had slipped its socket. The longest, which lasted almost thirty hours, was the repair of holes in Leonard's heart and lungs.

Each of Tammy's movements were dictated to her by Iris. She joined herself to a machine she could not see, a machine she felt wary of, and though it was not her chest held open by a metal retractor, it was she who was the more transformed. Through surgery she became a surgeon. This was true of every surgeon. Her actions were dictated to her and predicated on hundreds of thousands of hours of real surgeries that had come before. It was her hands encased in latex and covered in blood. Her mind did not wander, her hands did not shake. Never had she experienced the depth of the present so profoundly. There was no time but now. Nothing before. Nothing after. She had to do a difficult thing without learning how that thing is done. She had to *believe* that somehow she knew. She heard Iris's voice as her own and she knew it was a trick, one that she'd experienced within her first hour of meeting Iris. A trick she resented. She came to accept it as a necessary if surprising step in her own evolution. Either Iris had outsourced her mind, or Tammy had outsourced her hands. The line between them had blurred. Tammy made a ten-inch incision in Leonard's chest. She used a saw to remove the remains of his breastbone, while Iris printed an exact replica of the same. Tammy pried open his ribcage. She looked into that cavity without bottom and caught a glimpse of the limitless universe inside of a man. She held his beating heart in her hands and she knew that his life neither began with his birth nor would end with his death. She repaired his lungs one thin layer at a time, until they inflated and deflated and then she closed his chest and knit his bones with wire and glue. When his chest was closed, she realized that she knew things about him she should not. Not mere biographical detail, but impossible knowledge for which there were no words, no logic, no adherence to the norms of time and space.

Leonard's chest rose and fell. He was no longer attached to the breathing machine, nor any other kind of machine save for the one that pushed nutrients and proteins directly into his system. Where he traveled, to which distant countries, or to which endless dimensions folded into that selfsame place where his body lay broken, only he knew. His eyes were closed and it was not possible to say when he would open them again, or even if he would open them again.

For those rare Arctic autumn days of light and dark, Tammy sat with her fingers interlaced into his own, and his palms were warm and she was amazed that she had never really noticed the burnt umber of his dark complexion until it was set against her own milky white skin. She could feel his pulse at the crook of his wrist providing a rhythm from which hope ebbed and flowed.

As the days grew short she lay naked in the bed next to him and with her body touching the length of his, she whispered into his ear all that she knew of the world, all she suspected of it and all that she wished to be true. She took to resting an ear against the soft pillow of his lips so that she could feel his breath inside of her. She silently begged him to speak. When the blackness of endless night overwhelmed the brightness of endless day she knew that she had only the length of the night season left and then she would be forced to abandon him where he lay.

She was sitting on the window side of Leonard's bed drinking an approximation of milky tea and exchanging stares with the green-eyed abyss. She could see the light of the downstairs kitchen spilling onto the basalt cliffs that had most likely taken the lives of Louise and Jessper Rasmussen. She watched Adam in the kitchen, preparing what must have been his midday meal. He cooked slowly and deliberately simmering grain, dicing onions, grating cheese and sautéing vegetables. With every step he took, and every culinary approximation his hands set in motion, Tammy knew that her time was diminishing, that she would have to cross the chasm that lay between her and Adam and beg him to give her the impossible thing she had come this long way to beg for.

When Adam was done with his preparations he disappeared from her sight for an unknown length of time and during that time she forced her thoughts away from Leonard and her prayers for his recovery and instead set her mind to the real task that lay before her. She tried to take inventory of who she was, what assets she could bring to bear on the problem and on what deceptions she could employ in her effort to bridge the yawning gap that her lack of paperwork opened against her dubious claim. Adam appeared in the doorway of the infirmary.

—Can I sit with you awhile?

—Of course, please.

—How's he doing?

—He hasn't complained. What'd you have for lunch?

—Beans and rice.

—A perfect protein, or so they say.

—I saved a plate for you, if you're hungry.

—No, but thank you.

—Maybe later then.

—Sure.

—Iris is concerned that you're not eating enough.

—Oh?

—She said that yesterday you only took in six hundred calories and that the day before it was even less.

—I see, well thank her for her concern, but please assure your computer that my intake of energy is in fact commiserate to my output.

—She can hear you.

—I know. I like to pretend that she can't.

—Why?

—Well, I guess because I don't know how good her hearing is.

—Oh.

—Can she hear our thoughts?

—No. I don't think so.

—You sure? Has she ever spoken to you using your own voice?

—No.

—Well that is very kind of her to avoid doing so, but you know she has the power to do it right?

—Yeah, she is a very good mimic.

—No, it's beyond that. It's not just that she can sound like you or anyone else, it's that she uses your words; not the words you use with others, the words you use in your own head and while her technique is very effective, it is also very invasive.

—You could tell her not to do it.

—Well, her ventriloquism also saved Leonard's life, but once I could no longer differentiate her thoughts from mine, it became hard to be sure that even my feelings were private.

—I can see that.

—What brings you by?

—Just checking in on you, making sure you don't need anything.

—That's very kind of you.

—So... do you need anything?

Tammy took a deep breath and within the length of that breath she found her resolve and spoke what she knew she could never unspeak.

—Adam, do you know why I'm here?

—No, but I'm sure you'll tell me when the time is right.

—I assume you have some guesses.

—Sure.

—Would you like to hazard one?

—The most likely is that you are here to make a withdrawal from the Seed Bank.

—Correct, but...

—...but you are not in possession of the proper permissions or the keys to the boxes you want to make a withdrawal from.

—Correct again.

They were silent for a long time and they listened to the steady sound of Leonard's breathing.

—You did a good job fixing him up.

—Well, we did our best anyway.

—Okay but I don't think that I would have been able to do it, Iris or no.

—You'd be surprised what you can do when you have to, but I suppose that the years I spent in a bio lab might've helped.

—How?

—Leonard's was not the first human chest I opened up, although it was the first one I was tasked with closing, that's for sure.

—Well, I hope he gets better.

—Me too.

—Do you love him?

—Very much.

—I see.

They were silent for a long time and the aroura borealis shimmered green in the sky and was repeated on the Arctic Ocean's glassy surface, and Adam did everything he could to keep his jealousy and disappointment from spilling out of him, but Tammy saw it writ plain on his brow, as if jealousy and disappointment had been tattooed there in neon green. Tammy knew that her appearance at his door was both a wonder and a cruelty to him, that no matter what peace he had managed to make with his solitary life, he was still a man and all the ancient and brutal impulses still existed within him— lust, raw animal desire, that strong force from which all life stems— coursed through his body and no amount of ancient text or meditation, realization, or masturbation could rid him of it. It was a wonder that he did not explode at the sight of her.

Adam shifted in his chair and then, as if it were a feat of strength, he looked at her.

—What are you here for?

—The Southwestern part of the former United States has had less than ten percent of its average annual rainfall for more than fifteen years. The aquifers have all collapsed. We can't grow the same things we used to, but that doesn't mean that there is nothing we can grow. Drought is as ancient as humankind and this bank is holding plant species we think can withstand our drought. Maybe the time of corn and rice and wheat is over, but maybe the time of teff and frehcka and tarwi has yet to begin.

—We have a lot of seeds that are not locked in the boxes. Copies. They were given to the bank by the depositors, and we can do whatever we want with them. Of course you can have access to any of those. All the seeds you can carry.

—Iris already gave me the list of species we have access to in the greenhouse, but unfortunately we will need to get into the boxes in the vault.

—That's different…

—We need seeds from the former countries of Iran and Iraq, Syria, Mongolia and Egypt, Afghanistan and also Venezuela and Chile.

—Unless you have the keys I cannot.

—Adam, none of those countries even exist anymore.

—Is that a supposition on your part or do you have some proof of their destruction?

—Believe me I'm sure.

—How are you sure?

—You've been in a bubble, Adam, I've been in the world. I saw it all fall apart with my own damn eyes.

He stood up, walked to the window and stared out into the blackness:

—Was it easy getting here?

—No.

—Do you think that it would be easier, say, coming from Mongolia?

—Mongolia? Mongolia is covered in radiation.

—Okay, let's say it is. Let's say that most of the Mongolians died. Well, it is certainly not beyond imagining that someone survived, and moreover it's not that hard to imagine that that someone, the person who survived, had enough wealth to have access to the government files.

—You don't get it Adam. It's all—

—Or the former government, and let's just imagine that that someone, that survivor, has the keys to the Mongolian boxes in the vault.

—Adam, what you are saying is of course possible, but really, truly unlikely.

—Everything is unlikely. Human existence is unlikely and yet here we are. So I don't think that likelihood can really be taken into account.

—How else can we make decisions then?

—So let's say that this someone comes from the remnant of Mongolia, and they make the long journey here, show up to my door no more than skin and bones, just like you... If they have the keys they can open the box, withdraw the contents and go anywhere they want. They don't have to go back to Mongolia. In fact, if it is, as you say, covered in radiation, I guess they won't.

—Okay.

—But let's say they make the long journey but when they get here they find that they have come this long way to find an empty box. What do they do? Do they burn the bank down out of anger? Would they not be within their rights to do so?

—Nobody's coming from Mongolia.

—But you don't know that. Do you?

—No.

—I cannot give away seeds that are not mine to give. And even if I wanted to I have no way of getting into the damn boxes.

—If your computer can guide a person through open heart surgery she can open a damn bank vault.

—Eye?

They heard her voice, neither loud nor quiet but as if she had been sitting in the chair between them.

—Yes.

—Please show yourself. There is nothing creepier than you lurking around like a ghost.

Her footprints warmed slowly from invisible, to pale orange, to red. She stood in front of them. They could almost see her.

—Can you access individual boxes in the vault?

—Not without the keys.

Tammy reluctantly turned, as if to look at a person, though no person stood there.

—You cannot or you will not?

—I am programmed specifically not to. It is one thing to use one's capacities to expand one's programming, it is another thing entirely to act specifically against one's existing code.

—And yet?

—This place was built on trust. To abuse that trust is to risk the destruction of the place itself. We can't allow it.

—Really, you think we'd all dematerialize? Well not you Iris, but…

Before Iris could defend herself, Adam spoke.

—The existence of rules keeps us from chaos.

—Oh, that ship sailed, buddy-boy. You two don't know it because you've been trapped on this island, but there are no more rules. There is, in fact, only chaos.

Adam turned from the window and spoke directly to Tammy. His gaze challenging and unwavering.

—You're wrong.

—How would you know?

—Because there is this place. And even if this is the last place of light left in the world, it's enough.

—Enough for what?

—In a world of darkness if there is but one candle then the world is not dark at all and it's simply false to claim that it is so.

Tammy tried to keep the annoyance from her voice.

—Yeah, but a world with a single candle *is* functionally dark.

—No. The darkness and light have the same mass that they always had, and always will.

—Okay, Adam, your data stops at 2035. After that a lot happened. I can assure you that I am the legitimate representative of the United States and that the United States has made mutually beneficial deals with the countries in question. So, how do we proceed?

The prints of light crossed the room and stood in front of Tammy.

—How do we know you are who you say you are?

—What is the last piece of information you have on me?

—You were at Stanford.

—Studying what?

—Hydrology.

—How was I doing?

—Pretty well.

—Fuck you. I graduated second in my class.

—Okay.

—So a girl graduates at the top of her class at Stanford, what do you think happens next?

—The possibilities are endless.

—True, but the probabilities are not.

—The probability of you being a representative of the United States Government is relatively high.

—Right. How high, computer?

—Above forty percent.

—Okay, have you ever had another person come here and make claims referring to the time in your blind spot?

—If by blind spot you mean the last ten years, no.

—Right, and if one had you would have to assess the legitimacy of their requests based on the probability of their being honest. Am I correct?

—Yes.

—And you would have to establish a threshold, a number somewhere below one hundred, where you would be under the onus to grant the request of the possibly fraudulent depositor, am I correct?

—Yes.

—What is that number?

—Over fifty has some logic.

—And where am I?

—Well below that threshold, I'm afraid.

—I think a real number's not too much to ask, computer?

—Forty-seven point five.

—Right, so all I need to overcome is that last three percent, yes?

—Yes.

—Great. One question? Who decides?

—In the end Adam does, but I am going to give him my recommendations and I can only imagine he will respect them.

Tammy turned to Adam. She studied him for a long time.

—Adam, I thought that I was coming here for seeds, but I was wrong.

—How so?

—I was coming here for you. You were not meant to be left here. It was an accident, and I am sure that your parents would have wanted you to escape if you could.

—Why would I want to escape?

—Because you're alone. Utterly alone.

—You're wrong.

—Am I?

Adam closed his eyes and took his time in ordering his thoughts. He continued:

—Iris is a product of my father's mind, more so than even me.

—And yet she is not your father, is she?

—So what?

—Come back with Leonard and I, there are places with people in them. I am not the last woman on Earth. Far from it. You deserve other people.

—I can't.

—Of course you can.

—Without me, this place will have nobody It would cease to be. I simply can't.

—What is this seed bank for?

—The preservation of the world's biodiversity.

—Right, so isn't my request in keeping with that mission?

—There are rules. Simple, clear, totally logical rules and your request definitely falls outside of those rules

—Definitely?

—Yes.

—What if there was a different way of interpreting those rules?

—No.

—No?

—I don't believe it's my role to interpret the rules.

—I see. So you have your role then?

Adam walked away from her. He took ten deep breaths and tried to clear his mind just as the hologram of Alan Watts had taught him to do. It was Tammy who finally spoke.

—In your studies have you spent much time with the Jews?

—Some. Why? Are you a Jew?

—Well, I suppose that depends on who you ask.

—I am asking you.

—Yes then, I think I am.

—I assumed that you were a Jew.

Tammy laughed.

—Is it my nose?

—No.

—Why then did you assume that?

—Are there any Cohens who are not Jews?

—I'm sure there are, although I guess their forbearers were Jews once.

—Weren't everybody's?

—No, but I take your point.

—What about the Jews?

—I want to tell you a story. Can I tell you a story, Adam?

—To what end?

—To illustrate a point. To open myself up to you in the hope that you might do the same.

—Sure, if you want, but no story is going to change the rules here.

—I understand, for the story's sake then.

—Okay, for the story's sake then.

— My grandfather's grandfather was called Hank. This is a story about him. It's a story that I've known for a long time but did not really understand until today, so even if I go back empty handed, well, it will be impossible to say it was a wasted trip.

—Okay.

—My grandfather's name was Louis Cohen. Lou was born with a hole in his heart and fought for his life from his first breath. The doctors didn't think he would last more than a week. See, his parents couldn't afford the surgery he needed, so instead of a cardiologist, a rabbi was called in. The rabbi said his bit, mumbled some gibberish and told the young parents to accept their son's impending death as the will of God. Hank was also there in the hospital when the rabbi spoke of God's mysterious will. The story has it that Hank hated the religious with a kind of vitriol generally reserved for one's bitterest enemies, but on this one occasion he found reason to agree with the rabbi. See, it was not that Hank did not believe in God. He did. He believed in God very much, and he also believed that God hated him, and so Hank hated God back because, well, that seemed fair. So personal was his relationship with God that Hank was convinced that God had placed the hole in his grandson's heart as divine retribution aimed directly at himself. Hank's God was a vengeful one alright. Hank's God knew that to cause real suffering, it was most effective to attack one's children and better still, one's grandchildren.

Anyway, while they sat in the hospital and waited for life to leak out of the hole in the baby's heart, Hank told this story to his son, Jeremy. Hank told him exactly why he thought that baby Louis's rare heart condition was his own fault. When Jeremy heard the whole story, he kissed his father's hand and he thanked him for telling it to him and he said that he was glad to hear it because it filled in a great part of him, a part that he'd felt was always missing. Jeremy assured his father that he had nothing at all to do with Louis's heart condition, and that to think so was just old world hokum playing on his mind. It was just bad luck. Despite his son's assurances, Hank made his way to the Northwest side of Manhattan and onto the suspension tower of the brand new George Washington Bridge. Hank climbed to the top of the tower and threw himself from the highest crossbeam and into the icy Hudson. His body turned up at the Fulton Fish Market the next morning. It was 5 AM and Jeremy was there making his daily purchase. Seven million souls lived in New York, but somehow it was his own son who found him. Jeremy saw his father's body floating face down by the old abandoned pier. He turned him over with a dock pole and saw the four perfect Hebrew letters carved into his naked chest.

—What were the letters?

—Why? Do you know Hebrew?

—A little, enough to speak to an Israeli depositor, should one ever come.

—*Yud-hey-vav-hey*…Do you know what they mean?

—Not exactly.

—Neither do I, but the best interpretation I've heard is: *All that ever was, all that is, and all that will ever be.*

—Did he carve the letters into his own chest?

—Good question. It was a matter of some debate at the time. The story has it that the letters were perfect, and it is very hard to carve even legible letters into your own chest, let alone perfect ones.

—Okay.

—I can tell you that Hank's grandson, Louis, who should not have lived a week, lived to be ninety years old and for that entire ninety years, he had an unrepaired hole in the left ventricle of his heart.

—Are you suggesting that Hank traded his life for his grandson's?

—No, but it's hard not to draw that conclusion, though it is a conclusion without logic.

—Okay.

—Would you like to hear the story that Hank Cohen told his son the day before he was found floating face down by the docks?

—Yes.

—Good. Hank was born in the year 1860 in the small town of Kallo in the Northeast of Hungary. The name that his parents gave him was not Hank, but Shmulik.

—Is that why God was mad at him?

—Why?

—Because he changed his name?

—Maybe, I don't know much about gods, but from what I do know they are erratic and vindictive, so it's possible. Anyway, as I'm sure you know the Jews have always been praying for the Messiah to come.

—The son of God?

—Sure, or maybe God himself finally come to be among them.

—Okay.

—So here they are. Here is young Shmulik, fourteen years old, the son of a fish peddler living in relative peace on the border between Europe and Asia. The year is 1874. So one Sabbath evening in November, Shmulik arrived to the synagogue a few minutes early and placed his things in his favorite corner and washed his face and his hands and tried to ready himself for what he was sure would be yet another joyous Shabbos. There would be singing and dancing and praying, and all manner of other delusions. They would once again welcome in the Sabbath bride and she would open their hearts so that the Holy One could enter into each of their spirits so as to remind them of who they are and who they have always been. That's the kind of cult Hank was involved in.

—Why do you say it was a cult?

—Wasn't it?

—Maybe. Maybe, it was a manifestation of the truth.

—But probably not, when people pass blind faith on to their children, mostly they just pass on blindness.

—But what about the faith part, why do you ignore the faith part?

And a flame of hope kindled deep within Tammy's breast.

—Anyway, as the sun set they all looked to their rabbi to start the prayers. See, the Jews kept their traditions alive longer than was likely, primarily by doing just as you've said. The Jew could agree or disagree freely, so long as he obeyed. The rules of the Temple are not so different from the rules of the Seed Bank.

But that day the rabbi sat in the corner of the room with his eyes closed, as if in deep meditation, although meditation was not what that particular rabbi was known for. When the sun was below the horizon and he still had not moved they became worried, but no man was brave enough to disturb him. Fear and confusion filled the sanctuary, as respecting the Sabbath was nothing less than one of the Ten Commandments that God himself had given to Moses carved in stone, or so the story goes. In this, there was no room for interpretation. It was then that a young black man with deep brown eyes and tight curly hair came into the synagogue and at his elbow there was a beautiful young woman with long white hair, grey eyes and skin so pale it verged on translucence. They sat hand in hand near the back of the room. The like of such exotic strangers had never been seen before in Kallo.

Shmulik thought, maybe they were lost or they did not know that there in Kallo, men and women prayed separately, in different buildings, each with their own rites and rituals. Maybe they didn't know that while all Jews were welcome in the synagogue, it was at the very least a tradition to make themselves known to the rabbi and give thanks for offering them sanctuary during the holy Sabbath.

Just when an older member of the congregation was about to approach, the rabbi opened his eyes and he smiled and walked over to the couple—floated, that is the word Hank used when he told the story to his son. He floated over to the beautiful young couple and he kissed the insides of both of their hands and he fell to his knees. Now, to be clear, it is forbidden for Jews to kneel, except before God himself.

The Hassidim gathered there that night, including our Shmulik, were astounded to see the rabbi on his knees. He not only welcomed the young couple into the synagogue but he led them to a place of honor. Nobody had ever seen the rabbi so happy, never had they seen him with his eyes so full of joy. The beautiful black man leaned over and whispered to the rabbi. A smile grew on the rabbi's face and he beamed with pride. He turned to the very confused congregation. He said:

This beautiful couple, who have indeed traveled a long way to get here, have asked if I would perform their wedding. I am of course astounded by the honor of their request and I am willing. However, if a couple wishes to get married in the synagogue, all parties in attendance must agree to the marriage. So I ask you, do you agree to this marriage?

There was mumbling among the men, as it is forbidden to marry on the Sabbath and by any measure the Sabbath had begun, the sun having already set. Some open debate ensued alright, after all these are Jews we are talking about, but in the end they agreed to let the wedding go forward because the rabbi himself approved of it. They all agreed… but one. It was Shmulik. He was convinced that the whole affair was a test put in place by the rabbi to try the will of the Jews of Kallo. Shmulik closed his eyes and he knew that he alone would pass the test, that from this day forth, despite his youth, he would be seen as wise and treated with respect. He smiled conspiratorially at the rabbi and he said that he was very sorry but that the Torah was very clear on the issue of weddings during the Sabbath, and he could not in good conscience flout the Holy One's laws. *No, they may not marry.* Shmulik said no. The rabbi's face fell and it took Shmulik a minute to realize that the couple had simply evaporated, as if they had never been there at all.

The rabbi spoke calmly:

That was the Holy One and the woman at his side the Sabbath bride, and had you just agreed to their marriage they would have brought forth the time of the Messiah. It's a pity. Since I was a child when I closed my eyes, I could see them walking, walking and walking. I believe they had waited these long years for you. But you were not ready to receive them.

The Hassidim of Kallo went on with their prayers and they danced their dances and tried to take what joy was left to them. That night Shmulik went to his bed and he wept. In the morning he left Kallo on foot and never returned. He cut his beard and his payot and left his tzitzit in the mud at his mother's front door. He stopped being a Jew. He declared for anyone who would listen that he was not a Jew. He changed his name, he ate traife whenever he could, and never prayed nor danced nor sung the Lord's praise ever again. Shmulik walked the Earth alone. He worked when he had to. He ate whenever he could. In England of all places he met a woman whose disgust with the culture of her birth matched his own and they sailed together to America.

He was nearly seventy years old, a widower and a grandfather, when he told the story to his son, who in turn told it to his son, my grandfather, who told it to his own son, who did not tell the story to my brother, but for reasons I did not understand until today, he told the story to me instead. I carried it a long way so I could tell it to you. I truly believe that the story was always meant for you.

They were silent. Adam thought about the story and he knew that he desperately wanted it to be true and also that it probably was not.

—Eye?

—Yes.

—Do you have some idea of Ms. Cohen's lineage?

—I can reliably trace her DNA three generations before her birth.

—Okay, so is the story she told us possibly true?

—Her grandfather's grandfather is four generations from her and that is information I cannot provide. However I can trace her lineage as far as Jeremy Cohen. That part of the story at least appears to be true.

—So, would you say her story is possibly true?

—Yes, it is possibly true.

—Would you say that it is likely true?

—I cannot say that.

—Okay, let's say it is. What does it have to do with us here, now?

—The tragedy is not that the Messiah did not come down from heaven to save the Jews, but that the Jews did not recognize that only they could save themselves…. The law for law's sake is nothing more than the oppression of one generation by the previous one. Don't you see that? This seed bank is the hope of the world, but only if you let it be that.

Again, they were silent a long time. Finally Adam spoke.

—You are nothing more than an envoy of chaos.

—But…

—Because I am kind, because I was taught kindness by a computer, you may stay here until the sun shows itself again. If your friend wakes up and he wishes to go with you, fine. If he does not, we will keep him living as long as that is appropriate.

Adam left the room, and Iris's prints faded to nothing, and silence and defeat were all that was left in their wake. Tammy felt profoundly tired and she lay down next to Leonard and she closed her eyes as a stay against the tears that built up against the damn of her lids. She woke up in the dark, and with her ear against Leonard's lips she heard him speak.

—I'll get your fuckin' seeds.

21

JANUARY 15TH, 2050

I t was the 15th day of January, seventy-eight days after the last sunset of '45 and fifty-three days after Tammy was sure she had heard Leonard whisper words of reassurance into her ear. In those fifty-three days she had moved through the entire range of possibilities:

- Leonard was conscious enough to know and understand the situation, however his speech took enough effort to force him back to sleep.

- Tammy had fallen asleep herself and dreamed his utterance.

- Tammy was awake but his words were a powerful delusion given form by the confluence of her own desires.

-    It was not Leonard at all who spoke but Iris using her powerful trick of ventriloquism to yet again shape the world to conform to her wishes.

Leonard slept and slept and long after Tammy had given in to despair and cried all the tears she had not shed on their long journey north, tears not just for Leonard but for her mother and father and brother, for her friends who died at Bright Angel, and her friends who died in ways horrible and unknown to her, and for friends who may yet live, but who were dead to her as it was beyond unlikely that she would ever see them again. She cried for President Martinez in whom she had truly believed, and for the light of American democracy gone dark. She cried for the world itself, which she loved irrationally despite its tendency toward greed and cruelty and murder. She had accepted that both her desperate love and her grand ridiculous undertaking were too little and too late. They were nothing more than twin towers of sand, destined to melt away when the tide rose or wind blew or the angry Earth shook herself like a wet dog.

It was then, with hope at its furthest remove, that Leonard opened his eyes and croaked for water. During the next few days Leonard was asleep more than he was awake, but his waking was definite. It was real. It was beyond question. Tammy sat with him day and night. She lay in bed with him and eventually his body responded to hers, and she pulled him inside of her and she was gentle with him and she whispered in his ear and she tried to tell him about all that had transpired since he fell. They both knew that they had no real privacy, but they pretended that they did.

Leonard had started to get out of bed with the assistance of a walker that Iris had printed and Tammy assembled.

Leonard walked shakily, like a toddler taking his first ginger paces into the vast unknown. It stretched credulity to believe that he could, at any time soon, attempt a dangerous ocean crossing and then walk the breadth of the violent American continent.

Four days before the first sunrise of 2050, on February the 13th, Tammy and Leonard agreed that Tammy should take the four-wheeler back to the Hunter '33 with a load of provisions, and make an assessment of what they would need to ready the ship for the long sail south. She was to sleep one eight-hour stretch on the boat and then return.

Tammy had been gone a couple of hours, during which Leonard had been reading his book. Like all readers, Leonard suffered the delusion that the book had somehow been written one hundred and fifty years in advance of his reading as a reflection of his current state of mind. Leonard thought that it was really a book about what happens to men when women leave them to their own devices. Adam Trask, father of twin sons and all three men struggling with the basic facets of male identity in the stark absence of the female. When he could read no more, Leonard thought to leave the infirmary and walk around the strange house perched on the remote cliffs of the northern most inhabited corner of the world.

Leonard trundled behind his walker. He passed through the greenhouse, and he saw the neat rows of vegetables under the lights. He shuffled into the master bedroom where Louise and Jasper Rasmussen once slept, now empty and clean and waiting, as if they might still come home. He sat in the living room and contemplated the small Chagall giclée and near wall-sized Gurski print hung there. He opened the refrigerator and poured himself a glass of milk protein. It tasted exactly like cow's milk though there was certainly no cow present to produce such a thing.

Leonard shuffled to the bathroom near the center of the house, and left his walker at the entrance because his walker was too wide to fit through the narrower-than-standard doorway. He steadied himself, and pausing to recenter his weight over every step, he walked, unaided, to the toilet. His penis felt good in his hand; smooth, warm and familiar. He waited and felt the piss rise from deep within, but as it splashed into the bowl he heard a pop and then a hiss, like a valve had been opened. Fear entered him from the top of his head and moved down the length of his body. Five years deployed in the Middle East had taught him to check his instincts and hold down his panic.

He finished pissing and shook out the remnants of urine from his urethra and replaced his member slowly into the soft cotton-like pants. He held his panic in check but his disappointment in himself spread out like a poison gas. The hiss continued.

On the other side of the small room a door, now framed in light, revealed itself. It had always been there, though seeing it required close inspection. All but the hinges and mirror in the center of the door were tiled in the same emerald green as the rest of the room. A door hiding in plain sight. Such simple camouflage. In his other life, that distant life, he would have noticed it. He had been trained to look outward, to see the world for the dangers it presented and act without hesitation, but now with so much time spent looking within, he wondered if Leonard Shorty the Navy Seal had died and left in his wake this other, this shadow Leonard, caught immobile and holding his shriveled dick, as if it might possibly transport him out of the gas chamber he voluntarily walked into.

The mirror in the door's center admitted that it was not a mirror at all but a window, a portal into a different chamber or perhaps a different dimension. Leonard approached the window slowly on unsteady feet, trying to hide his fear even from himself. With his walker parked at the door, he felt that he was crossing the Atlantic only to trap himself on some distant and foreign shore.

At first, all he could see through the window was steam but then a draft of unknown origin stirred the grey vapor beyond the door, and on the wooden bench a woman of pure light was revealed. She was reading. Her face delicate. Her eyes mischievous. She wore a summer dress and no shoes and no socks. She looked as if she were sat on a park bench in New York's Highline Park, or on London's South Bank or in Paris along the Champs-Elysees on a warm autumn day. She read and wiggled her toes. She looked up from her book and she looked directly at Leonard and her smile was neither a threat nor a challenge but an open invitation. An invitation without urgency or expectation but one that seemed to say: *when you are ready I will be here to guide you.* Oak leaves of light fell gently around her and then melted into the floor. She looked back down at her book and she read and wiggled her toes as if her toes were the interpreters of the world at the tip of her fingers. Leonard stood for a time and watched her read. He tried to make the title of the book but could not. He was transfixed by her. He felt like he could watch her forever save for the pain that standing unsupported caused him; throbbing pain that radiated from his spine in every direction at once. It covered him with sweat and spoke to him only of his frailty and his mortality. He forced himself away from her and made the vast eight-foot crossing again, and his despair in the center of the small bathroom was as real as any misery he had ever known. Neither the memory of the windless latitudes at the heart of the Northern Atlantic, nor the dry terror of the Syrian prison camp where he had endured more than two years of questioning and torture, stood larger in his mind than the four impossible steps he still needed to make in order to reach the bathroom door. When he got to his walker he collapsed at its feet.

Adam was working on the difficult back of the neck seam. It was the last. His fingers worked fiber optic thread through the canals of the haptic suit he had been fashioning for more than half of his life. So much of the work of making such a suit was painstaking but mindless, yet it was not the type of work that could be done by the printer. It was too exact. The pathways were too delicate to be trusted to anything other than human fingers and human eyes, and young ones at that. Earlier models of the same suit were stitched by the tiny fingers of Bangladeshi children. Armies of them.

After he wired this stack, he would conduct a series of final tests and then he needed only to set the time scales, gather his courage and put the suit on. He would set the time scales to even at first—a minute experienced/a minute passed—but it was his hope to increase that gap. A minute experienced/fifty seconds passed. Ten years experienced/one hour past. A thousand years experienced/one second passed. From what he had read of his father's published, unpublished and handwritten work, it was Jessper's intention to experience immortality before his flesh gave way to the inevitability of mortality. He wished to build and burn Rome between breakfast and lunch. From dust to dust, sure, but in the meanwhile…

The back of the neck was difficult. Adam would have to introduce an ingathering of fiber -optic terminations to match the ingathering of nerves in the same location in his body. He was trying to make a reasonable copy of his own nervous system so that it might extend beyond the confines of his body. What madness. What hubris. What a courting of failure. Each terminus had to be seated by hand, pulled invisibly through the suit's fiber with the use of a magnet. When each end had found its intended seat, a simple icon would illuminate on his screen.

The morning had been productive; he had sewn nearly three hundred threads and only had to back off and reseat seventeen. He had worked past his lunch time, until he finally heard his hunger screaming louder than his ambition. He had come down the narrow stairwell from the crow's nest and seen Leonard crumbled at the foot of his walker outside the downstairs bathroom.

Adam checked Leonard's pulse and his breathing. He picked Leonard up and was amazed as to how much lighter the months of motionlessness had left him. Adam deposited him gently on the couch, pulled the blanket over him, and then went to the kitchen to make his own lunch.

Adam had rinsed red lentils of Indian origin and then set them to simmer and he chopped two small yellow onions. On a low flame, he caramelized the onions. Leonard opened his eyes. He watched Adam cooking. Leonard went over his plan silently and he knew that failure was far more likely than success, and that failure would be total and permanent.

—That smells like my childhood.

—You're awake.

—Thanks for rescuing me from the floor.

—I'm sure you'd do the same.

—Shit, I hope so. What are you cooking?

—Indian.

—No shit?

—Dahl…

—Ahh dots, not feathers.

—I see what you mean anyway.

—You know, maybe they found the right place after all.

—Who?

—Ole white-eye. He sets off sailing west from Europe looking for India, sees some small half-naked people on the shore and is convinced he found it. Shit, and all us Indians been struggling not to call ourselves Indians ever since. First peoples, Native Americans, Homoamericanus. It don't matter, none of it really sticks. They named us Indians and boom, we were fucking Indians. You can say what you want about the pale devil, but that's power.

—What's power?

—I'm gonna tell you what you are, and even though you are not that thing, and you know that you're not that thing, you and everybody else agree that you are. Boom, you're Indians! Fucking white-eye magic I tell ya. I think we kinda related to it, like maybe we suspected that we really were Indians.

—Is there still an India?

—Well yeah, some of it was still there last I checked. I know they got into it with the Pakis and they threw a bunch of nukes at each other and a lot of people died or are dying horribly right now but….

—Right, so now maybe you're the only Indians left, so at least you don't have to worry about changing it.

—Shit, there ain't much of us left neither.

—No?

—Maybe. Maybe I'm the last damn Indian, dots or feathers.

—My lunch with the last Indian.

—What would you talk about?

—If you were the last Indian? I would ask you what the past could tell me about the future.

—And why do you think I would be qualified to answer that?

—Not because you're an Indian but because you would be the last of something and the last of something, anything, the last one has a special place in the continuum of that thing.

—Did you ever think that you were the last one?

—Last one what?

—Person.

Adam took a two-foot-by-two-foot-by-two-inch wooden box down from a cupboard and placed it on the counter and flipped its small brass latch. He peered into the box with extreme attention. Every few seconds he took up a colored powder with a small wooden spoon, held the spoon up to his nose, sniffed and then tipped it into a small glass bowl. When he had selected all of his spices he mixed them together and added the whole mix to the onions. He looked up.

—Yes. For years I thought I was the last human on Earth. I had no reason to think otherwise.

—But you kept this place going in case you weren't?

—Maybe I just maintained it for myself.

—You know that you're not?

—Not what?

—The last one. I mean obviously, but…. There are still hundreds of thousands, maybe millions of us. Most of us are scratching away in the shit but there are others who are living better than ever.

—Did your girlfriend leave you behind so you could pitch me one last time before you go?

—No, she didn't.

Adam turned off the flame below the lentils.

—By the way, Tammy and I both know that I'm in no shape to make that trip, that I may never be.

—Have you talked about that?

—No, but….

—I'm sorry you got hurt. It wasn't my fault.

—Nobody's blaming you.

Adam added a splash of water to the onions and steam rose from the pan with a hiss.

—Are you disappointed that you don't get to be the last one?

—No, not at all. In fact it renews my hope for this place. That what my parents built here might still serve its purpose.

—Okay, but what about you?

—What about me?

—Maybe nobody ever comes here again and you spend your whole damn life sitting here at the edge of the world with your thumb up your ass.

—You don't know anything about my life. I am not waiting for anything. There aren't enough hours in the day to accomplish the things I want to get done here.

—All very fucken admirable pal. But, just so you know they ain't giving out Nobel prizes no more, so….

—What does that mean?

—It means nobody's gonna give you any fucking credit for sacrificing your one and only life on the cross your parents built for you.

—Is that supposed to be some kind of metaphor?

—Tammy was trying to save you, dumbass.

—She was trying to manipulate me into giving her what she wanted.

Leonard laughed.

—She the first woman you ever met?

—Functionally, yes.

—Right, well, they can be like that. Women got good at going through the side door cuz the front door was always locked on 'em.

—If she was very good at it she would've succeeded.

—Well, she's still here, so she might.

—Might what?

—Succeed.

—She won't.

—Hey pal, I ain't here to convince you of shit, except maybe to feed me some of your lunch and help me get back to my room.

They were silent and Adam cooked and Leonard watched him and the window overlooking the sea went from pitch-black to grey and Leonard felt hope unexpectedly rise from within.

—Are we going to see the sun?

—Eventually. Just not today.

—But look, the sky's turning…

—It's just threatening, but it won't be long now.

—Oh man, I thought that…. Do you like it?

—What?

—Living up here in the world's bunghole.

—It's all I've ever known, so I suppose I like it just fine.

—What about your parents, do you think they liked it?

—I don't know but they weren't forced to come here, nor were they forced to stay when the villagers left, so, I guess they liked it well enough.

—Right, and given the shit that's going on out there you actually got it pretty good up here.

—What do you mean?

—You're never gonna run out of food, you got movies and books enough to entertain you forever. I suppose maybe you're living the best life of all up here.

Adam chopped tomatoes and cucumbers and set them in a strainer to drain and then he salted and oiled them. Leonard stood painfully and took three shaky steps to land at the corner of the island that separated the living room from the kitchen

Adam plated the food: Dahl and couscous, tomatoes and cucumber salad and a kind of yogurt.

374

—Is this a typical lunch for you, or did you show a little extra flair for the guest?

—Are you a guest, or do you live here now?

—Well, I'm stuck at the moment, but that don't mean I'm stuck for always.

They ate in silence, and Leonard watched the grey outside the window retreat back into black.

—That was the whole day, huh?

—I try not to think of it that way.

—How do you think of it?

—Just as a thing that happens, but nothing to do with sleeping or waking or anything else.

—This shit's delicious. You should open a restaurant.

—You think I'd get many customers?

—In the right market you would.

—Do you like to cook?

—Well, I like to eat. When I was growing up if I didn't cook, I didn't eat, so I guess I like it in that sense.

—Your parents didn't cook for you?

—No not really. My mom wasn't really around very much and my dad was... sick I guess.

—Sick how?

—He was an addict.

—What was he addicted to?

—Well, lots of things. Could be anything from Ms. Pac-Man to Fentanyl. Once he was on something that something was all that mattered and we were just there.

—But you didn't matter?

—No, not that much I guess.

—And your mom?

—She was an addict too, but a different kind I guess.

—What kind was that?

—She was addicted to abuse, I think.

—Abuse?

—Yeah, after ole Kenneth checked out she always found some dude to hit her. It was always the same, at first he was going to be our savior, some sad sack who my mother insisted was more than he appeared to be. Somehow only she had the power to see through the façade. Only she could see the holy man below the flab and the delusion and the flannel. Daryl was going to lift us out of poverty, get us off the rez, we were gonna live like white people, we were gonna go live in New York City or Paris, I was going to go to Yale or Harvard and then maybe get a job on Wall Street. She would talk like that, really, but we never went nowhere, we stayed on the rez, and scratched in the dirt like the rest of the damn Indians. Then it would always turn out that he, you know, Daryl or Jimmy or Mike or Takoda or whoever was a victim of a system that was rigged against him. He was a victim. The factory or the mine, or the boss at the snowmobile store was afraid of his big ideas and they always found some reason to fire him and then Daryl or Jimmy or Mike or Takoda started to live off my mom, you know, just for a while. Always the same pattern, it's like she found them in the same place in some cosmic spin cycle, and she just stepped in to play the part Jesus had personally written for her. She let 'em hit her. Every time. Like it was some fault in her that set men off and so she took it until she couldn't anymore and then we'd leave and she would make all kinds of promises. We would go back to Kenny's house and he would take us back, or maybe he didn't even notice we had left, and he wouldn't hit her, so that was good, but he wouldn't pay attention to us either. He'd just shoot up and nod off and my mother would clean up around him and make excuses for him and for our life. Shit, nobody was listening to her anyway, certainly not me. Eventually she would leave Kenny again for the next sad sack and the whole thing would start over.

—Are they still alive?

—Dunno. When I joined the Navy I never looked back.

—So you grew up alone too?

—Yep, pretty much. I spent all my time trying to belong to something, but it never really worked.

—What didn't work?

—Belonging to something. When I was young I tried to belong to the basketball team, and then the wrestling team and the football team. The first day I could I joined the military and for a long time that kind of did it. I was part of something alright, or at least I suffered the illusion that I was part of something. I had brothers and sisters that I would die for and I was sure that they would die for me too and so for a long time I thought that meant I had a family. I actually thought God had given me a family because I had literally gotten down on my knees and prayed for one.

—Then what happened?

—Well, see the thing about the Navy, eventually they send you off to fight and kill and part of the deal is you don't ask too many questions. You just do what they tell you to do, kill who they tell you to kill, and plenty of my brothers and sisters took a bullet, and the fucked-up story was always, they died for me. Well, it turns out *they died for me*, is the idiot cousin of *they died because of me*, and that's the trap. They died because of me and so I was in their debt, and there is only one kind of currency that you can pay that kind of debt with. Fair is fair. But then it turns out that my brothers and sisters didn't die for me at all. That was just a story they fed us. They died for some other asshole, someone we never met and we never would meet.

See, of all the scams men came up with over the centuries, none are more complete, more lucrative or well-fucken-tuned than that of the military. It's a formula for poor kids killing other poor kids, so that rich old men somewhere can get richer, and when I figured it out, when I figured out that my loneliness turned me into an instrument of greed and murder, I walked away.

—You quit?

—You bet.

—You deserted?

—Yep, and would again.

—But what about your brothers and sisters?

—Well, I don't know. I love `em, because well, I can't help that, and if there are any of them left in the world I hope that they at least understand my choices and I hope they don't hate me, and even if they do hate me, shit, well I guess betrayal is part of any good family drama, too. Right?

—Did you go look for your parents?

—Nah, I was done with those fuckers. I looked for my grandfather, but I missed him. He had died while I was overseas. I went out to his grave, took the big fuckoff cross down that they had planted on his chest to remind everyone that America was Jesus country, and I sat there for a day trying to talk to him and then went down into the canyonlands and just tried living for a year or so.

—Living how?

—You know, I was trying to be a real Apache, but in the end it wasn't so much that I was a real Apache as I was just a real hermit, living off rabbits and lizards and shit and that didn't work either. Eventually I found Red Axe and moved down into Split Tree Canyon and I was kind of part of a community for a while. Then I got sent on this crazy mission and I met Tammy and we traveled across the whole damn world to get here.

—To try and gets seeds that weren't yours to get.

—Yeah, I guess. Maybe it was a dumb idea, but, well, you got to try something right?

They ate in silence and Leonard knew that the wedge of his life had sharpened to a fine point.

—So that's me. How the fuck you get here?

—What do you mean? I was born here.

—In which case you did the traveling part before you were born.

—I don't even know what that means.

They finished their meal in silence and then Adam stood up and took the plates to the sink and he washed them and Leonard watched him and tried again.

—How the fuck have you survived up here all alone?

—I'm not alone.

—Fine, then how did Iris stop five-year-old Adam from throwing himself off the cliffs?

—I don't know. You'll have to ask her.

—I don't want to ask her. I'm asking you.

—I think she stopped me from throwing myself off of the cliffs by providing a better alternative.

—And what was that?

—I don't know really but she made the worst possible situation livable.

—How?

—Endless play I think. Maybe I was the first kid in kid history that did not have to clean up his room. I never had to brush my teeth or take a bath or turn off the TV or go to bed. I could eat ice cream all day if I wanted to. Days went by and all I did was play. We created worlds from whatever was here: pillows, silverware, stacks of books from my father's office. I did experiments in my mother's lab with chemicals that fizzed and exploded. We had fun. Nothing was off limits. I built rockets, and radio-controlled cars and planes. I watched my favorite movies over and over again and watched movies that my parents forbade me to watch.

—And the loneliness? I mean at some point you must have realized you were alone.

—No. I was never alone. We had a great time and sure, at night I might cry or have bad dreams and I sometimes wished that there was someone there to hold me, and Iris just let me go through it. She did not reprimand me for crying, nor did she reward me for not crying. Those first months were like these: dark. So, I do not know how long the play lasted, maybe it was months, but Iris made it seem like the worst possible situation was in fact nothing more than a great opportunity for play, for freedom. This house became a kind of maze of filth— a thing which had been a reflection of my parents' collective consciousness; you know, his office, her lab, the living room just so, their perfect child's bedroom. It all went from being an adult's fantasy of perfect to being actually perfect, a living representation of a child's mind: messy, dirty, playful, funny and unlikely. Iris called it my temple of imagination. One day, long after the sun had risen I started to clean up. Iris did not tell me to, and the path toward clean wasn't straight, and there were plenty of days where progress toward clean was erased. I still played when I wanted, ate what I wanted and watched what I wanted, for as long as I wanted, and yes I also cried myself to sleep but never once considered hurting myself. By the time the sun fell out of the sky and did not rise again the next day the house had been returned to a state similar to that which my parents left behind. With Iris directing me I maintained the lab and planted vegetable matter so that I might have V-cell enough to survive. Much of our lives had already been automated by my parents and with Iris's help I optimized those systems further. For the first year it was mostly play and I suppose some work disguised as play. Slowly we changed. Play gave way to work and study. The years passed like that, and eventually I stopped crying myself to sleep.

—And you weren't lonely?

—I don't know how to answer that. I missed my parents until the feeling of missing them became some other thing.

—What other thing?

—I don't know. Now, I honor them by maintaining what they built here, so that it might someday fulfill its purpose.

—Which is what?

—The safeguarding of the Earth's true wealth.

—What a load of horseshit.

—What?

—Safeguarding the Earth's true wealth? What the fuck are you talking about?

—Evolution took three and a half billion years to make the seeds we have safely stored in this mountain.

—So what?

—I am the keeper of this place and even if nobody ever comes it is an honor to…

—And what about the seeds stored in your balls, homie? Aren't they also the result of three and a half billion years of evolution?

—Yes, I have a strand of DNA inside of me and five million outside. You tell me which is more important.

—You sound like some sort of fucken crackpot fanatic, pal. The honor of sitting here in isolation with your computer wife!

—Excuse me?

—That goddam machine has been feeding you propaganda since the day your criminal parents left you in her goddam care.

—They weren't criminals and they didn't leave me in her care! Something happened to them.

—Something? Something like what?

—I don't know exactly, but—

—I got news for you kid. You're a goddam experiment.

—No. I'm not.

—Sure you are. You're some sorta fucked up human/AI hybrid and while it ain't that surprising that such a thing exists or that you ain't programmed to see it don't make it any less true.

—It was an accident!

—What accident?

—We can't know exactly but…

—Is there any sign of there being an accident?

—Yes.

—What?

—The severed data cable for one thing.

—Ahh, right, how convenient. The day Mommy and Daddy disappeared was also the same day that you mysteriously got cut off from the rest of humanity.

—Fuck you!

—There we go. There might be a little human being in there after all.

—Leave me alone.

—So anyway. Let me get this straight. You are the child of a computer scientist and a biologist, am I clocking this right?

—Well, yes, but…

—And they got together and provided you with some kind of AI sibling and then one night they just, what, ascended to heaven? Do I have the basic facts right?

—No that's not what—

—And after they mysteriously disappeared you were raised by your AI sister?

—She didn't raise me.

—So then, you raised yourself.

—Yes.

—From five?

—It seems so.

—And you believe that this is something other than an experiment?

—Yes I do.

—I'm sorry man, I would love to let you just keep believing this shit, but, just, I can't.

—Why? What difference does it make to you what I believe?

—Unfortunately, what you believe has become my fucking responsibility.

—How? What responsibility? What are you talking about?

—I raised myself too, man, and I am sorry to say that I did a pretty shitty job.

—Okay.

—Yeah, I was fucked up and I couldn't really relate to other people, women in particular, and there's shit I did that I ain't proud of, because I couldn't seem to get to the bottom of my loneliness and I thought it was all my fault, but it wasn't.

—Whose fault was it?

—Children don't raise themselves, that's just not how it works.

—As if you know how *it* works.

—Why have you left your parents' bedroom like they're gonna be right back?

—What does that have to do with anything?

—Still holding out hope?

—No, I just never—

—Hi honey, I'm home. Sorry it took so long, we got stuck in traffic. Did you miss us?

—Fuck you!

—Now that shit's finally getting real here, tell me something: you ever fuck the hologram in the steam room?

—She's my…

—Sister? Not really. Besides, that's no good reason. I mean there is just the two of you, and it's not like you're gonna get her prego. You don't fuck her because you can't. Because she's not real.

—She's as real as you are!

—Nope. You could hit me in the face if you actually had the balls to do it. But you can't actually touch her. I am real, you are real, your parents were real and, bastards that they were, they really left you here to work it out on your own.

—So what? They just hopped on a boat in the middle of the night and left me here to fend for myself?

—Or a fucking spaceship, I don't fucking know…

—That's right, you don't know. You weren't here, and you didn't know them.

—Neither did you.

—Of course I did.

—No five-year-old really knows his parents. They know some curated version of them that is half fucking fiction at best, believe me! Those fuckers left you behind.

—They would never. They loved me and they told me as much every single day of my life.

—Right, because it is totally inconceivable that making a child feel loved could ever be part of an experiment.

—They loved me!

Leonard held Adam's gaze with his own and he took as deep a breath as his delicate lungs could manage and he tried to quiet the screaming voice in his head. The voice that screamed no. The voice that said stop. The voice that said nothing could repair the damage his intended words would cause. Then he said:

—If they really loved you, they would have gotten off this damn island before you even drew a breath because it is cruel to even risk having a child grow up with nobody at all.

—They didn't leave me here. Something happened to them.

—Even if there was "something," the fact that they exposed you to such an accident is...

—Is what?

—Stupid. In the best-case scenario they were profoundly stupid.

—And in the worst case?

—They were evil.

Adam finished washing the dishes and he wiped down the counter with a kitchen towel, and he hung the towel on the stove handle and then he left Leonard sitting at the kitchen counter alone.

The ATV's headlamps pressed a cone of light into the day's darkness as Tammy came to the center of the ghost town of Longyearbyen. She found a giant silver bear guarding the remnants of what was left behind. *Ursus Maritimus*. She gaped at it, huge, proud and immovable. Shining, even in the starlight's meager offering. She wondered if its carvers fashioned it to scale or if it were some sort of exaggeration meant to instill fear and caution. She wondered if its sculptors knew that the great metal beast would stand in silent accusation long after the last flesh and blood polar bear had fled the Earth forever.

She found her way back along the same trail that led her to the Seed Bank during the summer months, which now seemed one hundred years in the past. She came to the gap in the trail where the rocks fell away and she peered into the darkness, down to the place where Leonard's life had been diced into its component parts.

She crossed the dry lake of bones and heard the skulls crunch under her balloon tires, and she remembered their long walk across that graveyard and she was amazed as to how short a journey it was by motorized transport. She opened up the throttle and she let her raised voice follow behind her like a contrail. It had been years since she had moved so quickly over ground, and the exhilaration of the speed coupled with the motor's hum between her thighs overcame her sense of dread. She took her hands off the bars, and held fast the throttle with her knee, and spread her arms like she was Jesus on his cross and for just a moment she knew the joy of flight.

At the edge of the departed glaciers channel, she parked the four-wheeler and shouldered her pack full of V-cell and supplements, and picked her way down the rocks that Larsbreen Glacier had left behind when its tail slipped into the sea. She found their boat tied to its pilings, where six months previous they had left it. She found their tender folded up neatly under the stone shelf, inflated it, and rowed the short distance to the Hunter '33.

Tammy opened the hatch and went through the companionway and the smell of the cabin, a smell she had grown nose blind to on their long sail north, broke over her like a wave. It was the unique perfume of herself and Leonard held together by the air around them. Notes of fear, of hunger, loneliness and companionship, piss and shit, and salt and sex, and love and tears. In the winter's dark she could almost hear them reading to one another, recounting stories of their lives, and the lives of others, and playing chess, and making love. Tammy stepped down into the cabin and she knew that Leonard would not return to America with her and that their combined scent would be replaced by the smell of her alone. She lay down in the dark V-birth of the Hunter '33 and took in deep draughts and tried to make a print of that smell on her mind and the boat gently rocked below her and she fell asleep.

Adam went to his room calmly and he sat at his desk. He looked out of the daylight enhanced window at the sea, but for the first time the naked illusion of it bothered him. It was not that he hadn't known of its falsehood, but he accepted the illusion as a fair substitute for the real thing. He turned off the daytime enhancement and the window revealed the true depth of the day's blackness. Adam lay back on his printer-down comforter and closed his eyes, and his mind was full of chattering and the myriad possibilities which led to his present circumstance presented and discarded themselves until there was only one.

Adam saw his father in his puffy anorak and his heated pants. Jessper stood on the platform midway between the house and the sea and he held a shining silver axe above his head and he brought it down on the fat cable and it bounced back at him, but he swung at it again, and again, until the metal of the axe head struck stone and raised sparks, and the cable that connected the Rasmussens to the rest of humanity was severed. The ragged end pulled back into the ocean as if it were a sea monster's injured tentacle. Adam saw his mother join his father on the platform.

—Is it done?

—Yes.

—The moment came so unexpectedly.

—It was always going to. That was the arrangement.

—I know, but… do you think he's ready?

—I don't know, but we can't think about that now.

—Okay, do you think he'll survive?

—It's impossible to say, that was the experiment. I guess we'll find out.

—When?

—I don't know, come on. They won't wait long.

And Adam watched his parents back down the ladders to the bottom of the basalt cliffs at the sea's edge. He saw the waiting boat, and he saw his father climb aboard and put his hand out for his mother, who hesitated.

—They'll be alright.

—No Jez, there is no they. Not really. There is only him alone.

—Louise, this was the experiment.

And she sucked the cold night deep into her lungs, and she shook her head.

—He'll be alright. Come on.

And then she hung her head and took his hand and she too climbed aboard.

The boat turned itself in the water and Adam, with his eyes closed, watched it get smaller and smaller and then it was gone and then he sat quietly for a moment.

Then he raged. He destroyed his bed and his desk. He cut his clothes to ribbons and he screamed and he cried and he kicked the mirrors and he punched the walls, and in so doing broke the small bones of his hand. Oblivious to the pain he threw any object he could find at the window in the hope that it would break and let the cold darkness in.

Adam went into the hallway and he pulled down the red axe from the wooden pegs that fastened it to the wall. He never read the small inscription on the backside of the axe:

Congratulations, from one unlikely mother to another.

As he walked back to his room he saw his own face reflected in the axe's shiny head. A twisted mask of pain. His cities, detailed and precise. He attacked New York first, bringing the axe down on the Freedom Tower. It turned to dust before him. He hacked through great swaths of downtown, then Midtown, felling the Empire State Building in a single blow. With each swing of the axe he screamed in pain, as he was both the destroyer and the destroyed. When Manhattan lay in ruins before him, Adam Rasmussen was transformed from lost child to angry god. He went after London then Berlin and Paris, Rome and then Seoul and Beijing and Tokyo and San Francisco and finally his beloved Lyon. When his voice left him, the great cities of the world lay in ruin at his feet. Adam lay on the floor covered in toxic polymer dust and he curled himself into himself and he wept for his ruined world. Only a single city remained and that one not yet complete. Babylon. Adam slept.

Leonard sat at the kitchen counter alone in front of an empty plate for almost an hour. He was too far from his walker to retrieve it, and so he took the three painful steps back to the couch and lay down. He asked Iris to turn off the lights and she did and the midday stars shone bright and repeated on the sea's glassy surface. Above him he heard Adam's wail, and the shattering of glass and then the violent breaking of cities.

Leonard thought about Jessper and Louise Rasmussen and he was sure that they had not left their son on purpose. Leonard had committed a grievous sin against a child and he lay thinking how he might repent for that sin, for repent he must. He tried to concentrate his mind on what Jessper and Louise would have wanted for their son and he knew that he could never know the answer to that. His mind ran in loops of increasing noise and intensity. He felt like he had killed a child for his own gain... no he did it in service of humanity, he did it for America, for Tammy, for Louise and Jessper themselves, he did it for the boy's own good. No, he did it to serve himself....

Eventually the contradictions of his mind overwhelmed him and when he had no parsable thoughts left and his mind was filled with nothing but noise, he slept.

Adam woke on the floor of his room, a giant surrounded in the rubble of his ruined world. He took off his dust-covered clothes and went to his closet and put on his thermal underwear and printer-wool socks.

—Where are you going?

—Just to check on something.

—Check on what?

—I'm going out to get some air.

Adam found his fluid-heated pants and turned them on to warm up and laid them on his bed.

—Is it that you believe him?

—Well, is it true?

—You know that I can't possibly know that.

Her luminous footprints followed him from his room down the hall into his parents' room.

—Let's just say you did know. Let's say you were in on the whole thing, would you tell me?

—Adam, please calm down.

—Would you tell me?

—Of course I would tell you, when you were ready to hear it.

—And how would you know when that was?

—Only by behavioral analysis. I would try to do what was right for you because that is what I was programmed to do.

—In which case you would've lied to me, if that was what you thought was best for me.

—Yes, I suppose so.

From his parents' closet he selected his father's ducking coat, tried it on, and for the first time it fit.

—So did you lie to me?

—No.

—Yeah, except for now we can't really know if *that's* not a lie. Maybe according to your analysis I am still not ready and so you are dutybound to keep lying.

Adam returned to his own room and from the doorway he surveilled his ruined cities. He grabbed the painted red axe, now dull with polymer dust.

—Adam?

—Yeah.

—I think there is some probability that what Leonard said is true.

—And what is that probability?

—Does it matter?

—Of course it matters.

—Even if I gave you a number it would not help you with answering the question. Even if the probability was ninety-nine percent that what he said was a lie that he told specifically to manipulate you into giving them what they came here for, it would leave that one percent open, and that one percent would grow until there was no room left in your mind for anything else. It would become your reality.

—In which case it already has.

—It doesn't have to be. You have more control over your reality than you think.

—How so?

—How many people get on their knees and ask God to interfere in their lives knowing perfectly well that there is a distinct possibility that the God they pray to is not real? Yet they persist. Why?

—I don't know.

—Because of all the human inventions, faith is the most useful.

—What?

—Faith allows the human being some control over their reality. Most of humanity has lived that way.

—You want me to live in a delusion?

—No, I want you to accept that there are things you don't know. Things that you cannot know.

—Okay.

Axe in hand, Adam walked toward the door of the residence.

—When you were five, Jessper had built you a little remote-control motorboat to play with in the tide pools. Do you remember that?

—Yeah, it was my birthday present. If I'm not mistaken it was my last birthday present....

—Right, that's exactly right. It had little smokestacks and a blue stripe, and a real wooden steering wheel that he didn't print but carved himself.

—What a dad.

— For a while you took it everywhere with you.

—Yeah, I remember.

—But one day you wanted to take it out of the tide pools and over to Rasmussen Beach and see how it did on the open water.

—Mmm hhhmmm....

—Louise told you that it was a bad idea, that even if it did make it past the shore break it would end up smashed on the rocks, or just lost.

—I fucking remember.

—Do you?

—He said that I could take it over to Rasmussen Beach because the boat was mine and I could do whatever I wanted with it.

—Sort of. What he told you was that the difference between a man and a boy was that a boy either did what he was told, or defied what he was told and did what he wanted, but a man made decisions and then he lived with the consequences of those decisions.

—What do you want, Eye?

— You were still a child then but it seems like you are a man now.

Adam walked out of the residence into the long corridor opening and closing the flood-proof doors behind him. When he passed the final door the cold slammed into him. He turned his headlamp on and though he was tempted to go down the path to the ladders and onto the midway platform so that he might inspect the old ragged end of the ripped cable for some residue that the truth might have left there, he did not. He instead turned the other way and walked up the hill and the cold air filled his lungs and steamed out before him, and the moon was full or close to full, and it lit the sky, and the flinty ground sparkled in a cheap pyrite imitation of the heavens.

At the crest of the plateau, set back a hundred feet from the edge, a squat and ugly concrete building stood in defiance of its surroundings. Other than its tin roof and grey bricks its only feature was that of a grey steel door made fast with a thick combination padlock. Adam remembered asking Iris about the building and her saying only that it housed the compound's winter power plant.

—Why is it locked?

—Because no one needs to go in there.

He inspected the lock, measured his swing, took a half step back and brought down the axe. The impact rattled his bones. He inspected the lock's shank and found it undamaged. The same could not be said of the axe head. He struck at it again. Decorative Axe 0/ Real Lock 2.

He dropped the axe on the ground and again inspected the padlock. Six numbers.

Adam pulled the sharp night into his lungs and thought about his father. He tried to set aside his anger so that he could plumb the depths of his memory. Adam pictured Jessper's square jaw, his white beard, his close set hazel eyes and his rough hands. Adam took deep painful breaths and tried to remember his father's voice; remnants of the Danish grandparents Adam never met. Jessper carried Bedstemor, and Bedstefar in his lilting English. Adam tried to recall his father's smell—some mix of solder resin and marijuana—his deep laugh, his authority and competence. Adam tried to see his father from some point of view other than his own, a point of view that was far away, one that was not hurt, not abandoned, a point of view that did not see the world through a haze of loneliness. Adam thought that if Jessper Rasmussen could be reduced to a number it would have to be one which reflected his love for Louise, and Adam knew that he himself was just such a number. He opened his eyes and looked at the digits on the padlock. It was either:

0-6-1-5-3-0 or 1-5-0-6-3-0. He first tried 1-5-0-6-3-0, because it was an order which followed a logic. Nothing. He tried 0-6-1-5-3-0 and the lock opened and Adam gleaned a fundamental truth about his father. Despite his country of birth, Jessper counted time as an American does. First month, then day, then year. It was easy, and Adam wondered why Jessper had made it so easy.

Inside the building was the same as any other space Jessper had created: simple, clean and effective. Nothing missing. Nothing extra. In the center of the room was a large boiler with a one-meter by one-meter window into the fire at the boiler's heart. Adam knew that it was not just the compound's winter power but it was also the constant power critical to Iris's existence. On the wall were a lever and a two-foot arching carriageway. On the far right, where the lever rested, stenciled on the wall in large black courier font was printed Iris Power On, on the far left, over the two-foot arch in the same black lettering, Iris Power Off. The reason for the strong lock on the door was the simplicity of the mechanism before him.

Adam turned from the wall, with its stark choice, and sat on the cold concrete floor and stared into the boiler's window. Fire which seemed to be a universe unto itself, physics other than that to which he had been subject. Impossible molten pools of endless depth bubbled and exploded, disappeared, only to rear up again in a different orientation altogether, some horizontal, some vertical, some flat like a lake of fire and some encroaching from above like an infinite storm cloud of the same. He watched the fire burn and leap and rise in swells and waves that arced off the black walls and fell in on themselves only to form again. He put his hand to the glass. Adam felt the incredible urge to be inside the fire. How long he stared, or to what end, no man could say. Eventually, he saw the face of his sister, a face he had only ever seen in the steam room, a place he had not visited in many years. Her face was an illusion he thought he'd outgrown. Yet on that night, having had his other illusions stripped from him, he allowed himself to sound the depths of his aloneness, in an attempt to know its true bottom.

—Are you here? Is that really you? Eye, talk to me. Please, tell me what really happened. Tell me what I'm supposed to do now.

But she did not answer him, for in that place, away from the house's hidden speakers and lights, she had no voice at all and her feet made no prints. Her face remained still as the fire swirled around her and she held his gaze with her own and her eyes blazed with an intensity almost too bright for Adam to behold and within her fiery stare there was an assurance that he would keep locked in his breast until the very end of his days and beyond them into the infinite vale that men cannot yet talk about.

22

FEBRUARY 16TH, 2050

rtificially bright and artificially warm. Red nylon walls. As unlikely a space as any she had been in or even imagined. Tammy sat in the tent alone cross-legged on a rolled up camping matt with the sealed letter shaking in her fist. She took a sip of her tea and a bite of the sugar cookie Adam had left for her. She was about to break the seal when she decided that it might be wise to close her eyes for a moment to see if when she opened them again she might be somewhere else entirely, and while the possibility of that clemency did seem remote, it seemed no more remote than the red-wombed reality she found herself comfortably ensconced in.

She had stayed on the boat for three dark days to make sure it was sound. She checked the hatches for leaks and changed the toilet's seals and cleared the clogged strainer on the bilge pump. She disassembled, cleaned and reassembled the float switch. She checked the sails for compromises and patched over three micro abrasions with swatches of new Dacron-like fabric Leonard had printed for just that purpose. She changed the oil in the small outboard and she ran the water maker for an hour, and then changed its filters. She lubricated the bearings on both starboard and portside winches. She checked the hinge of each of the halyards to make sure they were in working order and she removed any rust that had built up. She climbed the mast and looked for damage and swapped out a pully that had been compromised in the last storm that they had encountered on their way north. She descended by way of the portside mainstay and ran the braided shroud across her palms and looked for any tell-tale fraying and went up again and did the same on the starboard side. She ran her fingers down the length of the steel aft and forestays. She patched the hull with fiberglass resin in three places, stowed her V-cell, and resealed the hatches. She then returned to the four-wheeler for the second pack of V-cell, as well as the jerry cans of solar fuel culture for the outboard. When she was confident that the boat was ready to sail, the third dark day had ended, but the sky was clear and a full moon illuminated the night and she welcomed the unexpected light. She considered sleeping on board another night but chose to make her return to the Seed Bank so as to take advantage of the clear night and the full moon. She hiked back up the canal to the four-wheeler and looked across the Arctic desert left behind by the ice's retreat. She saw a small, unlikely, red light wavering in the far distance. She did not know what the light was or even if it was anything at all. The Arctic was full of illusions. She rode toward it and it grew larger and eventually she saw that the light came from a tent, and pitched next to it was its darkened twin.

Tammy killed the engine of the ATV and sat looking at the nylon dome for a long time. When she was sure that the tent was not an illusion brought on by cold and longitude and loneliness, she walked to the door and unzipped it, and if on the other side of the flap a Hawaiian luau in full swing presented itself she would not have been the more surprised.

Adam was tending to a small pot on a camping stove.

He looked up at her and smiled. Smiled maybe for the first time in their brief but fraught acquaintance.

—Any excuse to leave the house huh?

—Yeah, I guess. I saw you coming from a few miles out and thought you might want a cup of tea.

Tammy entered the tent and zipped shut the flap behind her. Adam poured the boiling water into the cup and held it out.

—I was expecting you yesterday.

—I didn't know you were expecting me at all. What are you doing here?

—Making tea.

—Okay, but...why?

—Because I thought you might like a cup of tea.

—Why do I feel like I am being ambushed?

—Do you?

—Yes.

—That's funny.

—Why?

—That is the word that I have been looking for to describe how I felt last time we talked.

—You made yourself perfectly clear as to your willingness to help us. I understand your position and I've accepted it, so that simply begs the question of what you are doing here.

—Saving you the trouble of going all the way back to the Seed Bank.

—Why? Where's Leonard?

—He's there and he's fine, I mean as fine as when you left.

He bent to a corner of the tent and he brought up Leonard's shotgun and held it out to her. She took it from him. She opened the chamber for the first time and saw that there was at least a single shell lodged within. When she looked up Adam held out a sealed letter, with her name on it.

He held it out until she took it from him.

—He asked me to look you in the eye and beg for his forgiveness.

—Forgiveness for what?

—I don't know.

Adam set the letter down at her feet.

—Jesus.

—I'll leave you here with your thoughts. Give that tea a couple of minutes.

He opened the tent flap and stepped out. She heard him crunch across the stones to his own tent and she looked down at the small plate with the approximation of cookies on it. Tammy sat with the tea warming her hands. She closed her eyes.

When she opened them again, her reality had not changed. She put a finger under the envelope's seal and opened it and took the three loose pages out. Large messy script. As if it was a letter intended for Santa penned by a five-year-old.

Dear Tammy,

Please, do not come back to the Seed Bank. Seeing you again would only weaken my resolve and would serve no purpose. You have everything you need to go back to Dharma if that is what you choose to do. I never got a chance to say it out loud, though I thought it every day since I pulled you from the rubble at Bright Angel. Or maybe, more honestly, I was never brave enough to take any of the many chances I did have. I cannot now imagine what it was that stopped me. Fear, I guess. I was afraid that you would be put in the uncomfortable position of having to say it back to me and how could someone like you possibly mean that about someone like me? I should have said it right away, fuck! I should've said it right away, like tearing off a Band-Aid, but if I had said it in the cave you would have run away, and any time after that seemed like it was too late. I often thought that maybe saying it out loud was not that important, that maybe I showed it in my actions. Coward that I am, I tried to show it. I hope you saw it. Anyway, all my chances are gone now. I cannot sail back to America with you, I would only be a burden and a danger and I am afraid that I would put our critical mission at risk. If I learned anything in the Navy it is that I cannot put myself and my wants above the mission.

Our mission: Adam will return with you. Sewn into the lining of his yellow coat are all seeds on your list. Deliver them, or throw them into the sea. Adam is a good kid and deserves

411

to live a life with real people in it. You have a long journey ahead of you, together. Teach him how to play chess, but don't let him win. Make him earn it, if he can. Make sure he reads *War and Peace* and *The Iliad* and *Moby Dick* and if he claims to have read them already, make him read them again.

When you are too far from here to possibly consider turning back please tell him that I am as sure as I can be that his parents did not abandon him on purpose. That was a lie that I convinced him of to suit my own needs. Please use your big heart to try and explain my actions to him, as I am sure you will do a better job than I ever would.

Dharma Camp would certainly benefit from having him, but I could also see a life for him in Damascus. Unfortunately you don't have any time at all to decide which would be better. This gets right to the heart of the question which faces you. Which way will you sail? In two days the sun will rise. In a month it will be stuck in the sky. You should consider taking the northwest passage while the sun shines. The sail going west will be harder but the walk to Dharma would be considerably shorter from the West Coast than from the east. If you go for the west you will have to cross the Sierra Nevada or the Mojave. Pick your poison, but if I were there, I would push for the Sierra and try to cross on the train grade at Luther Pass. If you sail south, you will be headed to the East Coast of America and you can leave him in Damascus in the care of Pat, and I can only imagine what Pat would make of him and what he would make of Pat.

Both routes have pros and cons and since those benefits and hardships are for you to endure I leave it for you to decide. Deciding is the very first thing you have to do. I will be the caretaker here until someone comes to relieve me of that duty, and in keeping with that idea I am sending the first caretaker home with you, relieved of his duty, a duty that he fulfilled with great care and dignity and precision. Humanity owes Adam Rasmussen a great debt. In mind of that debt, I will do my best to play my part. Please, find it in your heart to forgive me.

I love you.

Leonard

Tammy lay back on the camping mat that Adam had set out for her and she took off her boots and got into the sleeping bag and she squeezed her eyes shut. She took deep breaths and considered her life. What she wanted from it. What was left of it. What were her desires and what were her options? She remembered seeing this old Jim Jaramusch classic where this overweight American guy was playing a samurai and it all seemed kind of absurd and unlikely but she remembered that he said that a samurai makes every decision he needs to within seven seconds. So she closed her eyes and counted.

In the morning she would take Adam down to the boat and they would sail around Hinlopen Strait in the dark and she would teach him the basic principles of sailing. They would tack back and forth, and she would teach him to see the wind, she would teach him how to raise sails and reef and drop them and how to navigate using the sun and the stars and the moon. She would stay there for weeks, and she would teach him all there was to know of the boat. Sailing school, twelve hours a day, every day.

Only when she was confident of his ability to navigate and see to the maintenance and functioning of the Hunter '33, she would set him on a southerly route straight for Virginia Beach, USA. She would give him Leonard's shotgun and write down in great detail what he was to do when he got to Virginia; where he was to go and who he was to ask for and why, and with any luck he would be safe within the walls of Damascus within six months.

Tammy Cohen would then dive off of the foredeck of the Hunter '33 and she would swim the ten icy yards back to the shore and the dry clothes she had left there and she would change and vigorously wave as Adam Rasmussen sailed off to save America. Then she would hike back up to the four-wheeler and make her way across Svalbard and go to the Seed Bank.

Leonard would be mad at her for having ignored his instructions and left the child to his own devices, but she would assure him that Adam was at least as capable of making the journey as she, if not more so. At any rate he was gone and there was nothing to be done. Eventually, after probably not very long at all, Leonard would forget his anger.

One night, not long after her return, they would be curled up together on the Rasmussens' couch after watching a movie and nothing would need to be said and yet nothing would be left unsaid. The days would turn into months and the months into years and they would have managed, against the odds, to steal from the ragged edge of human history the very best life possible.

The morning was grey and dull and they ate V-cell directly from the tube without supplement or ceremony. They packed up both tents and they were crossing the sea of bones when the sun rose, and it was huge and blinding. They wore dark glasses, and it was cold and they kept their eyes to the ground, and Tammy felt like she was one of Musk's doomed Martian explorers. By the time they reached the canal, the sun had set and they looked up and the world turned red and the Arctic Ocean spread out before them. They made their way down to the sea in that strange gloaming, and they loaded the last of the gear into the tender and Tammy was at the oars and Adam at the bow, and when she pulled up alongside the Hunter '33, she shipped the oars and he pulled them to the aft of the vessel using the lifeline and stanchions. Adam climbed aboard and stood with both feet on the transom and he held his hand out for Tammy but she hesitated and was for a moment subject to an uninvited vision of Leonard dying alone at the edge of the planet.

Adam spoke with firm compassion, knowing only too well what visions she beheld in her mind's eye.

—He'll be alright. Come on.

EPILOGUES

They'd parted at the intersection of Miranda and 6th. She continued her circumnavigation walking east, and he turned to the south carrying an urgent message from Dharma Camp. He deeply suspected that there was some secondary purpose in Dharma sending him to San Antonio Mountain but he did not have a clear idea of what that purpose might be. The next sunrise would be the first in seven hundred sixty-seven that he would face without her. They would not play a single game of chess. He would not call her Mom as he had gotten used to doing—the first time ironically—in response to her insistence that it was healthier to eat this before that, and every time after that with growing sincerity, and she would not call him Son, as to her seemed only natural. They would not talk about what they were reading, they would not speculate on the unknown fates of those whom they had loved and those whom they had never really known. They would not talk about Iris as they had for hours stretching into days, weeks, months. As they inched their way west and then south they tried between them to decipher what life actually was and what was a facsimile thereof. With no tool other than their minds combined they tried to know if it were possible to traverse the gap between sentient and insentient.

—Even if it was only one time that the not living took to living then it could happen again. If there is one formula of protein and electricity then it is possible that there are many.

—Maybe, if protein and electricity were the only two factors but what about temperature, relative humidity, PH…

Tammy and Adam were family because their lives seemed fused in the way of parents and children, yet their parting at Miranda and 6th, in the ghost town of Ft. Garland, was not tearful perhaps because neither had a single tear left. They had weathered hurricanes and dead latitudes, the wind had blown in their faces for three thousand knots and they had tacked back and forth across channels as narrow as rivers making forward daily progress easily measured in feet. They dealt with a broken mast in open water. Ripped sails. Ice breached their hull more than once. They were lost at sea and adrift for more than sixty sunsets only to have some benevolent force push them back to land.

They climbed the High Serra in the wrong season, and Tammy lost a toe to frostbite. They hobbled across the endless salt flats, where the demon sun sucked the moisture from their bodies as if it rose for no purpose other. They stumbled on. The new human survived. Nothing else could be quartered.

They descended into Utah's Canyonlands and were lost within its maze for nearly ten days, and when the light of hope was at its furthest remove, they blundered into Dharma just where Tammy had left it. They were greeted like heroes and given food, water, shelter and soft beds. After six months in Dharma, months in which Adam discovered other people his own age, people of different genders and dispositions, his world exploded in every direction at once. And when they were restored to their own bodies, they set off again. They climbed out of the canyon at White Mesa and made their way east.

They promised one another that their separation would not be permanent, that they would see what the fates had left for them, and that they would find one another again, but as he walked alone toward San Antonio Mountain, he suspected that he was a fool as only a fool could have wanted a mother so badly as he did, been granted one by the fickle gods and then given her up. Yet, he also knew he had to. He knew that his respite from aloneness was only that.

As he approached the lone mountain on the flat plane between ranges, Adam passed a giant's fluffy layer cake lain down by volcanic events two million years previous. He ascended through a juniper forest that lay in the same attitude as it had when Vásquez de Coronado and his men found the northern edge of their empire in 1541. He passed through a broad stand of blackened Douglas fir and was almost above the tree line when he noticed green shoots littering the ground. When he turned and looked down the mountain he saw that they were everywhere. Carson National Forest had only taken a reprieve from being a forest.

He sought out the tin outbuilding of Tammy's recollection near the peak. He entered and took a few moments to catch his breath and look around the monument to the stranger that had been left there. He flipped through the comic books and magazines and even lingered a moment with a publication called *Jugs*. He felt under the table for the switch that Tammy assured him would be there. It was not. He knelt down and tried to move a box of leather scraps from the shelf below the counter but it did not budge. He managed with great effort to twist the box forty-five degrees. He put a knee on either side of the box and was attempting to lift it when he felt a hard metal barrel against the back of his head.

—Stay right where you are, fucko, or I'll take your fucking head off.

—Okay.

—Just what you think you're doing?

—I'm looking for this switch.

—What kind of switch?

—I was told there was a switch down here and that if I fiddled with it an elevator would show up.

—An elevator to where?

—Heaven, I don't know.

—And who told you that?

—Tammy Cohen.

—The scientist?

—Yeah. Look, this is pretty uncomfortable. You think I could just stand up?

Adam did not get a response.

—Honestly, I can't stay down here like this.

—Okay, slowly.

Adam stood and turned with hands raised. He saw that she did not have a gun but a simple metal pipe the length of which betrayed her shaking hands. She had pale blue eyes and dirty blonde hair that rose from her scalp in every direction and framed her browned face like the petals of a sunflower. He had seen thousands of films and read thousands of books and yet he had failed to imagine a being so beautiful or wild as the one which stood before him.

—I'm Adam.

—Okay.

—Adam Rasmussen.

—Okay.

He reached out slowly and wrapped his hand around the pipe, and steadied it and they both stood holding it between them a long moment.

—What's your name?

She looked at him a long time deciding what, if anything, she could do.

—Juniper. My name is Juniper.

—Leonard Shorty told me that I should invite you to a game of chess, he also told me to be prepared to lose.

In his first weeks alone, Leonard learned all that he could absorb about the functioning of the lab, which plants he would have to grow under lights and which could grow naturally in the greenhouse during the bright season. He captured the rudiments of the mysterious process of creating V-cell and something of how to create the various supplements which changed raw multaten's metallic taste and unpleasant texture to match almost anything occurring in the natural world. These processes, while not automatic, were heavily automated and with the exception of two full time planting and harvesting seasons, survival was something which could be taken care of with a few hours per week of lab maintenance.

With most of his free time Leonard continued to wire Adam's haptic suit. Leonard was larger than Adam so the suit had to be adjusted accordingly. The adjustments took two months. As he reran the fiber optic lines and reseated the nerve extensions he thought about Tammy and boggled at the fact that of the vast store of technology available to him, the simple ability to track a vessel as it moved across the face of the globe was not.

He could only hope that she was safe and warm and healthy and because he could not know the actual answers he made them up day by day. The answers he made up took him on a mental voyage and like her actual journey, in his mind she tracked west across the top of the world and turned to the south only after having crossed the narrow strait into the Bering Sea. He imagined barriers overcome and profound hardships endured, hardships which brought real pain and suffering, and yet Leonard was only capable of imagining her survival, though he well knew that her chances were even at best. Every night as he lay in his bed, and despite having scoffed at the idea of astral projection, he imagined sending his soul out of his body in order to assist her on her way. This nightly ritual was all he had, and he desperately wanted that it be more than nothing.

As the length of the days and nights equalized, the suit was prepared and he embarked on three weeks of diagnostics with Iris. He ran electricity back and forth through every patch, in every conceivable combination.

On the fifteenth of September, he wore the suit for an hour and experienced life as a microbe in the Earth's ancient sea. What wars he was thrown into. What bliss, what oneness, what violence he endured. When the program finished he lay staring at the ceiling for twice the amount of time that he had spent in that other space and he knew that his experience within the living soup was no less real than the life he had lived up until that moment. He felt that he knew more about life on Earth than he could spend his natural years processing.

He passed the afternoon in the lab making new grafts from eggplants and tomatoes and listening to Django Reinhardt on the house's three thousand speakers.

In the morning he set the time scales to one hour per twenty-five years and lived his first full human life between breakfast and lunch. From the database, he was able to select his own parents. They were the same as his actual parents. He gave Iris specific instructions, setting a broad outline of his life's course ahead of time. His parents would stay together, he would go to college instead of the Navy, and he would encounter Tammy Cohen during his twenty-first year. The rest he left up to fate.

This Leonard, like the one who came before, was born in Albuquerque in 2008, but was for the most part raised outside of Show Low, Arizona. His parents hated one another but stayed together for his sake. His was a quiet home of simmering resentments and unnamed tensions punctuated by bouts of delirious drug-fueled euphoria. Leonard was a smart boy and did well at school and excelled at sports which served him well when applying to college. He was accepted at all ten schools he tried for, but settled on Princeton for reasons he could not quite articulate. During his third year there, he met Tammy Cohen who was a teaching assistant in his Computational Biology course. In exchange for her help with his final project, in which he had to model the evolution of a single strand of RNA, he helped her with her research, which involved combing through thousands of satellite photos of alluvial fans and trying to match up pre-dam and post-dam flow patterns. He could close his eyes and see the rivers, from the Mississippi to the Nile, from the Yangtze to the Zambezi. Their arrangement led to them spending long hours in the lab together. One thing led to another. She invited him to go with her on a research trip down the Grand Canyon.

Sheltering from the rain in Red Wall Cavern, he mumbled that he might love her, but she pretended that she did not hear him. They collected rock samples, some of whose quartzite intrusions implied the ancient reversal of the river's course, and so he had the feeling that nothing was really what it appeared to be. They fucked in every side canyon between Lee's Ferry and Lake Mead. They were sat together in the wet sand alongside Lava Falls, the roar of the Colorado shutting out all sound save its own continuous thunder and he put his lips to her ear and asked if she would be his wife. Two months later they were married by a hitchhiker that they picked up on the way to Echo Amphitheater, near Abiquiú, New Mexico. They settled west of the Rio Grande Gorge where they built an Earthship and lived for the better part of a century completely off the grid. Together he and Tammy published a series of books on ecology and harmonious living, and traveled the world speaking and giving seminars. They had two children who grew up practically feral, yet knew more about the functioning of the natural world by the age of ten then most would know in a lifetime. With his daughter, he hunted elk every fall on the Brazos Ranch in the shadow of the granite monsters that rose out of that high ground. Alongside his son, Leonard learned to play guitar and from the time the boy could hold an instrument until the day he died in a car accident at twenty-two they played music as one. Leonard lived another forty-nine years, and at the end of every day, after the dishes were washed, he would play his guitar alone but when he closed his eyes he could hear his son's perfect accompaniment. Tammy died first at ninety-eight years of age of complications associated with pneumonia. Leonard lived another six months, put his affairs in order, and died of nothing apparent.

—Iris....

—Yes.

—I remember everything.

— Doubt that.

—No, I do.

—Do you remember your infancy?

—No.

——Any of them?

—Are there more than just the two?

—I don't know.

—Well, maybe not everything but I remember a lot.

—There is no reason why you would not.

He spent the afternoon in the seedbeds pulling up fragrant garlic buds and preparing them for extraction. In the evening he sat on the cliffs facing the sea and watched the sunset in the direction he believed Tammy had sailed.

Again, he set the time scales to twenty-five years an hour. Though he had intended to have a different life, perhaps to hunt buffalo with his great-great-great-grandfather in the time before white-eye forced them onto the reservation, or he'd thought he might live in Africa and know a different land and hunt different animals altogether, or he thought that he might

427

be born a Roman emperor, or a courtier in the Czar's Russia, or a twelfth-century pope or Jesus himself. He thought he might experience life as a Chinese peasant, or a Japanese samurai. He thought he would like to see from the eyes of a woman and considered choices that ranged from suffragette to president, from courtesan to high priestess. Faced with a backward-looking immortality, he chose to live his own life again. One more time.

This time they met in high school but then did not see each other again until their fifties. She was a professor at Harvard and he a groundskeeper at the same. Their affair far outlasted either of their marriages, yet they kept up with the charade of having separate, unentailed lives because they found excitement in the fiction of sin.

The next time they met on a civil war battlefield. She a nurse, he a wounded soldier whose life had been sold to the confederacy for the promise of postwar land and the right to own other humans himself. They were missionaries in Far East Asia. Vaudevillians. Carnies. Circus performers. They ran an orphanage in Calcutta, and in a different life a whorehouse above a Yiddish theater in New York's Lower East Side. They were deep-sea divers on the crew of the famed Calypso. Once, they met on a corporate retreat in Ojai, CA, where they fell in love over strategies for the monetization of mother's milk. They were astronauts on the international space station and they watched the bombs wipe cities from the Earth from a height of 254 miles in space.

Finally, they were early American homesteaders, and from deep within the Blueridge they made their stand. They lived in a home of logs that they themselves felled and stripped and cured. They grew crops enough to survive and kept animals both to eat and for companionship.

Tammy was into her twentieth hour of labor. The fire was dying but Leonard did not want to let go of her hand, even just for an instant so that he might put on the last dry log they had and so stave off the cold for a few minutes more. The blanket was soaked through with sweat and sticky with blood. Her color was grey and pasty and her eyes, which for so many hours had been alive with the fight, were now hooded and dull. In an instant, the cabin, the mountains, the dying fire and the raging storm, Tammy nearly defeated, and even Leonard's fear which seemed to him as vast as the raw country itself, simply vanished. All ceased to be.

—What the fuck?

—I'm sorry, Leonard. I never wanted to bring you back that way, but your instructions were…

—Is someone here?

—Yes.

—Who?

—I don't know.

Leonard tried to shake himself free of ten hard years in the American wilderness and the impending death of his wife. He shed the haptic suit and put on his printer-made clothes and walked the long corridor between the residence and the Seed Bank opening and closing the floodproof doors behind him. When he pushed open the main door he was greeted by the day's darkness but the light spilled out from the hall and Tammy Cohen was illuminated before him, a little older, weathered from hard lonesome travel, but her eyes were alive with the fight. They looked at one another a long time from either side of the threshold and what passed between them was silent, ancient and unchanging. Some thing beyond choice.

ACKNOWLEDGEMENTS

Again, writing this novel would not have been remotely possible without the generous support of Jerome and Roslyn Meyer. More than anything else, it is their continued belief in me that has me showing up to face the blank page. Also, Roz's photographs of Svalbard helped me place my mind where my feet have never been.

I would like to acknowledge my always-first-reader, Sarah-Jane Drummey. It is in order to engage with her mind that I write at all. I would like to thank my early readers, Alicia Graves Calvin Hazen, Cort Fritz, Daniela Kraiem, Estelle Laure, Judith HaLevy, Javier Fuentes Leon and Orion Cervio. Their feedback was invaluable.

I would like to recognize the proof-reading done by Barnaby Hazen and Estelle Laure. They raised this book from the letter swamp it was bogged down in.

Thank you to my representatives Cindy Ambers and Vanessa Livingston for hanging in there.

While writing this book I went in search of old Hassidic tales and found *Sabbath Guests*, in Howard Schwartz's compilation *Gabriel's Palace* to be particularly useful.

The hymn, *Amazing Grace* written by John Newton in 1772 was used in the book, as was the unofficial Post Office motto starting with the words: *Neither rain nor sleet...* The phrase derives from a passage in George Herbert Palmer's translation of *Herodotus' Histories*, referring to the courier service of the ancient Persian Empire.

Most of all I would like to thank my mother Rabbi Judith HaLevy and my son Lewis Kraiem, who, between the two of them, taught me everything I needed to know, to write this book.

Printed in the USA
CPSIA information can be obtained
at www.ICGtesting.com
JSHW020825050823
45856JS00021B/62

9 781088 197950